PRAISE FOR

The Rhythm of Grace on Standalone Mountain

"Jeffery Deal has written a page-turning tale that spans centuries and cultures and faiths and, most importantly, the matters of life and death that drive history itself. This novel is part murder mystery, part historical fiction, part military suspense, but when all put together, it's above all a marvelous story of the power of love and family and identity. This is a meaningful and entertaining book full of heart."

—Bret Lott, author of *Gather the Olives: On Food and Hope and the Holy Land*

"Intricately linking five centuries of mountain culture one puzzle piece at a time, Jeffrey L. Deal tantalizingly paints a canvas with mystical intrigue and murder mystery. With stunning scenes that parallel biblical floods and now-familiar images of a raging Appalachian river, *The Rhythm and Grace of Standalone Mountain* is a vivid reminder that our present and past are one and the same."

—Lon Wagner, author of *The Fever: The Most Fatal Plague in American History*

"Jeffery Deal is a great storyteller who wrote a book that is hard to put down. The characters are drawn realistically and with great empathy. I wanted to meet them and know them and felt like I knew them at the same time. This is no mean feat for a storyteller. The empathy and grace with which Deal drew the characters is one of the great strengths of the book—and this is true even for those characters you initially have little empathy for but come to know as real people, with real needs and with their own view of life."

—Thomas Leatherman, PhD, professor emeritus, University of Massachusetts, and distinguished professor emeritus, University of South Carolina

"Alternating first- and third-person narratives, Jeffery Deal composes the most exquisite symphony of voices from the past and present; compelling inner monologues of ancient, forgotten souls resonate into modern-day lives, walking the reader through a timeless adventure.
"Narrative layers unveil similarities that linger through the centuries, as well as eternal human challenges. The author shows his expertise by weaving a magical, timeless, legendary hero's journey into the fast-paced action scenes of a contemporary detective-story scenario. Combining his skills as an accomplished anthropologist and an outstanding storyteller, Jeffery Deal is able to share a breathtaking literary experience."

—Heloisa Prieto, author of *The Musician*

The Rhythm of Grace on Standalone Mountain
by Jeffery L. Deal

© Copyright 2024 Jeffery L. Deal

979-8-88824-500-2

All rights reserved. No part of this publication may be reproduced, stored in a retrieval system, or transmitted in any form or by any means—electronic, mechanical, photocopy, recording, or any other—except for brief quotations in printed reviews, without the prior written permission of the author.

This is a work of fiction. All the characters in this book are fictitious, and any resemblance to actual persons, living or dead, is purely coincidental. The names, incidents, dialogue, and opinions expressed are products of the author's imagination and are not to be construed as real.

Published by

köehlerbooks™

3705 Shore Drive
Virginia Beach, VA 23455
800-435-4811
www.koehlerbooks.com

The Rhythm of Grace on Standalone Mountain

Jeffery L. Deal

VIRGINIA BEACH
CAPE CHARLES

circa 972 BCE

Now there was a famine in the days of David for three years, year after year; and David sought the presence of the LORD. And the LORD said, "It is for Saul and his bloody house, because he put the Gibeonites to death."

So, the king called the Gibeonites and spoke to them. Thus David said to the Gibeonites, "What should I do for you? And how can I make atonement that you may bless the inheritance of the LORD?"

Then the Gibeonites said to him, "We have no concern of silver or gold with Saul or his house, nor is it for us to put any man to death in Israel."

And he said, "I will do for you whatever you say."

So, they said to the king, "The man who consumed us and who planned to exterminate us from remaining within any border of Israel, let seven men from his sons be given to us, and we will hang them before the LORD in Gibeah of Saul, the chosen of the LORD."

And the king said, "I will give them."

II Samuel 21:1–6

CHAPTER ONE

8:32 a.m., July 3, 1974

Three years, four months, three days, and fifty-eight minutes until failure

Dinah did not believe in chance encounters. When she met the other woman, she sensed a restlessness that drew her like a hound to a blood trail. They had bumped shopping carts at the Clover Farm, a local grocery and "everything else" establishment wedged between the railroad tracks and Clemson Highway. Living in the same small town of Toccoa, Georgia, they went through the typical formalities, which lasted much longer than an outsider would have considered necessary.

Soon they were meeting weekly for early coffee and talking about everything from their marriages and children to local gossip, a favorite topic in Stephens County. When Christmas drew near, Dinah surprised her new friend with a set of earrings shaped like a stylized bird of prey.

"Oh, thank you, but you shouldn't have," the woman said with a smile. "Is this supposed to be Rock Eagle?"

Dinah nodded. "Yes, it is. Have you been there?"

"Not since my Girl Scout days, and I won't say how long ago that was," her friend chuckled.

Dinah laughed politely, then eased the conversation into

local myths and legends that involved Rock Eagle and the myriad other Native American artifacts found in the hills and mountains surrounding them.

"How do you know so much about the Indians around here?" the woman asked.

"What Indians?" Dinah replied. "We're all gone."

"We?" The woman cocked her head.

"I meant 'they,'" Dinah replied with a nervous chuckle. "They're all gone. Trail of Tears and all."

"That was a shame," the woman replied. "I think we're better than that now."

"Perhaps," Dinah mused. "A lot of good that does anyone."

"Well, it can't be fixed now, is all I'm saying."

"But wouldn't it be something if it could? Imagine if we could . . ." Dinah trailed off. She glanced at the other woman, gauging her reaction.

"I'm afraid my imagination is a bit rusty," the woman said.

Dinah looked down at her own hands and was surprised that one of them had formed a fist. She abruptly changed the subject, and the other woman relaxed.

They continued to meet for coffee, usually at an establishment outside of town. For some reason, the woman was keeping her relationship with Dinah a secret from her husband, as if she needed it to be for her alone. Dinah sensed this and was pleased. Soon, the conversations drifted toward religion. The woman seemed excited when Dinah said she was "involved in leadership," as such things were not allowed in any of the other local churches. She was even more excited when, a month later, Dinah told her she had taken over some of the preaching duties from her husband. When the time was right, Dinah invited her to one of her weekly gatherings. After the first meeting, Dinah knew the woman was hooked.

One warm Wednesday evening, Dinah stepped to the pulpit and looked down on an expectant congregation. Her new friend sat in the first row. Dinah's husband rested on an ornate wooden chair to her right, his eyes closed.

"Many of you are aware of my husband's condition," Dinah said to a hushed audience. "He has ordained me to take his place, for now."

As one, the congregation looked at the row of deacons, who sat alone to one side. They could have been made of stone.

"I want to lead this church into a new age of righteousness and redemption," Dinah said.

She paused and scanned the congregation for signs of rebellion. She saw none.

"What would you do for God?" she shouted suddenly. "What gift could you bring, what devotion could you offer, what sacrifices would you make?"

She peered about expectantly.

"Would you give your fortune?" she asked.

Many of the congregation mumbled, "Yes, I would."

"Most of you already have," she said softly. "Would you give your time, all of your time?"

"Yes, we will," they responded in unity.

"We shall see," Dinah said. "We shall see."

She paused, gazing down at her hands as if in prayer.

"Would you give your life for God?" she asked.

Congregants shouted, "Yes!"

"Amen!" several men added as the women nodded.

"Last week, we read about how God visited a severe famine on Israel because of the sins of the nation," Dinah continued. "A famine in a time without grocery stores, without trucks to bring us food from far-off places, meant widespread death. Leading up to that famine, we saw how each generation of God's chosen fell further and further into sin. Do you recall?"

"Yes, we do," the deacons intoned.

Dinah expounded upon other verses, read and reread them, each iteration growing louder and more urgent. She paused as the congregation gazed down at their Bibles, each one from a translation personally approved years earlier by Paul and Dinah. Dinah took a dramatic and loud breath before continuing.

"Preachers don't talk about the stories where God asks for—no, *demands*—sacrifice, do they?" she challenged.

Several men muttered in agreement.

"They don't preach on this chapter, do they?" Dinah proclaimed amid more sounds of agreement. "They pick and choose what they preach on, don't they? They do not preach, like the apostle Paul preached, that there is no forgiveness without the shedding of blood."

Murmurs escalated to a crescendo.

"No," she continued. "They only want to talk about the kind parables, sweet stories, green pastures."

More utterances of approval.

"Here, we speak the truth—all of it," Dinah said, spreading her hands.

She waited for silence to slowly settle.

"Close your Bibles for a moment while I read for you," she said. "Perhaps also close your eyes and focus on my words."

She held her breath as the prayers and the rustling of pages faded, then began to read.

"Then God said, 'Take your son, your only son, whom you love, Isaac, and go to the region of Moriah. Sacrifice him there as a burnt offering on a mountain I will show you.' Early the next morning, Abraham got up and loaded his donkey. He took with him two of his servants and his son Isaac. When he had cut enough wood for the burnt offering, he set out for the place God had told him about. On the third day, Abraham looked up and saw the place in the distance. He said to his servants, 'Stay here with the donkey while I and the boy go over there. We will worship, and then we will come back to you.' Abraham took the wood for the burnt offering and placed it on his son Isaac, and he himself carried the fire and the knife.'"

Dinah closed her eyes and stood with her hands stretched out to the congregation as if to bless or curse them. No one moved as a deathly stillness fell. A child in the back of the church whispered to his mother, who silenced him with a withering look. Someone coughed.

"You've told me you would give your lives and fortunes for God," she continued.

"Yes, we will," came the reply. "Yes, Lord. We will."

"Now, let me ask you. Can we muster the courage of Abraham?" Dinah asked, staring across the crowd. "Would you offer your only child for God?"

This time no one responded. Dinah sighed and closed her Bible. A few women, including Dinah's guest, sobbed.

"Maybe we don't deserve God's grace," Dinah suggested.

People shouted, "Amen!"

"It's true, we cannot earn that grace," Dinah said. "But if we right a wrong, stand up for justice and righteousness, perhaps He will offer us a bit more than a small sip of His kindness. Perhaps He will rain down mercy and goodness all the days of my life. For this, perhaps we will need sacrifices of our own."

Some people responded, but most stayed quiet. Dinah noted the ones who voiced their support of her message and those who remained silent.

"Right here in Toccoa, we are surrounded by the ghosts of people whose blood cries out for justice," Dinah continued.

Now the congregation cast questioning looks toward Dinah and one another.

"The very name 'Toccoa' is borrowed from them. No. Not borrowed. Stolen," Dinah said. "If you have Indian ancestors, raise your hand."

Men and women glanced around for a few long seconds before a dozen raised their hands.

"Like King David and the other prophets before us, my husband and I have inquired of the Lord," Dinah said. "He has told us that the day is coming when the apostates will drown in the very waters that they stole. He has told us that when that day comes, we will know He is with us and none can stand against us."

People shifted uncomfortably in their seats.

One of the deacons stood and declared, "I have a word from the Lord!"

All eyes turned to him.

"God also tells me that this country, our country, has a blood guiltiness that runs deep," he bellowed. "Too deep to be cleansed by anything but sacrifice. David did not commit the sins that threatened Israel, but David sought and found the sacrifice that could heal it."

As he sat, another deacon stood.

"I too have heard this same word from the Lord," he said, then immediately sat again. More deacons stood to declare that they had received a message from the Lord as well, as if vying to profess the most profound revelation.

Throughout the congregation, people began to call out "Amen" or speak softly in languages that could only be understood by the angels they presumed to be with them. The room filled with shouts and songs of praise. Some stood and swayed, while others sat with their heads bowed.

Dinah surveyed her congregation and smiled.

CHAPTER TWO

11:39 p.m., November 4, 1977

Upper Tugaloo River

One day, thirteen hours, and fifty-one minutes before failure

Thunderclouds lumbered in from the northwest, their turbulent guts illuminated by silent flashes of lightning. The smell of rotting wood and electricity filled the deep woods. Two men carried a large bundle, following a tall woman with flowing black hair as she led them down a narrow trail toward the distant singing. They bore no lights, and the damp ground muffled their steps. An observer inclined to such beliefs could have mistaken them for ghosts or forest sprites.

They continued up the trail until they made out a bonfire winking at them through the trees. Shapes moved in the firelight as the singing grew louder and more urgent.

The woman did not know the specific path they followed, but she knew the land and was comfortable in the dark. Her black jeans and gray T-shirt made her almost invisible in the weak light. As she glided noiselessly across the forest floor, the men behind her saw only a moving shadow and the occasional sparkle from the silver barrette in her ponytail. When she paused to listen, the two men lowered their burden to the ground.

"They're closer to the river this time," Yochanan whispered. "I hear water going over Yonah Dam."

Ben Edmonds and Isaac Holland breathed heavily from their labors and did not respond. Another flash of lightning revealed the concrete wall looming over them. Almost one hundred feet tall, a thousand feet wide, and streaked by decades of moss and lichen, the ancient dam radiated pent-up energy and peril.

"We're too close," Ben said. "If they release the gates, the trail behind us will flood."

"We're on high ground," Yochanan replied. "If they decide to open the gates, we'll hear the alarm in plenty of time to get back. We do not pick the ground and the time."

"I hear it rained pretty hard up on Rabun and Burton," Isaac said. "River's already high and rising. They'll open the gates tonight. I guarantee it."

Yochanan could barely discern the two men in the darkness. A nearby whippoorwill called rhythmically, answered by another further into the woods. She turned her head slightly toward the sound.

"You worry too much when you should be trusting God," Yochanan said.

For one of you, it will not matter, she thought.

"Why are we waiting?" Ben asked.

Her soft sigh went unnoticed.

"We are making history," she proclaimed in a hoarse whisper. "Don't you think it's worth taking a moment to savor this?"

"I want to get on with it," Ben said gruffly.

"Such a hurry," she said, not moving.

"The others are waiting," Isaac said. He leaned down to lift one end of the bundle. Without a word, Ben hefted his end, and the three of them continued up the trail.

As they approached the clearing, the voices ahead grew quiet. The trio stepped into a circle of firelight, and the crowd of around twenty men and women stopped dancing and turned to stare at them. The ground around the fire was trampled flat and denuded of vegetation.

"There is no death, only a change of worlds," Yochanan declared.

As one, the crowd replied, "There is no death, only a change of worlds."

Ben and Isaac set their bundle on the ground as the others resumed dancing and singing. A woman came forward between them and the fire. She was small and lithe, with glossy black hair that trailed down her back in a thick braid. She wore loose jeans and a checkered shirt tied in the front with a knot at her navel. Though her face was in shadow, they sensed she was smiling at them. The two women embraced, then stood facing one another and holding hands.

"This is your sister?" Ben asked.

"Yes," Yochanan replied. "This is—"

"Here, you will use my real name, Miriam," the woman softly interrupted as she released Yochanan's hand and turned to face the men.

"Miriam," Ben repeated. "Older sister of Moses and Aaron. A prophetess that helped bring Israel out of Egypt."

Miriam laughed. "Very good," she said. "Isaac and Ben?" she then asked. The two men nodded in reply. Miriam and Yochanan exchanged glances.

"I'm Ben," said the short one. He was barely five feet tall, with a barrel chest and a thick neck. Black, oily hair shrouded his broad face.

Miriam looked past Ben to Isaac, who stood staring at them. He was tall, over six feet four inches, with close-set eyes, a long neck, and spindly limbs. In the light of the fire, his hawklike face looked frozen, a mask of indifference. She guessed he had been chosen.

A moan came from the bundle.

"Take her out," Yochanan said.

Ben and Isaac carefully unrolled the old carpet to reveal a semiconscious young woman. She had closely cropped brown hair and wore red shorts and a revealing white halter top, with no shoes or socks. When they grasped her arms to sit her up, her eyes flew open, and she worked her mouth as if attempting to speak.

"Should I dose her again?" Ben asked.

Yochanan considered for a few seconds. "I think so. There's no need for her to be awake—just alive."

Ben pulled a plastic case from his front shirt pocket and extracted a syringe and needle, already loaded with a cloudy liquid. The woman on the ground saw the needle and struggled feebly.

Yochanan leaned forward and whispered to her, "Do not be afraid of those who want to kill your body. They cannot touch your soul. Fear only God, who can destroy both soul and body in hell."

Seconds later, the woman slumped to the ground. The men spread out the carpet and carefully lifted her onto it.

"Turn her so that her head is to the west," Miriam instructed them.

Ben glanced at Yochanan and shrugged his ignorance. Yochanan pointed toward the splashing of the river, and the two men dragged the woman to face the direction she had indicated.

Ben took another syringe from the box and looked at Isaac.

"Not now," Isaac replied.

Ben replaced the syringe and went to join the dancers. They moved with abandon as if dancing only for themselves, but the refrain echoing off the nearby dam was coordinated and rhythmic. Isaac settled next to the unconscious woman. As he did, he noticed the two oblong holes dug beside the fire. He crossed his legs, put his hands on his knees, and closed his eyes.

"We should get ready," Yochanan said. Miriam nodded, and they went to the edge of the clearing and retrieved two burlap bags. From inside the bags, they withdrew a dozen or more pouches, which they placed on the ground. Discarding the burlap bags, each took up a pouch.

The two women leaned forward as one and carefully poured lines of powdered charcoal in a circle around Isaac and the unconscious woman. The crowd grew silent and gathered to watch. When the women had finished, Miriam used a pouch containing finely ground pigment the color of red clay to draw a figure that would enclose the circle. When she was done with one side and starting the other, Yochanan selected a pouch of blue powder and began to pour a line following the outline Miriam had started. The fire crackled, and thunder resounded in the distance. Nearby, a barred owl called plaintively for an answer that did not come.

Yochanan and Miriam stepped back to inspect their work. The effigy of a large bird of prey outlined in blue and red surrounded Isaac, the unconscious woman, and the two holes.

"There is no death, only a change of worlds," Miriam said, and the crowd repeated the words back to her.

One by one, men and women came forward and took up the remaining pouches. Staying outside the bird figure, they bent and poured various colored powders into intricate shapes and characters on the ground. Soon, scores of images filled the clearing. When the dancers were finished, they returned the pouches to the burlap bags and stood silently at the firelight's edge.

Yochanan retrieved a final bundle and walked across the images, careful not to touch the lines of powder. She approached Isaac, who still sat staring at the ground.

"There is no death, only a change of worlds," Yochanan said softly.

Isaac did not respond.

"Are you ready?" she asked him, barely loud enough for the others to hear.

The fire threw sparks into the night. More lightning flickered on the horizon, and the creatures of the dark ceased their calling. The night grew silent and still. After a long moment, Isaac lifted his eyes to meet Yochanan's.

"There is no death, only a change of worlds," he said in a voice that carried both conviction and doubt.

Yochanan unfolded the bundle to reveal a flint knife with a handle wrapped in leather. She proffered the knife to Isaac, who took it hesitantly, as if he did not know its purpose. From the shadows, Miriam broke the quiet with a sob.

Yochanan shot her a warning look.

Isaac rose to his knees. Pressing the knife to his palm to test the sharpness, he was rewarded with a trickle of blood.

Lightning struck nearby, and thunder rolled across the forest. A siren blared.

"They're opening the gates," Ben said. "This place will be an island soon, and we'll be trapped, maybe for days."

"He needs time," Yochanan said.

"Time we can't give him," Ben replied sharply.

Yochanan frowned at him, and he fell silent. The siren continued to wail, and people in the crowd shifted nervously.

Isaac looked up at his audience. Without warning, he lifted his arms and drove the stone knife into the chest of the woman lying before him. Blood spurted upward and coated his hands. He withdrew the knife and stared at it for a long few breaths. Turning the point toward his own chest, he grasped the blade with both hands. His blood mingled with that of the dying woman as the razor-sharp edges of the knapped stone cut into his fingers.

Isaac fell forward, his weight burying the knife into his chest. He let out a moan, and his legs twitched for a few seconds before he went still.

The crowd observed in silence as the siren drowned out all other sounds of the night. Then they heard metal creaking, followed by rushing water.

"They opened the gates," Ben shouted. "We need to go now!"

"Help me get them into the graves," Yochanan said. "Quickly!"

Ben and another man entered the effigy and hurriedly carried the woman's body to one of the shallow graves, taking pains to ensure that her head continued pointing west. Lifting Isaac's lifeless body next, they placed him in the parallel grave, but with his head to the east. They spread the carpet over him and saw Miriam staring at the bodies. When they called to her, she shook her head as if waking from a dream.

"Go ahead," Yochanan finally said. She stepped forward with two shovels she had retrieved from the brush and handed one to Miriam.

"Get everyone back to their cars," she directed Ben. "Make sure they leave a few minutes apart. Go now. Miriam and I can finish here."

Ben glanced hesitantly at the drawings. Sensing his question, Yochanan said, "A hard rain is coming. All of this will wash away."

Ben nodded and joined the others, who were already disappearing down the dark trail.

Yochanan hastily shoveled dirt onto the two bodies. After a few moments, Miriam bent to help. Metal scraping across metal again pierced the dark forest, and the roar of rushing water grew louder.

"They opened the second gate," Miriam cried. "Hurry!"

They shoveled and scraped dirt into the graves until filled, then stomped across the loose soil before adding more dirt.

"That'll have to do," Yochanan finally said. The sounds of the rising river seemed closer.

"We've got to move fast," Miriam said.

Clutching the shovels, they ran to the path but had to slow to a fast walk once they lost the firelight. The risk of being spotted by night fishermen or young lovers looking for seclusion had been too great to allow for flashlights.

They had traveled a few minutes when they came to a low part of the trail that was already flooding. Neither hesitated to wade through frigid thigh-high water pulled from the bottom of the mountain lake above the dam, and they soon began to shiver. The trail was rocky and kept them from sinking into the mud, but the surface became slick and treacherous, and they slowed further to a cautious walk. Twenty minutes later, the trail turned upward, and they climbed free of the rising waters. The churning river grew faint until they could barely hear it above the din of the siren.

Both women were drenched in sweat and floodwater by the time they reached an overgrown logging road. This they followed for half a mile before arriving at a well-traveled dirt-and-gravel road. Yochanan led Miriam to where they had hidden the pickup. Ben was nowhere to be seen, and they assumed he had hitched a ride with one of the others.

Yochanan unlocked the door and let Miriam inside, then climbed into the driver's seat. She inserted the key in the ignition but did not start the truck. Instead, she turned to Miriam. The truck cabin filled with a chilly, musty smell.

"Your first is the hardest," she told Miriam, who responded with a soft sniffle. "They are in paradise." In the darkness, Yochanan detected the slightest of nods.

She sat back and closed her eyes. When she sensed Miriam had settled, she continued, "He wouldn't tell me, but I think Isaac knew the woman."

"Is that a problem?" Miriam replied.

"I don't know. I don't think so," Yochanan said. "Even if they connect Isaac to her disappearance, they can't connect anything to us. They'll think he took her somewhere. Since they won't find him, they'll assume they ran away together to Alaska or something. It's happened before. It just makes me nervous that we didn't have time to clear out the site."

She leaned forward and squinted up through the windshield as more lightning split the night sky.

"Rain's going to wash all of it away tonight," she reassured them both. "This time of year, it should rain a few more times before they let the river go down. Till then, nobody will try to cross over. I don't think we have anything to worry about."

Yochanan started the truck, turned on her lights, and pulled onto the road.

"Another couple ran away last night," Miriam said. Yochanan did not reply, but Miriam heard her shift in her seat and saw her look out the window.

"Some of the men tracked them to the Bible College," she continued.

"Seems the place to go," Yochanan replied. "They get a hero's welcome. The true believers who escape the evil cult, and all that."

Miriam did not reply.

"We've made plans to deal with them," Yochanan continued.

Miriam turned to her companion. "Plans?"

"Ever been to Kelly Barnes Lake, just up the creek from the falls?" Yochanan asked.

"Many times," Miriam replied.

"There is no death, only a change of worlds," Yochanan said, smiling.

CHAPTER THREE

5:55 p.m., November 5, 1977
Seventeen hours and fifty-five minutes until failure

Sheriff Tom McClain parked his cruiser beside his office at precisely 7:35 a.m., the same as he did every day except Sundays and Wednesdays. He took his usual stroll down West Tugaloo Street toward the courthouse, where he turned south on North Alexander. Passing the Toccoa Police Department, he wondered for the thousandth time about the inefficiencies of having two separate law enforcement organizations on the same block of a small town.

He turned east onto Doyle Street at the next corner. As usual, he walked a little faster past the storefront office of the local newspaper, hoping to avoid Terrance Head, a furniture salesman turned investigative reporter. Somehow, Terrance always knew about overnight crimes and accidents before anyone else, and the sheriff hated being ambushed by questions concerning cases he knew nothing about. Few of the incidents were significant by any other standards than those in Toccoa—rabid dog sightings, watermelons stolen, someone bitten by a rattlesnake.

As he skirted by, McClain peeked through the glass windows and past the proudly displayed words Toccoa Record. Established 1873. He saw movement in the back, but no one burst through the door with a recorder and notebook in hand. Today, perhaps, he could eat in peace.

The town was quiet after the big storm. The streets glistened with rainwater that would turn to steam within an hour or two. Gazing up at a sky awash in red, the sheriff knew more rain was on the way.

McClain continued down Doyle Street to the Southern Charm Café. Like the newspaper and all other downtown establishments, the Southern Charm Café's front window boasted of its opening date: ESTABLISHED IN 1961.

McClain removed his hat and entered with a tinkle of the bell over the door.

"Sit anywhere, Sheriff," Pearl Stowe called from behind the counter. She finished pouring coffee for an elderly man, brushed a strand of light-brown hair from her face, and picked up a laminated menu. The sheriff settled in a back booth, and she brought him the menu and a glass of ice water. Turning the ceramic mug on the table upright, she filled it with coffee without asking if he wanted any.

Sheriff McClain did not look at the menu. In fact, he had not looked at the menu in years.

"Scrambled eggs, bacon, and whole wheat toast," he told Pearl when she finished filling his mug. She smiled and nodded, as she did every morning.

The years had been kind to Pearl. In high school, she had been the homecoming queen, captain of the cheerleading squad, and the object of every male student's desire. She had warm brown eyes that crinkled slightly in the corners when she smiled, which she did frequently. Though slightly rounder than she had been in her youth, she filled out the waitressing uniform in all the right places. Pearl knew that the sheriff and every other man in the restaurant eyed her when she turned her back to them. As long as they kept their language civil and their hands to themselves, she did not mind.

McClain wasn't doing too shabby himself in the aging department. Thanks to regular runs and occasional boxing practice, the uniform still fit well, and his hat hid the fact that his brown hair, once thick and a source of boyish pride, had receded and thinned.

Still, not bad for fifty-eight, he thought.

Already, at least a dozen people were scattered about the café, drinking coffee and eating. A cluster of men huddled around the table in the corner, where they sat every morning. Four of them formed the core of the Toccoa Men's Coffee and Discussion Club, a name they made up on the spot when Terrance Head interviewed them the previous year. No one knew how or when it started, but the men had been meeting to solve the world's problems for at least twenty years. People came and went from the group, but the core remained.

Roy McBee, the retired basketball coach and now full-time house painter, was the most reliable member. Tall and thin with dense, slightly graying hair, he sat sipping coffee from his own cup to avoid paying thirty-five cents for a new one. Every morning, Pearl chastised him for being so cheap, and a couple of times a week, Roy made a great show of putting a one-dollar bill in her tip jar.

Next to Coach McBee sat Robby Towns, part-time farmer and retired superintendent of schools. Robby was a short, jovial man who never had an unexpressed thought in his life, and his friends knew to interrupt him if anyone else was to have a chance to talk.

The sheriff's favorite of the group was a pulpwood worker they all called Tiny. At a few inches over six feet, he had muscled arms and a protruding stomach that strained at his bib coveralls. He rarely spoke, but when he did, he spurted words in staccato cadence to quickly say what he needed to before he lost everyone's attention.

"Tiny is one of those people who needs to talk for a while before he knows what he wants to say," Robby liked to joke.

Tiny was quiet now as he gobbled down an egg sandwich. Steve Davis, the local director of the Fellowship of Christian Athletes, stood next to the table. It was football season, and he could not stay long; he said so repeatedly. Like most of them, he had played one or more sports for the Stephens County Indians. He carried almost as much bulk as Tiny, along with a shaved head and thick neck. A couple of farmers unfamiliar to the sheriff also sat around the table.

With a sigh, Sheriff McClain picked up his coffee and went to speak to the group. It was an election year, and getting the Toccoa Men's endorsement was always useful. After greetings and nods all around, Roy asked whether McClain wanted to sit with them.

"For a few minutes, until my breakfast comes," the sheriff replied as he pulled up a chair. "Any news I'm missing today?"

"Well, we're all worried about Tiny," Robby said with a mischievous smile.

Tiny stopped chewing to frown at Robby.

"Seems he's losing his appetite. He only ordered four sandwiches today," Robby said.

The joke had been entertaining the first few hundred times. Now they just laughed in compliance with the unspoken pact to pretend each other's jokes were funny.

"Nothing new from us, Sheriff," Roy added. "Of course, we don't dwell on things that tamper with natural ignorance, right, boys?"

They all chuckled.

"But we hear you've got a challenger this year," Roy continued.

"You worried?" Robby asked. All eyes turned to the sheriff.

The cooler temperatures and rain had slowed the fishing to a standstill, and with deer season a few weeks away, there was nothing to hunt except crows and raccoons. The discussion group would, as always, dissect the last high school football game while carefully avoiding criticizing the coach—in the offseason, he was one of the group. With other current events being as dull as they were, a contested election for the sheriff's office was big news.

"Not real sure," Sheriff McClain replied. "Should I be?"

"Before you retired, I would have said no," Roy said. "But people seemed to get used to another name over that badge. Why would you want the job, anyway?"

"Can't say that wanting the job is the way I'd put it," McClain replied. "What I want to do is to serve the people of this county. I think this is the best way."

He had nailed the answer, and he knew it. The members of the Toccoa Men's Coffee and Discussion Club nodded enthusiastically, and just like that, the sheriff had their endorsement. He was grateful to see Pearl bringing his food, and he used the excuse to return to his booth.

When Tom McClain had retired as sheriff three years ago, he thought he and his wife, Carol, would pull their camper around the country for a few months, then return to a life of fishing and hunting with their children and grandchildren. Those plans all changed on a particularly balmy weekend in June, less than four months after he retired. McClain had driven with Coach McBee to Columbia, South Carolina, to watch two members of the high school basketball team compete in a summer league. When they returned late that night, Carol and her car were gone. McClain waited until almost midnight, then began to call her friends. No one had seen or heard from her. He then called the sheriff's office. Since he was still a much-beloved character around the department, they immediately sent out notices to surrounding counties and across the border to Seneca and Clemson.

Two days after she disappeared, a Clemson University security guard found her car and reported it to the local sheriff. There was no sign of Carol, no sign of foul play. Just the car. The Georgia Bureau of Investigations sent detectives to interview McClain and other close family members and friends. They asked him the usual: "Were you having any marital problems? Any unusual activities in the days prior to her disappearance? Has she ever left without letting you know before?" McClain endured the questions and kept his hopes up for two months.

As time passed, so did his faith that she would return safely. He compiled a large file of everything related to the case and traced and retraced every possible place Carol might have gone that day. He climbed down ravines, posted her picture in grocery stores and gas stations, and interviewed everyone who knew her. No one had any idea where she went or why she had left. It was as if she had stepped off the planet.

The next year, the man elected to replace him was abruptly fired by the county council. While no official cause was given, rumors flew that he was either caught with illegal drugs, found raiding the department accounts, or both. A few phone calls later, and the mayor appointed McClain as replacement until the next election. The sheriff put up the proper level of resistance but then agreed to return to office. He did not hide that he was glad to again have a purpose.

Now a former high school football star had returned from a stint as an Army Ranger and was running against him. The sheriff had no clue how to manage a campaign, a duty his wife had always handled.

Sheriff McClain had just taken his first bite of eggs when Deputy Adams entered. Doug Adams was so thin that he always appeared to be on the verge of losing his pants. He kept his khaki uniform starched and pressed, his shoes shined to a warm glow, and his badge polished, and yet he consistently looked disheveled, his clothes actively resisting all order. The gun and other implements sagged on his belt, and he would pull them up with one hand while the other fiddled with his hat.

Doug graced the Toccoa Men's Coffee and Discussion Club with a curt nod as he strode to McClain's booth. By the time he had settled, Pearl was pouring his coffee. She lingered a bit longer than necessary and asked about Doug's mother. He replied with a big, silly grin. She returned the smile and brushed away the same strand of hair, which at once draped back across her left eye.

McClain sipped his coffee and watched them flirt. Both were single and in their early thirties, and he assumed they would soon be a couple. The cook rang the bell for a pickup, and Pearl excused herself.

"Something can't wait?" McClain asked as both men watched Pearl retreat.

"Just thought you should know early, Sheriff," Doug said, taking a sip of coffee. "We may be stretched a bit thin today."

"What's happening?" McClain asked.

"Well, Perry's out today and likely for the rest of the week," Doug said. "His wife went into labor last night, and he drove her over to

Gainesville. I told him I could cover most of his shifts. But that was before the calls last night."

McClain took another bite of his eggs and nodded for Doug to continue.

"Got two reports that need immediate attention," Doug replied. "You remember Cory Cantrell, the girl we caught last year hauling liquor for her uncle, Chester?"

"I do," McClain replied.

"Seems she went missing a couple of days ago, and Chester's real worried something's happened to her," Doug said.

"Chester's out already?" McClain asked.

"He spent six months in Warrendale, but a judge let him go early for bad health, or something like that," Doug said. "Cory only got thirty days for her part. Chester's her only living kin. He says she's been working as a nurse's aide at the hospital and never came home from the evening shift. I checked with her supervisor, who said she clocked out at 11 p.m. Monday night. Her car's still in the parking lot. I think Chester's got good reason to be worried."

"You put out notices yet?" McClain asked.

"Finished up just before coming over here. I notified all of our deputies, the town police, and the sheriff's offices in Franklin, Habersham, Hartwell, and Rabun Counties. I think we should impound her car and see if GBI will send a forensic team out."

The sheriff thought for a few seconds, then said, "Impound her car, but let's wait the morning before we call GBI. What's the other problem?"

"You know Roddy Cobb, don't you?" Doug asked.

"Known him for years," McClain replied. "Lives up on Prather Bridge Road with his wife, Dora, and a couple of kids. Does he still work for the power company?"

"He does," Doug said. "Last night he was standing a shift up on Yonah Dam. With all the rain they've had upstream, they've been watching the water levels pretty closely. Last night he said they had to open two of the floodgates."

"He called to tell you that?" McClain asked.

"No, Sheriff. He says that he sounded the alarm, but then right as they were opening the gates, he looked out and saw a campfire on Eel Island, that high spit of land close to the South Carolina side of the river."

"I know the spot," McClain said. "A little hard to reach for most campers, but a great place to party if you can get in and out."

"That's the problem, Sheriff. Roddy tells me they can't close the gates for a couple more days. He's worried someone's stranded out there on the island. If they get desperate, they'll try to swim across. He says with the river like it is, no one could make it."

The sheriff took another bite of eggs while Doug fidgeted and stole glances at Pearl.

"Why don't we go down to Big A Feed and Poultry and ask Leroy to borrow his boat," McClain finally said. "I'm sure he won't mind. It's a shallow-bottom aluminum rig that should be light enough for us to lower down the bank. I'll finish up here and meet you at the office in about half an hour. Let's drive out together and check it out."

Doug left, but not before stopping to chat with Pearl. He always seemed to stand straighter when he was around her.

McClain finished eating, settled his bill, said his goodbyes to the Toccoa Men's Coffee and Discussion Club, and headed to the office. He took a different route back and spoke to as many people as possible, reminding them that he would appreciate their votes this fall.

Sheriff McClain managed to get into his office and close the door with only a few nods and curt greetings from his staff. They knew to leave him be for the first few minutes of the morning.

He sat heavily, tugged a large folder from a desk drawer, and spread the contents across his desk. Clipped to the first page was the last picture he had of Carol. He had taken the photo on the banks of the Chattooga River days before she disappeared. He had said something silly to her, and he could almost hear her laugh, see her shaking her long brown hair in the wind, for an instant still alive. Each time he relived his memories of her, they seemed to have deteriorated just a bit, and he worried that one day they would decompose into a pile of dust only vaguely shaped like her.

McClain's aging mother, who had lost all of her friends and most of her family, had warned him against dwelling too long on such things.

"These memories, you can't cage them," she said during one of her more lucid moments. "They're such unruly, dancing things, likely to show up when you are trying to enjoy a bowl of pudding. No matter how we turn it, there is a cost to mourning that can never be fully paid. The best we can do is to keep their memories alive, but at a respectable distance."

From what he and investigators had determined was missing from the house, he had pieced together what she was wearing when she disappeared. Short-sleeved yellow blouse. Jeans. White cloth shoes with no socks. Wedding and engagement rings. Sterling silver necklace with a sea turtle pendant, memento of a trip to Charleston, South Carolina, the year before she disappeared.

As he did every day, McClain read through each page of the thick folder. He had long since committed the entire file to memory, but the daily ritual comforted him; she had not and would not be forgotten. Someday, he told himself, he would find her. When he finally looked up, the clock on his wall read five minutes until nine.

With a final glance at Carol's photograph, he left.

CHAPTER FOUR

11:04 a.m., November 5, 1977

Fourteen hours and twenty-six minutes before failure

Deputy Adams drove Sheriff McClain down Big A Road in the department's white Chevrolet Bronco. The feed store was owned and run by Leroy Davis, who lived with his wife in a double-wide trailer up the hill behind the store. He was expecting them.

McClain and Adams entered the store to the smells of feed dust and farming chemicals. Leroy sat at his desk in the back, puffing on a cigarette and sipping black coffee from a cracked mug sporting the Ralston Purina Feeds checkerboard logo.

"Morning, Sheriff. Deputy," he said as they entered. He did not rise to greet them, expecting them to sit for a while and talk. He was a tall, powerfully built man, used to stacking feed sacks and manhandling farm equipment. In his early sixties now, he was still handsome, with blond hair just starting to thin, striking blue eyes, and weathered skin that gave him a rugged look. Leroy and McClain had served in the Marine Corps together at the tail end of the war in Korea. Leroy came across as a gentle soul, but folks around town knew better than to cross him.

"Leroy," McClain said as he sat across the desk. The smell of tobacco tugged at him. Doug stood in the doorway.

McClain and Leroy chatted for a few minutes about family, the election, and the uncommon nature of so much rain at this time of year until the sheriff got to the point.

"Any chance we can borrow your boat, Leroy?" he asked.

"You men have some official fishing to do today?" Leroy asked with a grin.

"We have reason to believe there are some stranded campers on an island up near Yonah Dam," McClain replied. "Water's up, and there's no other way to get to them. Sure appreciate it if you could see fit to let us use your boat. The county's still not bought one for us."

"Anytime, Sheriff," the other man replied. "Haven't used it since early spring, and I'm afraid she's overgrown with honeysuckle. You'll have to cut some of it away. Take my bush axe with you. The motor's in the shop. There's only a little gas, but I've kept it out of the weather, and it should start just fine. I'd try it out here before you drop it in the river, though."

"We'll take good care of it," McClain assured him as he stood to leave.

"On second thought, maybe I should just go with you," Leroy said. "Fall planting season is over, and all I'm doing now is selling a few pesticides and flowers."

"We don't mean to take you away from your business, Mr. Davis," Doug said.

"Hell, son," Leroy replied, "Walmart up the road's already taken my business. I just sit around here, pretending to work. I could use a little time on the water. Just let me call to see if Katrina can sit in here. She's studying for some sort of nursing diploma, and she can read here as well as anywhere. I'm sure it'll be fine with her. Besides, my son, Mike, gave me a new camera for Christmas this year. I've been wanting pictures of the river. Maybe with it high like this, the *Toccoa Record* would even buy them."

MINUTES LATER, DOUG was backing the Bronco to a boat and trailer overgrown with weeds. While he did, Leroy used the curved side of a bush axe to cut away most of the vines. McClain lowered the trailer onto the hitch ball, attached the safety chains, and ignored the trailer light connections, which he assumed did not work anyway.

They pulled the boat to the sheet metal building, where Leroy manhandled the eight-horsepower motor onto the transom. He then set the red gas container inside the boat and attached the fuel hose.

"Current's pretty hard on that part of the Tugaloo. We'd better make sure she starts fast before we go," Leroy said.

He fastened a spring-loaded flushing device to the cooling system intake and attached a water hose. Doug climbed on board as McClain opened the faucet and water shot in all directions.

Doug pulled as hard as he could on the starting rope, thankful he was not trying this on a boat being swept down a fast-moving river.

Standing beside the boat and ignoring the impromptu shower, Leroy pumped the bulb of the fuel line a few times, adjusted the choke, then told Doug to try again. After two more pulls, the engine roared to life. They let it run while they stowed some old, dirty orange life jackets, a paddle, and a small anchor and rope. When they stopped the motor, Leroy topped off the tank from a dented metal fuel can and added a little oil.

Katrina drove up. She parked and made a show of not looking at them as she stalked into the store, carrying an armload of books.

"She'll be fine," Leroy replied to the unspoken question. He stopped by his trailer and retrieved an expensive-looking 35 mm camera small enough to fit in his front pants pocket.

They drove to the dam through old homesteads and pastures along a road that mostly followed the Tugaloo River as it flowed from the northeast and formed the border between Georgia and South Carolina. A few state campsites lined the river, most of them empty and flooded.

"It's high," Doug commented. "Not sure I've ever seen it with both gates open."

Roddy Cobb met them as they pulled up to the picnic area just below the dam. After brief greetings, the four of them wrestled the boat off the trailer, down the steep bank, and into the waters of the Tugaloo.

"If they're still there, they should be on the north side of the island where I saw the campfire last night," Roddy said. "From up top of the dam, I can still see a little smoke this morning."

"I would have thought the rain would put out the fire," McClain replied.

"Didn't rain here," Roddy said. "It's not unusual for it to rain here when the rest of the county is dry and for us to stay dry when it's raining everywhere else. The state hydrologist says this little gorge is some sort of what he calls a microclimate. Rained plenty upstream, though. They say there's more to come tonight. Even with both gates open, the lake is still rising. It's going to breach the spillway later today. Nothing we can do about it. I figure you've got till about two o'clock before that entire island will be underwater."

"Any danger for the people downstream?" Sheriff McClain asked.

"No, Sheriff," Roddy replied. "The islands this far up get covered every ten or fifteen years. There's plenty of riverbed between here and Hartwell Lake to handle it just fine past this area. The Wicker family's pastures will get a little wet for a week or so, but nothing more. I already called Josh, and he's moved the livestock to higher ground."

They thanked Roddy and boarded the small boat. The engine started with the first pull, and Leroy guided them into the rapids.

The current immediately swung the boat downstream, and even at full throttle, they made slow headway. Fortunately, the island was only fifty or sixty yards from the bank, and they were soon nudging the bow to shore. When they had tied off, they clambered up the short bank and pushed through rhododendron and mountain laurel bushes lining the island, flushing several grouse that glided across the river and out of sight. Doug made a note to hunt here when the season opened.

Breaking through the dense brush, they found themselves under a canopy of chestnut oaks and white pine trees. A wisp of smoke filtered upward, and they followed it toward a clearing. They called several times but heard only echoes and the beating of wings in reply.

When they stepped into the open area, all three stopped to stare.

In the middle of the clearing, the remains of last night's fire still smoldered. The vegetation had been flattened by footprints from dozens of people. It took a few seconds for them to see it, but they were standing on the edge of a minimalist drawing of a bird at least thirty yards wide from wingtip to wingtip. The image appeared to have been made from colored powders. Surrounding it, scores of other colorful symbols covered the ground.

"What the hell," Leroy exclaimed.

"Everyone stand still and don't disturb anything," McClain ordered.

"I've heard plenty of stories about witches and stuff in these mountains, even encountered a few myself," Leroy muttered. "Never seen anything like this. Not sure we should be here."

"We won't stay long," McClain assured him. "Doug?"

The deputy did not reply, and they turned to see him staring across the clearing. McClain followed his gaze, and he too froze.

"Are those graves?" Leroy asked in a hushed voice.

They all looked up as thunder rumbled down the gorge. Directly above them, the sky was bright and blue, but from the west, a wall of black approached at an alarming speed.

"We don't have much time," McClain called out over the increasing wind. "Leroy, start taking pictures of everything, especially those symbols. Doug, start notching trees around this clearing. If that storm hits us, we might have trouble finding this exact spot again. Especially if the river covers it over for a few days. Hurry!"

McClain took out his notebook and sketched everything as fast as he could while Leroy walked in circles, clicking photographs. Minutes later, the first large drops fell just as Leroy announced that he was out of film. Gusts of wind struck them and scattered the colored powders into the air.

"It's all we can do now," McClain shouted as the squall spiraled down the gorge. "Let's get out of here."

CHAPTER FIVE

1:45 p.m., November 5, 1977
Eleven hours and forty-five minutes until failure

Rain pelted the sheriff, deputy, and Leroy as they hauled the boat up the slippery bank. Once the boat was secure on its trailer, Doug started down the winding road away from the dam as water began to cascade over its spillway behind them.

"Is that camera of yours waterproof?" Sheriff McClain asked Leroy.

"I guess we'll find out," he replied. "What the hell was all of that?"

McClain swallowed his suspicions, resisting starting a rumor he would have no hope of controlling.

"In a few days when the river is down, we'll come back and conduct a proper investigation," he said.

"Those two holes," Doug started. "They looked like—"

"I know what they looked like," McClain interrupted, a bit more brusquely than intended. "Let's just keep our suspicions to ourselves for now."

Doug and Leroy nodded.

"Leroy," McClain continued, "you okay for us to swing by Walmart before we take you home? I'd like to get those pictures developed as fast as we can."

"Hell no, I'm not okay with that," Leroy growled. "I hate that place. It's killing all the local businesses, mine included. Take it to Troup's. He'll get to it right away if we ask him. Especially if he knows it's official sheriff business. He'll also know how to keep his mouth shut, if you ask him."

They passed a few empty picnic areas as Doug drove them along the river and back toward town. Slowly, the rain let up, to be replaced by a dense fog that wiped colors from the trees. They rode quietly for a few minutes until Leroy spoke.

"I think I've seen some of those symbols before," Leroy said. "Or something very much like them."

"Me too," McClain replied.

"So, what were they?" Doug asked as he peered intently ahead, following what little of the road they could see. "And who in hell would go to so much trouble to put them way out there?"

The three sat in tense silence as they passed through small streams overflowing their culverts and spilling across the highway in rippling sheets. To their left, the usually peaceful Tugaloo flowed with palpable ferocity. Leroy lit a cigarette in the back seat, then offered one to the sheriff. Knowing he would regret it, McClain accepted. He cracked his window and blew smoke into the afternoon air of the Blue Ridge Mountains.

"So, are either of you going to fill me in?" Doug said.

McClain took another deep puff of the cigarette and felt the nicotine infuse and relax him.

"I think we should get some help with this before we speculate further," he finally replied. "Leroy, you good?"

"I know how to stay on my side of things, Tom," he replied.

"Doug?"

Deputy Adams shrugged. "You're the boss."

"You know where that Old Estatoe village is?" McClain finally asked after another long stint of quiet.

"Sure, Sheriff," Doug replied. "It's on Bill Hayes's place. We'll pass it shortly."

"They're doing some excavating again," McClain said. "You should see trailers along the riverside. Pull in there when we get to it."

Doug cast a questioning look at the sheriff, who ignored it.

"We're almost there," the deputy said a few minutes later. "I've been out here a couple of times with people from the Historical Society. They've been negotiating with Bill to buy the place and turn it into a historical park or something like that."

"They want to start calling it the Tugaloo Bend Historic Site," Leroy added.

"I've heard," McClain replied.

Through the fog, they caught sight of a collection of shiny silver trailers pulled into a rough square at the end of a low field. The muddy road into the site was churned up with deep tracks. Doug stopped and engaged the four-wheel drive before proceeding. Small patches of blue peeked through the clouds as the men pulled up into what served as a parking area. A few people sat under tarps stretched between trees to shelter a collection of tables and chairs. A large white tent with open sides sat astride a mud-streaked plywood floor. No one looked up from their books or conversations to acknowledge the new arrivals.

McCain and Doug stepped out of the car and immediately sank to their ankles in muck.

"I'll just wait for you in here," Leroy said.

The sheriff and deputy made their way to the shelter, the mud sucking at their feet. When they were at the edge of the closest tarp, they introduced themselves to the pair beneath. The man and woman were engaged in intense conversation and made a show of not noticing the sheriff and deputy. The smell of marijuana lingered in the air. McClain pretended not to see the smoldering stubs in the mud nearby.

"What can we do for you, Sheriff?" the man eventually replied. He was maybe in his late twenties or early thirties, with dense black hair and a beard. The woman with him seemed much younger. Long brown hair spilled over the shoulders of her ragged Army-fatigue jacket. Both wore jeans coated to the knees with mud.

"I was hoping you could direct me—" McClain was interrupted by a delighted squeal behind him. Through the sticky mud, a tall African American woman somehow managed to run to them and threw her arms around him.

"Sheriff Tom McClain," she said as she buried her head into his shoulder. "As I live and breathe."

"Louise," McClain answered. He held her at arm's length and looked her up and down. "As beautiful as ever, I see."

"I've only been here for a couple of days and was planning on looking you up," she said. "Now here you are. And Doug Adams. Good to see you too."

She stretched up to plant a soft kiss on Doug's cheek.

"Louise," Doug replied warmly.

Louise Morris Beatty, PhD, was barely shorter than the two men. She wore her black hair in a tight ponytail that made unruly patterns on her shoulders and back, and her smile briefly flashed the slight unevenness of her upper front teeth, an odd feature that added to her attractiveness. Sheriff McClain could never decide the color of her eyes. Sometimes brown, sometimes hazel. Occasionally, when the light was just right, he could swear they were blue. Today, they were something special—brown specked with gold.

"Is that Leroy Davis I see sitting in your car?" she asked.

"Says he doesn't want to get mud in his shoes," Doug said.

Louise stepped into the tent briefly, then brought out a pair of knee-high rubber boots.

"These'll fit him close enough," she said, handing the boots to Doug. "Tell him to get his butt over here. I haven't seen him since I played ball with his daughter, and he's not getting away without a hug."

Doug slogged back to the car while Louise led McClain to a circle of rickety wooden chairs surrounding an equally rickety plywood table.

"I got a grant to do more excavating here," Louise said. "I took it so I could be with Dad."

"How's he doing?" McClain asked. "I've not seen him in a year, maybe two."

"Starting to show his age," she replied. "Still driving, but in the daytime only. Rey and I have been staying with him. She loves her 'gampa.'"

"And Rey?" McClain asked.

"She's doing great," Louise said. "Like any other child with Down's Syndrome, she's got some challenges. Looks like we're done with the heart stuff. The rest are just nuisance issues."

McClain knew better but did not challenge her. Even though Louise lived in Athens near the university, word got around. Toccoa was a small town where everyone knew you were at the doctor's office before you had your prescriptions filled. He knew that Louise's daughter suffered from colon issues requiring daily treatments, recurrent ear infections, and the inevitable speech and language problems.

"I haven't heard you mention your husband," McClain said. Louise shifted slightly in her chair. "Sorry, didn't mean to pry."

"No. It's okay," Louise replied. "We're fine. Still together, I think. It's hard when a husband and wife have separate careers that pull us in so many different directions. I think Rey's illnesses have been hard on him. He's off setting up a lab in Greece. Been there four or five months with no end in sight. The university supports him well, and he has grants from the Smithsonian."

"The digging and studying of ancient civilizations that you do makes sense to me," McClain said. "I'm not sure I'll ever really understand what Paul does."

"It's called archaeogenetics," Louise said. "Most of his work is an offshoot of the Human Genome Project. You've heard of that, I assume."

"I get *National Geographic*," McClain replied. "Read about it there and in a few articles in the *Atlanta Constitution*. They're going to make a map of human genes, or something like that."

"Close enough," Louise said with a polite chuckle. "Anyway, archaeogeneticists like Paul have developed ways to extract ancient DNA from remains that are tens of thousands of years old. Sometimes even older. They use the information to trace how humans moved across the globe, interbred, evolved. It's really quite exciting—in many ways more so than digging up old pots and bones."

"If you say so," McClain said. "Anyway, I'll stop in to see your dad in the next day or so."

"That would be great," Louise replied.

Leroy strode over, and Louise hopped up to hug him for a few long seconds. Doug followed, cussing under his breath about the mud, his shoes, his dirty pants legs—just about everything that had to do with the weather.

"I didn't know you were here, or I would have visited earlier," Leroy said.

Louise motioned them all to sit. A young man with long hair parted in the middle and wearing a dirty white apron brought them large ceramic cups and a pot of coffee. Once they were all sipping the stout brew, she asked him to return to his work.

"Grad students," she said when he was out of earshot. "Gotta love 'em."

Leroy talked a bit about how slow his business had been, feed prices, and the local basketball team. McClain and Doug talked about the rare changes to the town that had occurred over the last few years.

Having grown up near Toccoa, Louise knew that discussing the trivial was a subtle way many locals announced they had something significant to discuss. Here, you warmed up by talking sports or something else before starting important conversations. She also knew how to shift in her chair in just the right way to suggest that time was short.

"I'd love to catch up soon," she said. "But these rains are flooding some of our dig sites, and we've got to trench and cover as many as we can."

"We'll try not to keep you, Louise," Sheriff McClain said. "But I need you to look at something."

He pulled his notebook from his pocket. It was wet, and he took care not to shred the paper as he opened it. Louise gingerly leafed through the pages with a frown.

"That shape is definitely Rock Eagle, or close to it," she said. "The flint mound up in Putnam County's the best known of these sites, but there are others around. They date back to around a thousand years BC."

"Yeah, we all recognized that one," McClain said. "But what about this?"

On the next page he had drawn a narrow rectangle with its ends collapsed inward. Above and below the rectangle were two triangles with their points touching the edges.

"Have you seen this before?" he asked.

"Of course," Louise replied. "It's the emblem of the butterfly. You'll find it in the symbology of almost all Native American cultures. Why?"

"Does it mean anything?" McClain asked.

"Just a minute," she said. She squished over to one of the trailers and returned with an object in her hand, which she carefully laid on the table. "We found this piece of pottery a few days ago."

The broken clay surface was slightly curved, and the convex side displayed the exact symbol McClain had just drawn.

"We're finding that symbol on lots of artifacts," Louise said. "All across the region. Here, in the mounds, at Rock Eagle. Everywhere."

"Is it just pretty, or does it mean anything?" McClain asked.

"Among present-day Cherokee, it's the sign of everlasting life," she said. "In fact, it has the same meaning across the continent and even a few other parts of the world. The butterfly is the symbol of the soul, which the death of the body cannot destroy. In its expanded definition, it can mean change, resurrection, and transformation. All of these concepts are intertwined in most Native American philosophies. You want to tell me why you're asking about this?"

"Later," McClain said. "We'll get together and catch up soon. Maybe then I'll be freer to tell you more about it."

"Whatever you say, Sheriff," Louise replied. "I have another project at the Rock Eagle site down near Eatonton, so I'll be out of town for a week or so. I'll find you when I get back. I want to take Rey with me. Maybe you can check on Dad while I'm gone? I worry about him."

"Of course," McClain said.

"Ridge and I go back a long way," Leroy piped up. "I'll check on him too, maybe even get him out of that house. The river's running too hard, and the lake is too muddy to fish much, but it won't stay that way forever. I'll take him out."

"You know he's starting to—"

"We've got him, Louise," McClain interrupted as he stood to leave. "You needn't worry."

Tears flowed from Louise's eyes as she hugged them all goodbye.

When the men were back in the Bronco and headed toward town, Leroy asked, "Can I see your sketches?"

The sheriff again carefully removed the wet writing pad from his front pocket and handed it over. Leroy squinted at the images.

"I've seen a couple of the other symbols somewhere else too," Leroy said as he handed it back.

Sheriff McClain nodded. "So have I. I pulled over a car from one of the people living up in that compound near the falls. His car had a bumper sticker with the same bird shape."

"That may be," Leroy replied. "But I saw the same thing on some rock carvings up behind Currahee. I was following my grandson around a trail on the backside while he was scouting for deer. Odd thing is, I've lived here all my life and never heard of it, but my grandson said lots of people have seen it. He says the university even sent a team of graduate students up to document and preserve the site. Damn poor job of preserving it, if any old coot like me can just walk right up to it."

"You sure it's the same?" McClain asked.

"Looks the same to me," Leroy replied. After a moment, he added, "I've also seen some Rock Eagle earrings."

CHAPTER SIX

6:25 p.m., November 5, 1977
Seven hours and five minutes until failure

"But if you had known what this means, 'I desire compassion, and not a sacrifice,' you would not have condemned the innocent," the itinerant evangelist read with a loud, dramatic flair.

The strange woman was sitting two pews back from Ridge Morris when he heard her gasp. In fact, most of the congregation of Shiloh Baptist Church heard her, and she put her hand over her mouth and lowered her eyes to avoid their stares. As the only White person in a Black congregation, she stood out, and Ridge thought the woman looked vaguely familiar.

The preacher hesitated ever so briefly before continuing. He was a tall man, made to appear even more so by the low ceiling and elevated stage. To his left hung the Stars and Stripes, and to his right hung the Christian flag: white with a red cross inside a blue square at one corner. Behind him, the choir sat in white robes with bright-blue sashes and gold trim.

Tracey Ariel sat at the electric organ, ready to overlay the pastor's final words with mournful tunes. At fifty-eight, Tracey was one of the younger members of the congregation. Half a dozen small children sat with adults too old to be anything but grandparents. They whispered loudly and were repeatedly shushed. Occasionally, one would start to cry, only to be quickly carried outside.

Rey Beatty sat beside Ridge with her hand in his. As instructed, she sat as still and quiet as her seven-year-old body would allow. She looked from her grandfather to the preacher, silently wishing the sermon would end and they could go home. Questions came and went from her mind before they could be given voice, though she tried with little success to store them to ask Gampa later.

Ridge looked down at her, and their eyes met. Rey smiled, and his heart melted.

When she had first been diagnosed with Down's Syndrome, Ridge prayed that God would heal her. But in his deepest moments of reflection, he realized that had God granted his wish and removed the extra chromosome, the new Rey would not be the Rey he loved so dearly. He would be asking God to give him a different grandchild from the one now squeezing his hand and making silly eye gestures at him. In those moments, Ridge chose gratitude.

As the sermon ended and he rose for the final hymn, he glanced back at the woman who had been so moved by the earlier passage. Others around him did the same and saw only the back of her head as she left. He noted the long black hair bound by a silver ornament.

Rey whispered to her grandfather, "R'k Eagle." She was pointing at the figure slipping out the back of the sanctuary.

Leaving the service was a slow ordeal as Rey hugged everyone they met. Ridge maneuvered her into the back seat of the crew-cab pickup he had bought the day he learned that Louise was pregnant and began the arduous ordeal of getting Rey properly buckled into her rear car seat. She sat patiently until he took a short break to stretch his aching back. She then deftly buckled herself into the complex device.

"All done," she said, smiling.

"You are a smarty-pants," Ridge said. He checked the straps, and as usual, they were all done correctly.

Ridge drove to the mixtape of cartoon movie tunes Louise had made, all picked out by Rey.

"I'm ungry," Rey said. When her gampa did not immediately respond, she said it a second and a third time.

"I hear you, Rey," he finally replied. Experience taught him that she could repeat a request more times than he had the patience to tolerate. "What would you like to eat?"

"Hmbug," she said.

Ridge heard but did not at first understand, so Rey repeated herself two more times with escalating loudness. Not angry or demanding, just assertive.

"Let's go get your mom first," he replied. "Then let's find some hmbugas."

Rey laughed at him and shook her head. "No," she said. "Hmbug!"

For the hundredth time, Ridge was reminded that what his granddaughter heard and what she said were not the same. To encourage Rey's language development, Louise had asked him not to speak baby talk to her, and he usually resisted doing so.

"Okay, okay. Hamburgers," Ridge said.

"Yeah," Rey replied. "Hmbug."

"But after we pick up your mom," Ridge reiterated. "Would you like some Goldfish to tide you over?"

They turned away from town and any places to buy a "hmbug" and onto Prather Bridge Road, named after the family who had owned a large plantation and residence along the Tugaloo in the 1850s. Built with slave labor and timber from their plantation, the twelve-columned Greek-revival antebellum home was called Riverside. Descendants of the builders still occupied the house. On most Saturday afternoons, the old guard of Toccoa gathered under its wraparound porch to smoke, drink, and play chess and gin, all the while deciding the course of Toccoa's key institutions. Judges, lawmen, attorneys, and superintendents of all sorts participated—if they were invited.

Ridge passed the house just as the two cars ahead of him turned in to the gravel drive. He continued through dense woods peppered here and there by small houses or trailers discreetly set back from the highway. Barbed wire fences surrounded the few flat areas where cows grazed on dark-green Bahia grass. Through gaps in the trees, he saw the river rushing toward Hartwell Lake and already spilling out into some of the lowest farmland.

When he came to the dig site next to the Old Estatoe village, he pulled into the muddy drive but stopped short of the trailers to stay on what looked like solid gravel. A young man he had met before but whose name he did not recall emerged from a trailer. The man wore cutoff jeans, a baggy tank top, and knee-high mud boots. When he spotted Ridge's car, he came over.

"Morning, sir," he said. "You here to see Dr. Beatty?"

"I am." Ridge let the statement hang for a moment.

"Randy," the man replied. "My name's Randy Cash. We met last week."

Randy, like all the University of Georgia students Ridge had met, wore his hair long and shaggy to match his immature beard.

"Of course," Ridge replied. "Could you tell Dr. Beatty that her daughter is waiting in the car, and she is quite hungry?"

"Hmbug," Rey called out from the back seat.

Randy waved at Rey, and they exchanged goofy looks before he excused himself.

A few minutes later, Louise came squelching through the mud to meet them.

"Momma!" Rey exclaimed. She fiddled with the buckles of her seat until Ridge stopped her. Louise settled into the front seat, and Rey said, "Hmbug."

"Just what I was hoping for," Louise said. She reached back and brushed the hair from Rey's face. "Sorry about the mud, Dad."

"A pickup needs a bit of dirt every once in a while, to remind us why we drive 'em," he replied. "Your loafers are still in the back. You can change when we get to Sosbees."

"Dad, remember, Sosbees closed years ago," Louise said softly.

"Of course," Ridge replied. "I meant to say Applebee's."

"We need to make it quick, though," Louise said. "I'd like to get settled at Rock Eagle before dark so I can check on my team's progress."

Louise and Rey played a confusing game of I spy while Ridge drove them back along the river. The alternating patterns of rain and sunshine produced explosive shades of green across the rolling hills, dotted here and there with red and yellow. Ridge made his habitual comment when he passed the wooden Prather Bridge, which crossed into South Carolina.

"There it is," he said. "The oldest wooden covered bridge in the state."

While Louise knew this to be not exactly true, she let it go without comment.

"You know, the Prather family built the first one at this exact site back in 1804," he continued. Louise leaned back and gazed out the window. Experience told her it was best to let her father finish the story, even if it was one she'd heard dozens of times.

"Back before they built the dams, the Tugaloo would flood, and it kept washing the old bridges away," he continued. "They built the last wooden one in 1920, near the same time they built Yonah Dam, which is probably why it lasted so long."

Louise studied her father as he talked and drove. His gray hair and beard rippled slightly in the breeze through the open window. She saw the bags under his eyes and the slight tremor in his right hand when he adjusted the rearview mirror. As he retold the story, she wondered how long he would be able to drive and, more importantly, how long she could trust him to be alone with Rey.

The early-evening crowd was thinning by the time they reached the restaurant. The waitress, a petite girl with hair shorter than Ridge's, seated them. A few friends waved and chatted briefly. Louise smiled, waved back, and pretended to remember them all.

They ordered hamburgers and fries. Rey gobbled hers quickly and spent the rest of the time coloring unicorns on a children's place mat.

"You going to be okay while Rey and I are gone?" Louise asked as they ate.

"I'll be fine," Ridge replied. "Any word from Paul?"

"I get a letter most weeks," she replied. "He's fine. Working hard, all that stuff."

"What is it he's doing over there?" Ridge asked.

"That's too long a story for now, Dad," she replied. "I've got casseroles in the freezer, the pantry and refrigerator's stocked, and Mrs. Harper said she'll check in on you most days."

"No need," Ridge said. "You'd think I've never fried an egg. I'd just as soon—"

"Oh, I forgot," Louise interrupted. "Sheriff McClain came by today. He had Doug Adams and Leroy Davis with him. They all said to say hello and that they wanted to visit you soon. Leroy said something about fishing."

"That'll be fine. Just fine," he replied. "But please, let's keep Mrs. Harper away. She's been around a lot lately, and I'm not interested in what she's offering."

"I'cream?" Rey asked.

Before Louise could refuse, Ridge had already called the waitress.

CHAPTER SEVEN

11:14 p.m., November 5, 1977
Two hours and six minutes until failure

John Maples and Jerry Rexroad had no real understanding of how to inspect a dam. They were volunteer firemen, after all, and poorly equipped for the task. But near constant rains had caused concern for the college campus downstream, so school officials asked John and Jerry to take a look.

Rain pelted them as they worked their way down the steep slope to the lake, the light from their flashlights swallowed up in the gloom.

"Not sure what to look for," Jerry shouted over the wind and rain.

John grunted a reply.

"Should we see if those Fellowship of Faith people will let us come in from the other side?" Jerry asked.

"Can't see how that'll change anything," John replied. His oilskin jacket offered little protection from the rain, and a trickle of water intermittently wound down his back from his neck. "It's just as dark over there as it is here. Let's just tell the safety officer at the college to expect some flooding, then go home."

The two men climbed back up the bank, sending old river rock sliding down behind them. Partway up, Jerry stopped and cocked his head. John frowned back at him for a moment, then continued.

Jerry listened for a few more seconds, then decided the voice he thought he heard was either a night bird or his imagination.

THE TWO MEN skulked in the laurel thicket until the flashlights disappeared into the night. They had placed the small charge as far beneath the edge of the earthen dam as they could reach from the top. When they heard voices, they retreated and waited.

Once they were alone again, they crept out to the dam until they found the fuse they had secured beneath a rock.

"How long?" one asked.

"Slow-burning fuse," the other replied. "It'll be a couple of hours until it blows."

He took out a lighter and sheltered it from the rain with his other hand. With a flick of his thumb, he ignited the fuse and watched it sputter for a moment before transforming into a slow-moving glow that snaked into the void.

CHAPTER EIGHT

11:34 p.m., November 5, 1977
One hour and fifty-six minutes before failure

Every time she walked from the bathroom and down the short hallway, the old wooden floor sagged just enough for the kitchen door to rattle once. She would glance back to check whether the doorknob was turning and then gaze worriedly at the windows, praying that no one outside looked in. This had been her routine for years, and tonight was no different. Except that it was. Tonight, she knew, was her only chance.

Lightning silhouetted the trees outside. The old oaks swayed in the wind, whispering secrets into the night as their leaves rustled and rippled. She lingered for a few tense seconds before heading down the hallway.

She felt sure they suspected she would run tonight. She was never good at lying or keeping secrets. The only thing guarding her thoughts was that the others could only stand to look at her for a few seconds; her ugliness was her shield. Earlier, during chapel, she had not been able to keep her hands from shaking. Her heart raced as she knelt in prayer. They had to know. But when she peeked at the deacons, their faces were blank and unmoving. She cast her eyes down rather than chance that they could read her intention. She did not want them coming to her house again. Not tonight.

Martha slipped back into the bed she shared with her sister, who mumbled something in her sleep, her beautiful face barely visible. What Martha did tonight, she did for the girl beside her.

Their elderly cat lay motionless in the spindled chair beside the dresser, cushioned by a folded quilt. His pace had slowed over the years, and he had long since stopped depositing mice on the porch steps. Gray fur lined his face and seemed to spread further each week.

The deacons had already threatened the cat once to keep the sisters obedient, and she felt sure they would do so again if the old cat did not simply die in his sleep or slip out one day and never return. Each night, she left a table lamp on by the dresser so she could detect his chest rising and falling, praying that when he passed, she would find him before her sister woke. Tonight, she could not see him breathing, so she coughed and was rewarded with an ear flick.

More lightning flashed, and thunder rumbled through the mountains. The rain might help or hurt her tonight, but it did not matter. Martha's path was set.

They had no clock in the room, so she guessed the time by listening as people walked or drove through the compound. Eventually, even the most distant sounds died away, leaving only those of her sister's breathing inside and the wind shaking the world outside.

When she could wait no longer, she snuck from the bed and quietly changed into a long dress, one of the two she owned. Martha pulled the case off her pillow and took it to the closet, which she had left open. In planning for this night, she had laid out all she needed in a back corner. These things she put in the pillowcase. She peeked over her shoulder, glad to see that both the cat and her sister remained motionless.

Martha pulled on her flat shoes, then sat on the edge of the bed for a few breaths. She looked again at her beloved sister and resisted the urge to kiss her brow. The cat cracked open one eye for a long second, then drifted back into oblivion. She was alone.

She crept down the hall past her mother's room and through the kitchen. The old house creaked and popped with every step, but the noises blended with those of the coming storm. She waited for the lightning to show her that the yard was empty before slinking through the back door. After searching in the darkness for signs she had been seen, she walked quickly to the next house. If caught, she would have no explanation for being outside at this time of night, and she knew well where they would take her and what they would do. Tonight, she saw no one, and she hoped the ominous weather would keep everyone indoors.

Only a few windows remained illuminated, and Martha carefully avoided their pale light. The wind picked up, and large drops of water pelted her, harbingers of the storm. In her doubt, she felt the heavens were spitting at her for what she was doing.

She bolted from shadow to shadow until she reached the fence at the edge of the compound. A well-worn trail led to a breach in the barrier that every child and many adults used to enter the forest beyond. As she pushed her pillowcase through the gap, an outside light from the nearest house flicked on. She glanced back when someone shouted her name, then shoved through the fence and into the blackness in a panic.

The violent storm slammed into the forest. Martha ran, dodging limbs and branches that reached for her with wet, limp fingers. Rain pummeled the trees, for a moment drowning out all other sounds except the thunder. She paused behind a massive oak and held her breath. She knew they were back there somewhere. She knew they were coming for her and that they would not stop until they had taken her back—something she would not allow at any cost. Not again.

After a few minutes, she left the shelter of the tree and moved down the muddy trail, this time cautiously. The pillowcase over her shoulder caught on a thorny branch, forcing her to halt. She steadied her hands to untangle it. As she worked, a bundle slipped from the bag into the mud. She scooped it up and carefully wiped it clean before replacing it. Draping the bag over her shoulder, she continued along the trail.

The land fell off more steeply as she walked. Martha's flat shoes slipped with every step, and she struggled to stay upright. The soaked dress clung to her thin frame as she shivered against the cold. When the rain slowed, she paused to listen.

A dog barked in the distance. Beyond that, no other sounds but those of a wet forest and her labored breathing reached her ears. The rain picked up as she resumed her trek.

A few paces further, the trees gave way to a black nothingness. It was too dark to see the lake that lay somewhere ahead. Rain pattered its surface to her right while water rushed over an earthen dam on her left. She lingered in the shadows at the edge of the forest.

Months of planning had led her to this moment. She had hoped to sneak away, gain a lead on her inevitable pursuers. She was not sure whether they could track her in these conditions, but some of them would likely guess her intended destination and come directly after her.

Martha heard voices to her rear and crouched as a flashlight beam cut through the trees. After an eternity, the voices and the light turned from her and back into the forest.

She felt as if she stood on the edge of a precipice, her past behind her and the unknown future ahead. The freedom she craved was so close yet cloaked by a palpable darkness. Her heart raced as she strained to hear movement beyond the soft drum of raindrops. Then, suddenly, a soft sucking sound came from the edge of the forest near the pond—like the suck of someone's boot pulling out of the mud. She cocked her head, praying that it was just dirt sliding off the bank.

"Come back, Martha," someone called from the darkness to her right. "You know you are part of our family, and family is forever."

Martha jerked her head in the direction of the voice. She saw no one. Her hair fell in her face, and she shook it from her eyes. Stepping sideways, she eased closer to where she believed the earthen dam crossed the ravine. If she could make it to the other side, she had a chance.

The rain began to pour even harder, masking all other sounds. She took another step toward the shadow of the water.

"Please, Martha. Just come back with us. All will be forgiven."

This time the voice came from her left, downstream of the spillway—or at least where she thought the spillway should be. The blunted noises of the rain gave her the sense of a vast abyss in that direction.

Lightning cracked the sky, revealing the scene for an instant. Two men stood thirty or forty paces from her. The water had already risen level with the dam, with small rivulets forming on its red clay surface. Halfway across the dam, water roiled through the narrow spillway. She did not believe she could jump over it, nor did she think she could stand against the rushing current to wade across. But she had to try. She had no choice.

I cannot go back. Not again.

With the scene seared into her mind, Martha bolted. When she felt soft clay beneath her feet rather than water, she knew she had guessed correctly and was on the narrow dam. Shouts erupted in her wake. She pulled her long skirt above her knees and moved faster.

If she reached the other side, she could find help at the sleeping college downriver. Others had done it. People there knew her, knew her situation and her family. She could be free. She hoped and believed that the men pursuing her would not dare violate the boundaries of the campus.

After a few dozen steps, she slipped in the mud and fell hard. She felt the earth shift as she scrambled to her feet. Now she was running.

Martha arrived at the roaring spillway, a vague white smear across the blackness. She did not hesitate but leaped as hard as she could for the other side and surprised herself by landing face down in soft mud. She crawled through the muck a few feet, then rose and dashed for the bank and the freedom she prayed lay there.

When she was only a few long steps from solid ground, something moved about her in the darkness. She heard, or rather felt, a deep boom followed by a rumble. She willed her legs to move faster, but it seemed that the earth itself was falling away, tempting her to fly. A ragged, dark shape loomed ahead—how far she could not tell. With the last bit of strength in her failing legs, she dove for it, and in an explosion of water and mud, her world disappeared.

CHAPTER NINE

483 years and eleven months until failure

I make these words in Tsalagi, the symbols of the First People. If anyone finds them in this hidden place, I ask for you to bring the wisest of you here so that they can know my story and, through it, I may live. It is difficult work for a woman like me, laboring away in this dark and silent place with no knowledge of the passing of the sun, no idea of time or seasons. I could be at work for days or most of a year without knowing which. Only by careful scrutiny of those who attend me can I tell if it is cold or hot in the world beyond this cave and guess how long I have lived here.

My nieces bring me food each day, and only the most trusted warriors stand guard on the trail that leads here. These I will kill when I am finished with the story, but that is perhaps several seasons to come. For now, I need the food, firewood, and materials to make paint that will cling to the smooth rock walls that surround me. For now, I can put my story on these walls in peace. For now, this is my home. Dark, sullen, and no more than I deserve, or so the gods would have you think.

Mya, my oldest niece and daughter of my sister by adoption, found this place while searching for berries far from our home, or so she said. I knew she was looking for her soul. In the deepest ravines, if you shout loudly enough, you can hear your own voice repeated from the cliffs. Some say souls live in such places, only partially crossed over to where death takes us, and that they wait there for us to rejoin them and be whole. They say you should not look for souls in these places, for if found, they could drag you to the dwellings of the dead before your time. Even worse, they say, would be to find your own soul and be driven to madness by it. Mya never heard a warning she heeded or a rule she would not break and often slipped away to search where she should not venture. Berry bushes do not grow in these patches of eternal shadows, so I only pretended to believe her story.

She told me about this place in whispers by the fire when most of the camp slept, and she swore me to secrecy. The next morning, she took me to this place. I did not know then that I would rest here until the end of time. We entered the cave only as far as we could still see where we placed our feet. The air and rock were strangely warm, as if we stood in the very womb of Standalone Mountain. We both thought we heard stirring in the dark and left quickly.

A few days later, when red blotches appeared on Mya's skin and she burned with fever, I worried that someone's soul had poisoned her. The next day, when she died, I knew this place to be sacred, guarded by gods or perhaps the spirits of mortals.

I did not know then why a hidden part of me rejoiced in Mya's death. I only knew that she kept secrets no more than she kept rules, and I wanted this cave to remain hidden for a purpose that, at the time, had not been revealed. I know now that these writings were that purpose. I also know that I would not want this place discovered by others before I turn to dust and before all I have loved are dead or far away. Only then do I hope against hope that these words can be read by men wise enough to judge my story, judge my complaint against the gods of these mountains. If there were justice between gods and men, I would put my faith in the gods. Since there is not, I will trust in my own judgment and that of those who read these symbols.

In my early years, I was called Atsila. They tell me that in the language of the First People, it is one of their many names for fire. *Atsila* is the beautiful fire around which families gather. In my youth, it seemed to me a good name, though in later years it seemed like my own family had joined God to mock me with it. When I passed into adulthood, I took many, more noble names. For now, I will use Atsila alone, for it is the name I can write in the language of the First People.

I was the oldest daughter of the chief, a station that would normally come with great advantage except for one inescapable fact. It was this thing that I suspected as early as I began to understand people's speech but did not know for certain until I was old enough to recognize the whispered comments and stares. I was ugly. It was not just a lack of beauty that dominated my life. I was ugly in a way that felt like punishment.

Beauty is an enormous, unmerited gift given randomly and foolishly by the gods to those who just as foolishly squander it. I was not encumbered by such a burden. My mother told me from the time I could understand her that God—for she worshipped and believed in a single God—created only beauty, and that the hand of the creator placed in me a type of beauty that waited to be awakened.

For most of my early life, I ignored the crude comments of adults and age-mates and waited patiently for this awakening. As adulthood edged closer, I realized that God's hand must have slipped when he made me and there would be no awakening. When I had seen but twelve seasons, I heard my father pray to make me wise, for a body and face like mine would be of no other use. This knowledge, once awakened, played the tyrant for the rest of my life and forever scarred my soul.

I write this in part to ease the pain, but I could no more heal my spirit than I could make my face beautiful. Men link beauty and goodness together as if one cannot exist without the other. Since I could not be beautiful, I chose to embrace my ugliness and decide good from evil for myself.

In the year I received the woman's curse, I came to understand that I would never know love from men nor gods, for it seemed that in such things, the winners and losers are marked out from birth. Since I could not know love, I would know fear and power, and the trade was enough. The blindness of love shows us who we want to be. The clarity of combat, even a subtle war, shows us who we are and compels us to tell our stories to justify what we have done, whom we have killed. As I write these words from this dark place, I see my life clearly, though you would think the tale is yet too brief for any to guess its ending. For me, I am choosing how this story ends and will not trust the gods to make it for me.

MY GRANDFATHER WAS still a young chief when our people came to this mountain. In a story repeated countless times, the elders say that we came from a land far to the north, where lakes form the end of the world and winter's cold is so deep that people walk on frozen rivers. They tell of a great war that split the nations into more tribes than can be counted on twelve hands. My grandfather fought for someone called Montuk, a spiritual leader he believed would rule the world and bring heaven to earth. In the end, my grandfather watched our enemies strip the skin from Montuk while the holy man screamed repentance. From that time, we became mice without boroughs under a sky darkened by hawks.

Our people fled south, always skirting the edge of the mountains. The migration took more than three years, and many lives were lost to starvation, beasts, and almost daily raids by savage bands of strangers. One morning, after a hard push southward to flee the particularly fierce warriors who ravaged our flanks, my grandfather first spotted this mountain. As a fog lifted above the trees, it appeared as a single peak among undulating green hills, standing alone and keeping watch. Currahee, the Standalone Mountain as it was called, beckoned, and my people came to her. On that day, the raids stopped.

My grandfather kept our people moving and gathering supplies as this mountain grew larger each day. When he approached her base with a scouting party, Grandfather found himself surrounded by over a hundred silent warriors armed with hatchets, clubs, and bows. They made no move to attack but stood in silence.

Then a painted man approached. He was unarmed and naked but for a leather necklace laced with strange shells. My grandfather placed his weapons on the ground and stood to meet this stranger. The man spoke to my grandfather in a language he had never heard. He then spoke again, this time in a different language. He appeared puzzled when my grandfather did not respond. He tried again and again, adding hand signals to the words and gesturing for my grandfather to respond. By now, the warriors from both bands had laid their weapons aside and sat or stretched out on the ground. Finally, the naked stranger spoke a few words my grandfather understood, and both men laughed with joy.

This was our initial encounter with the First People. Within months, my grandfather and a few elders could converse in the language in which I now make symbols on this dark wall. The First People allowed us to move into a land they claimed as their own but did not occupy, for they said it was inhabited by ghosts. These ghosts, they claimed, would not harm us, but they were mischievous and dangerous to the First People.

After much discussion and a few ceremonies, our people believed them, and we came to this place of hardened beauty. The land banked against the Currahee—a stone-faced knob guarding the way toward the larger Blue Wall mountains in the distance. Soon it came to mark the western edge of our territory. A river marked the eastern border. The First People called the river Tugaloo, which means "a place in the river that forks." All rivers fork, so the name made no sense to me.

"You will not be of the First People," the chief told my grandfather. "It is because we already have the sacred number of seven tribes. We cannot have eight."

So, we stayed the Abittibi, saved most of our gods, and preserved some of our speech and customs from being absorbed by the might of the First People. The bottom land we occupied was rich, and our gardens overflowed with beans and maize. The First People shared other seeds with us, showed us the many forest plants we could eat. Most of them we already knew, but our women were polite and grateful. This pleased the First People.

The most valuable thing we possessed my grandfather shared in abundance. The First People yearned for stories almost as much as they craved tobacco or food. With every new moon, Grandfather would take a few of our warriors to their camp, where they would spend days telling the First People of the north country, especially of the fierce Iroquois and their efforts to form a single nation under one chief. Grandfather told them of white bears and other fearsome beasts, open plains filled with so many bison and elk that a man would be tempted to walk across their backs. This delighted the First People, and Grandfather always returned with flint, pelts, and other goods.

A large and ancient settlement of the First People sprawled across the western bank of the Tugaloo, and we traded freely and peacefully with them, always returning to the Currahee and rarely venturing farther into their lands so as to never appear to be a threat. Over time, some of our warriors took wives from among the First People, and they took wives from among us. They sold us slaves taken from battles with other tribes. Gradually, though we were not of the First People, one could hardly tell the difference.

"Your coming had been foretold," an elder of the First People had said to my grandfather. "That is why the chief did not kill all of you. I foresaw that a splinter of the People of the Longhouse would come to us, and I was advised by a spirit child that we should meet you in peace."

That is the story of the origins of the Abittibi people and how we came to live at the foot of Standalone Mountain, as told to me. What follows is the story of how the gods used me to destroy them.

CHAPTER TEN

Twelve days from the beginning of Dehaluyi
502 years, four months, and nine days until failure

I sat on the rounded edges of the great stone precipice, looking out at an ancient forest that stretched to the ends of the world. Small patches of bright green marked where my people had cut or burned the woods to plant amid the giant oaks and chestnuts. The sun was low in the sky behind me, and the shadow from the mountain crept slowly across the land below.

I knew I should go back, spend the remainder of this day in my place, however humble.

"Every morning, God shows us a world made new," my mother would say. But she was not marked as I. She refused to see anything but beauty, and it made life sufficient for her.

My mother would not believe that the few blueberries and papaws in the woven-grass basket beside me had taken me this much time to collect. She would know that I had again climbed Standalone Mountain to see the world, something the elders believed to be a waste of time and effort.

"My daughter," my father would say, "Unetlanvhi is everywhere."

Wohali, my father, was named for the Great Eagle that protected our family, and he taught me that Unetlanvhi lived in the earth and sky and that the mountaintop did not bring us closer to him. I do not know how Father gained such knowledge, but some, I suspected, he drew from his friends among the First People.

Below, in the perpetual shadows of the forest, I did not feel Unetlanvhi as I did from atop the mountain. Here I could almost see the edge of the great sea in which the world floated. On some days, where the light cut across the low clouds of a winter morning, I believed I could see the ropes that held the world in place. Only on Standalone Mountain could I see more than a stone's throw away from my own feet, and I loved it like I might a silent grandmother grown old and feeble but full of wisdom.

I began the long walk down the mountain, across loose stones and dust. I moved slowly, dreading the stares that always followed me as I entered the camp. I was the only one of my age group who had no suitors, and no one in my family expected that to change. I loved my people and wanted them to love me in return, though it was a false hope born of youth's false humility, which is itself a sort of pride. I know now that my hope and the raw pain of rejection created a deadly poison that would not be denied. How much of this did I know at such a young age? Some, I now think. The knowledge lay in my heart, unformed, unspoken, but hard and relentless.

I passed by the stand of poison ivy at the base of the mountain.

"My friends," I said. "Let me pass."

The words of conciliation worked just as Mother had taught me, and I squeezed through the narrow passages between the vines without them reaching out to touch me. Mother knew many things about plants—which ones had souls and demanded deference, which ones you could crush to use as medicines or seasoning for food. Her favorite cure for almost any ailment was tea made from the bark of the black gum, but she knew of many more. Lemon balm for a sore throat. Burdock for scraped skin or the rash from poison oak. Ginger for an unsettled stomach or poor appetite. She hinted occasionally of darker uses for some of the plants—particularly manchineel fruit, elderberry, and water hemlock. She told me how to properly prepare these to be useful and how to avoid making them lethal. But in the things she did not tell me, I found the dark secrets that would serve me in my later years.

I came to the village from the north side, walking through the row of huts with thatched roofs and mud walls. The huts created a broken circle around fields where our women grew beans, corn, and squash. Through gaps in the trees, I saw other clearings, all cultivated by women with wooden adzes and spades. Small guard huts dotted the edge of the woods. At night, they would house the young men, who would run off the opossums, deer, and raccoons that frequently raided our fields and stole our precious crops. On occasion, a bear snuck in, and the guards called for help. On these nights, our men lit the torches around our fires and ran to the fields to drive out or, better yet, kill the bear. Mother had special uses for the gallbladder of bear, and we all used bear fat to ward off mosquitoes.

As I moved through the clearing, I saw a hunched figure limping down the hill. He was dressed as a man of the First People but carried a basket on his hip like a woman, something that men of the Abittibi would not do. His head was shaved on both sides, leaving a scalp lock of black hair in the middle that stood straight, likely held in place by opossum grease. I swung my path to intercept him. As I approached, he stopped and stood as straight as his bent frame allowed. I acted as though I did not see him, a game we had played since I could walk.

"Ho, Atsila, my love," he called out to me. A few nearby girls snickered at the comment, and we ignored them.

I stopped, pretending to notice him for the first time.

"Sequoyah," I replied. "How are you and the rest of the women doing today?"

He laughed. No other man would take such an insult so lightly.

"We are well," he replied. "The sisters have grown big. We will eat well tonight."

"I am grateful," I replied.

He tilted the basket to show me the bounty of squash, beans, and maize we could cook together. In the way of the First People, we called them the Three Sisters. Sequoyah limped toward me, dragging his left leg slightly. I was told that in his youth, he had explored the mountains far to the west, finding strange people and animals. He discovered useful plants and brought their seeds back to his people. He gathered knowledge and remembered everything. On one of his trips, he slipped from a steep embankment and fell to the rocks below. His friends carried him to camp, where women skilled in medicines cared for him until he could walk.

I could not say what of this was true. I knew only that he was now a slave, or something close to one.

When he was free, Sequoyah had learned from some distant people how to make pigments of many colors, which he began to use in abundance and with great skill. People came from far away to ask him to paint scenes, people, or totems on their shields and leather goods. The trade made him wealthy and powerful—overly so, he would learn.

Even limping as he did, Sequoyah had continued to travel the lands of the First People, collecting strange implements and skills. One such skill was how to place stories on sheets of scraped animal skins or bark by painting small symbols representing the sounds of our speech. In such a way he could send a story across all the lands to be repeated by any who knew the secrets of his markings. This, his greatest achievement, eventually cost him his place with the First People.

He taught a few holy men the writing skills, and they gave the knowledge to others. As the years passed, Sequoyah's fame grew, as did his vast collection of painted skins, which he kept stacked inside a dry cave near the Tugaloo. He learned too late that not all knowledge should be preserved in such a way. Some secret sects within the First People hoarded understandings of poisons and evil potions that could drive a person mad in days or kill them in a few heartbeats. They kept and passed down the secrets of demons. As the understanding of such things entered Sequoyah's keeping, the knowledge came to dominate him. Such power, once unleashed, could not be restrained, and Sequoyah began secretly to kill—first those who taunted him, and then those he deemed unworthy to be one of the First People.

By the time Sequoyah shook himself free of the lure of this dark power, the elders of his clan had begun to suspect he was a witch. The choice to send him to us was an easy one, for they could not take the chance that such a man could dwell with them, nor could they kill him without risking the wrath of the demons he controlled.

Sequoyah, "sparrow" in the language of the First People, came to us when I was but a child. He was a servant or hostage, meant to solidify the bonds between our people. In exchange, we sent to them a male youth and distant cousin of mine. The transaction made no sense to me. The boy, now a man, was strong and handsome, fierce in battle. Sequoyah was none of those things, and I as yet did not understand his power.

Sequoyah built a small hut close to ours and lived under the protection of my father. Word of his dark deeds had made its way to our tribe, and our people avoided him. Father believed that anyone could be redeemed, and he welcomed Sequoyah to our fire. We quickly became great friends.

On this day, I left Sequoyah and continued to my family's hut. Ahyoka, my mother, sat roasting a deer quarter over smoky coals. She smiled at me with kind eyes, and I smiled back. Mother always tensed when I smiled at her. She tried to hide it, but I could tell that my face did not become more pleasant when I smiled, though I resolved long ago to smile when others smiled and to frown when others frowned. It was my rebellion against them.

My father was not to be seen, and I assumed he was with the younger men, teaching them to hunt. I sat across the fire from my mother and studied her while she turned the charred meat as if it required great concentration to do it properly. She smiled again at me and then looked back at the fire. Sometimes, in unguarded moments,

I caught Mother's face clouding over, drawn into confusing shades of emotion. At such times, she looked diminished, stripped of some vital part of herself. I knew that in the night, she shed tears for me, and each year her worry for my future chipped away at her.

My younger sister, Sehoy, sat at the door of our hut, weaving feathers into her hair. Sehoy was everything I was not. Where I was bent, she was arrow-straight and tall. Where my face turned people away, hers drew stares. She had a slight frame with narrow hips and the first hint of breasts forming beneath her dress. Men lusted and women feared that she would steal their husbands and suitors. Her eyes were deep pools like those of a fawn. She was as beautiful as her name suggested.

She had been born in late fall, five years after my birth and long after our mother hoped for a child. Even covered with blood, she came out mewing sweetly. As I washed her for the first time, I knew that this was a girl whose beauty would dominate her world and perhaps even mine. When I handed her over to nurse, Mother glanced at me, then at her new daughter, and a look of relief washed over her face. Her new child was not deformed like me. When Father saw her and sang his songs of praise to Unetlanvhi, he sang of the beauty she would become and the children she would bear, and I rejoiced with him.

Then he sang praises for what she was not. His words were a knife driven into my heart until I realized that I too felt relief that Sehoy was not like me. On the night of her delivery, I slipped outside to the forest edge. There, I lifted my ugly face to the full moon and spread my arms to embrace it. I sang softly the same songs as my father, and on that night, I fully accepted my fate.

I did not resent Sehoy's beauty but rather delighted in it as if it were my own. I loved Sehoy, and she loved me. She was my primary source of joy. It is in a mother's nature to love her children, but sisters do not need to love, and, in fact, many find themselves in bitter wars over family affections or men. We had no need for such rivalry.

Sehoy proved to be a most attentive and affectionate sister. What the gods kept from me, they gave to her in abundance, and that was enough for me. When she looked at me, she showed no hint of revulsion or shame beneath her bright smile. On most nights, we would lie side by side, our faces almost touching, sharing warmth on cold nights and whispering secrets until Mother scolded us to go to sleep.

On this day, as Sehoy wove turkey feathers into her shiny hair, she looked at me and smiled, and I smiled back. She should have been crushing the beans piled on the deerskin mat at her feet or tending the fields. There were many tasks that a woman should do instead of weaving her hair, but none of us cared, for tending such beauty fed us in a way that many families could never know. I saw a few early squash in a stack beside her. At least she had done that much, I thought. I planned to pick our part of the field later.

I looked past my sister, where, in the distance, a small band of young warriors approached the camp. They dragged a travois. They carried their weapons strapped over their backs and walked quickly with their heads down. Chitto, the handsome young man who courted Sehoy, walked beside them. He glanced at my sister briefly but then lowered his eyes again. She did not see him.

They would not make a travois except to carry a large kill back to camp, and such a feat should have inspired dancing and singing. I could not reconcile this contradiction until I saw my cousin carrying a spear bearing my father's colors.

My mother had her back to them and did not notice their approach. I looked at her again, and she smiled for the last time. When she saw the worry in my face, she turned and cried out.

CHAPTER ELEVEN

1:37 p.m., November 6, 1977
Seventeen minutes after failure

Chaos roared all around. Martha scrambled away from the rushing water just below her feet and felt a small, solid opening in the muddy bank. She pushed into the blackness. Looking back, she made out the water cascading into the abyss below. The ground rumbled, and she slithered deeper still. Gradually, the noise lessened, and she inched forward until she felt a hard wall on one side and dry ground beneath her. There she huddled, afraid to move for fear of slipping into the abyss—or worse, being discovered by those who pursued her.

She took a thin, wet sheet from her bag, spread it on a flat part of the cave, then rolled it around herself. Shivering, she whispered prayers into the night as a troubled, exhausted sleep stole over her.

IN HER DREAMS, Martha saw Eve, her younger sister, in a dazzling white dress. They were in the sanctuary of the Fellowship of Faith. Eve struggled against a tall man who was leading her down the aisle. On one side of the aisle, people sang hymns, while on the other side, they screamed obscenities and shook their fists. Eve kept turning to

Martha, pleading for her to come with her or kill her. Martha's hand lifted of its own accord. In it, she held a gun as cold as ice. She tried to shoot the man dragging Eve down the aisle, but her dream fingers could not make the trigger budge no matter how hard she squeezed. Martha moved behind Eve and the man while the congregation raged at her. As she passed, some took off humanlike masks to reveal the faces of wolves, dogs, and other beasts. These began to howl. Martha tried with all her might, but still, she could not pull the trigger.

They will kill me when I shoot this man, Martha thought. *For Eve, I would do this thing.*

In her dream, a great commotion flared up beyond her periphery. She refused to turn for fear that if she so much as glanced away from Eve, her sister would somehow be lost.

Her fingers ached from pulling uselessly at the trigger. The rage building in Martha's chest came out as a scream that was drowned out by the crowd on either side of her and the growing commotion. With one hand holding the heavy pistol, she brought her other hand to her own face. She felt something cold and rigid where she should have felt warm flesh. With a start, she realized that she too was wearing a mask.

MARTHA AWOKE FROM the dream and lay still, trying to remember where she was. In seconds that felt like hours, the memory of her flight through the woods and the rushing water came to her. Her stone surroundings seemed strangely warm, and the sheet had begun to dry. For reasons she could not fathom, she felt cradled in the womb of the Currahee—protected, safe, and ready for a new birth. She shifted slightly in the thin sheet, and though her joints and head ached, she was no longer cold. In seconds, she dropped back into the sleep of babies.

Hours later, a beam of light traced across her forehead, and she woke abruptly. The peaceful trickle of running water filtered into the cave. Martha tried to stand and hit her head on the low ceiling. She wished she knew more curse words.

As her eyes adapted, she saw that she had fallen through the narrow opening to a large cave exposed by the sudden deluge. She drifted toward the light to peer outside. The gap in the mud and stone barely reached her shoulders, and she wondered whether it was the power of water or of God that had pushed her inside.

Outside, a gash in the earth that could have been made by the knife of giants stretched below her and out of sight in a tangle of trees, brush, and displaced boulders. The broken body of a man stripped naked by the water hung wedged in the crotch of a bent oak, his white buttocks pointed obscenely at the sky. To her left she saw where the dam had failed. Where the spillway should have been, a large crevice now gushed water. Martha stared and listened. She neither saw nor heard anyone else, and slowly she relaxed.

As she did, she felt the copious bruises and strains her body had sustained during her fall.

I am alive, and maybe I am free, she thought.

The bank below the cave entrance dropped more than fifty feet, littered with soft mud and smooth rocks, and she knew she could not get out that way without assistance. She thought she heard a far-off siren and possibly a helicopter. Neither was for her, she knew. The only people who knew she was in the woods were either dead or had returned to the compound with stories of seeing her washed away in the flood. More than likely, the sirens were for others downstream, perhaps from the college.

Martha turned and wobbled deeper into the cave, peering through the darkness. Then she remembered the flashlight in the pillowcase, which had miraculously remained in her clutches as she fell. She pulled it out and flicked on the light.

At first, she saw only a dark passageway that widened as it extended into the mountain. She edged forward, keeping a hand on the wall for balance against the slick floor. Before she could react, her feet slipped beneath her, and she slid on her backside down a short, rocky slope and into a shallow puddle. Her light flickered, threatening to plunge her into total darkness.

She gently tapped the end of the light, and it flared to life again and onto the face of a monster.

CHAPTER TWELVE

Twelve days from the beginning of Dehaluyi
502 years, four months, and nine days until failure

"None of us saw the Great Snake until it struck Wohali," one of the older warriors told my mother. They stood useless, ashamed, and terrified as my mother applied a poultice of ashes and freshly chewed plantain to my father's leg. He lay still and pale against the failing light. If not for his labored breathing, I would have thought him dead. Sehoy sat beside us and cried silently. Others from the village built fires around us so we could see and to keep dangerous spirits away.

My mother did not acknowledge them but kept to her work. She lifted the poultice to examine his ankle, now swollen to twice its normal size. When she probed the wound with a bone needle, hoping to bring out some of the venom, Father stiffened. He opened his eyes and looked at my mother with a calmness signifying either bravery or madness. He tried to sit up, but she pressed him gently back onto the deerskin mat.

The old woman, Yonah, always brash and nosy, pushed through the men and stared down at us.

"He will not live the night," she said with a cruel casualness. "You waste your time on him."

Without looking at the old woman, my mother responded: "It is my time to waste, old one. Is your life so empty that you seek joy in our pain?"

Sehoy touched Mother's arm in gentle warning. The old woman had powerful friends among the other women, and it was unwise to arouse her wrath.

Yonah turned without answering and shoved her way back through the warriors. A few of the younger ones who loved my father bumped her shoulder with theirs as she left, an indiscreet show of contempt and disdain. Knowing Yonah as I did, I suspected she took notice of those who showed her this disrespect and was already plotting a war of gossip against them and us.

"You two," my mother said to the oldest of the warriors who had brought Father to us. "Help me move him into our hut. Sehoy, go and find Sequoyah."

I held aside the skin covering to our mud-and-stick hut as they carried Father inside. When they had laid him on a pile of furs, they stood awkwardly, uncertain whether they should stay or go.

"Leave us now," Mother told them. "But for tonight, keep at least one of the young men nearby in case we have need of something else."

They both dipped their heads in acknowledgment before rushing outside. We heard low murmurs and the shuffling of feet as the crowd left, each to their own huts.

Sequoyah entered silently, took one look at Father, then left. He returned later with a basket of various herbs, the testicles of a buffalo, and the scent glands of an elk. He sat beside Mother to mix and crush some of these in a shallow clay bowl. I thought the smell of it would make me vomit. Mother nodded her appreciation and took the bowl when Sequoyah had finished.

Mother spent the night tending my father's leg while I fed the fire from twigs Sehoy had stacked against the wall. Sequoyah sang a soft song that felt as clean and gentle as a young dove. He sat in the corner, his face barely visible in the flickering light.

Once, while I fought to stay awake, I saw through the smoke the shadow of the Great Eagle. First the eagle stretched out his wing and stroked the faces of Sequoyah and Mother. He then turned toward Sehoy, stretched out his great head, and gently rubbed it across her chest. Sehoy stirred slightly in her sleep but did not awake. He did not touch or look at me. Then the giant bird leaned forward and covered Father with his wings, and immediately my mother rose up and cried out in despair.

When I saw Unetlanvhi take my father that night, I knew that the gods were real and that we could never escape them. From that day, I sought to enlist them to my cause, which was still just a whisper in my own mind.

The next morning, my aunts took Father's body to a stream, where they carefully washed him and rubbed him with scented herbs. Mother, Sehoy, and I watched from a distance. Mother rocked back and forth, her eyes dark, wet stones. Waya, the shaman, sang, danced, and waved implements over him as they worked. Waya spoke in the old language of the Abittibi, using words not known to the First People, who have no shamans of their own.

Later in the morning, the young warriors who had brought Father home wrapped him in a deerskin and carried him to the Tugaloo. Word had spread that the great Wohali had passed, and I heard the crying and wailing of voices across the valley and echoing from the face of Standalone Mountain. I kept my eyes down as I walked with Mother behind my father's body, occasionally glancing up at the forest to see people alone or in groups of three or four, watching. Some stood still as stone, while others swayed or danced in respect.

When we made it to the Tugaloo, we stopped by a mound of dirt and rock. I was told that the mound had been built by a lost tribe who had lived there before even the First People, vanquished now from all but the deepest crevices of rarely spoken memories. Across the river, hundreds of the First People lined the bank in silence. One young man caught my attention, and I had to stare. He stood facing us across the river, holding the arm of an older woman. Distance made it impossible to read much of his face, but I had the impression that he was handsome, with long, shiny hair that spilled across his shoulders. His thin frame was taut with muscle.

He moved his face in shallow circles as if trying to catch the scent of something. I could not tell what his eyes sought, only that they did not rest upon me or anyone else around him. It was a strange thing to see. I remember glancing many times at the young man across the river until my mother took note of my distraction and squeezed my arm.

My memory of the ritual is faded by time and grief. I recall standing with Mother as people sang, wailed, and danced for Unetlanvhi. I did not believe the Great Eagle was in the dance any more than I believed that the body wrapped in the skin was my father. Both had left us and watched from a great distance, perhaps atop Standalone Mountain.

Four warriors stayed with Father's body while the rest of us made our way back to camp. I do not know where they buried him. Perhaps in the mound. Perhaps in a deep ravine. Maybe even under the waters of the Tugaloo. The warriors would never tell.

The village returned to a sullen routine of hunting, gathering, building, and repairing. Families left food outside our hut, not wanting to embarrass us for our need. Days later, my father's scent had left the hut, and we began our lives again.

CHAPTER THIRTEEN

1:52 a.m., November 6, 1977
Twenty-two minutes after failure

Martha dropped her flashlight and stumbled back, fully expecting the monster to seize her and drag her to a fiery hell. When nothing happened after a few long seconds, she leaned forward and listened carefully. She heard nothing but dripping water and her own breathing. No roar of the monster, no rush of sulfur-scented breath. She crawled to the flashlight, which was sending a beam to the wall to her right, and reached down for it, keeping her eyes up and straining against the darkness. When the light was secure in her hands, she gradually raised it to point at the frightening apparition.

The monster sat on a stone seat. The seat itself rested upon a slate platform rising three feet from the cave's floor. Martha fought to steady the wavering light in her hands as she edged closer. She knew she was looking at a skeleton, but the proportions were sufficiently off to question whether it was human. The empty eye sockets staring back at her were not at the same level, as if the skull had been shattered and reassembled by an incompetent mortician. A strip of metal, now green with corrosion, wrapped around the skull and had drooped over time to reveal nasal slits, also deformed.

She dared to peer beneath the mask and saw that while most of the creature's teeth remained, the upper teeth sat far back under the skull, and the lower jaw protruded a finger's breadth forward. She could also confirm that a gap ran from the nasal slits and divided the upper jaw like the mouth parts of a giant grasshopper. Martha's hand drifted to her own face, and she wondered if this was how she would also appear in death.

Whoever this person was, their face in life would have been as frightening as it was in death. This strange detail inspired in her a sense of kinship to the skeleton. She was certain that these were the remains of a woman who, like her, had led a life of sorrow. The bones seemed to radiate sadness, for what else could have drawn the woman to this cave and this end?

In an instinctive show of respect, Martha dropped the light from the long-dead woman's face, and the beam fell across the torso. Dusty bands wrapped around it, binding it to the seat's back and explaining how the skeleton remained upright. Martha hesitantly touched the cold bands, brushed the dust away, and saw the glint of tarnished green metal. She rubbed more dust away to reveal a shiny band no thicker than a leather belt and about two inches wide.

Suddenly, the skeleton shifted forward, almost touching Martha's face, and she screamed and jumped away.

When she had collected herself, the skeleton was still in place but was now leaning outward, its head tilted to one side as if to question Martha's intent. Martha resolved not to disturb it again.

She shined her light around the rest of the cave and saw flint tools—knives, hand axes, hatchet heads, and arrowheads. Partial skeletons of small animals littered the floor around the tools. Behind the skeleton's throne, for that was how Martha found herself thinking of it, the cave widened into a chamber as big as a basketball court, with a ceiling at least twenty feet high. The walls were smooth and mostly flattened and adorned with symbols and images in careful rows and columns.

More flint implements lay in stacks against the wall or meticulously arrayed in patterns of circles and starbursts. Other than the animals, Martha saw no additional skeletons, and she relaxed a bit.

"Hello," she called softly—and heard only her own voice.

Convinced she was alone, Martha moved along the chamber wall, careful not to touch the markings or disturb the objects. She stepped around a small rockfall from the far wall and there found a narrow passage from which she felt a faint draft of air. She turned off the flashlight, and a weak light filtered from the tunnel beyond.

Martha rested against the wall near the passageway. The slight movement of air reassured her, and she slid down to a seated position and again wrapped herself in the thin blanket. Within seconds, her head dropped, and she drifted once more into a fitful sleep.

The pale light from the passage was brighter when she awoke. Hungry and thirsty, Martha ate soggy bread and a sausage from her bag, then quenched her thirst with the water trickling down the rock wall. This time she slept the deep sleep of one who has been through hell and back, and in her dreams, she found the first promise of healing.

When Martha next opened her eyes, she felt refreshed and alert. The stone wall was unexpectedly warm and comfortable. She ate a little more before returning to the narrow cave entrance to peer outside. The wail of sirens and engine noises resounded down the gorge. She briefly wondered if she was a fool not to call for help but assured herself that rescue would not come from that direction even if she tried. Worse, her pursuers might be up there, searching for their own survivors. This she could not risk, at least not in daylight.

Martha relieved herself in a corner just inside the entrance, out of sight of the throne, then returned to the larger chamber. She sat to think and plan. Doubt flitted across her mind as she recalled her escape. *Had the risks been worth it?* Then she saw her sister's face.

She again lay down on the strangely warm rock, wishing she could stay there forever. Somewhere between wakefulness and sleep, the torturous path that had led her to this moment and her desperate flight filled her thoughts.

CHAPTER FOURTEEN

June 27, 1962

Fourteen years, four months, and nine days before failure

Joanne Morris had always been a seeker of that which others might have missed. Martha, her oldest child, had a cleft palate, a deformity Joanne was convinced was the result of a dietary deficiency. As a consequence, instead of milk, Joanne fed her children a concoction of brewer's yeast, crushed sesame seeds and herbs, and whatever had been most recently touted in *Prevention* magazine. Secretly, the children and relatives called it "tiger's milk." When the children did not grow as Joanne thought they should, she fed them even more. She distrusted doctors and hospitals, believing them to be factories of death designed to make money and weed out the undesirables. Her husband, Wayne, went along as much as possible.

After Martha, Joanne gave birth to four boys. One died in childbirth, and another of cancer when he was five. Martha was too young to remember much of what happened, but her father later told her about how the tumor silently grew in her brother's abdomen and he cried in pain all the time. Meanwhile, Joanne continued to study natural cures and ointments and used them all.

In the midst of this turmoil and sadness, she gave birth to Martha's sister, Eve. She immediately turned the beautiful girl over to Wayne's mother and rushed back to her ill son.

Their mother never lost a beat in trying to heal him. She prayed fervently, often with those from their church, that God would heal him in a way that no one could doubt was a miracle and that God would take all the glory.

A stranger came to one of these prayer sessions and convinced their mother that the mass in the child's abdomen was a devil that could be driven out by a shouting session. She and three other women of the church spent hours screaming at the child and the demon in him, and the boy shrieked back. Wayne pleaded with Joanne to take the child to the doctor, and she refused. When in desperation he finally took the screaming child to the local emergency room, the doctors told him that while this sort of tumor usually responded to chemotherapy and radiation, it was too late to save him. They would treat if he wanted, but it was likely that the child would die soon. Wayne urged them to try.

They put in lines and filled the child with chemicals. Martha's mother came to the hospital and grumbled and barked at the staff, all the while casting critical looks at her husband. For the first few weeks, the therapy appeared to be working. The tumor shrank, and the child began to eat again. Then, on the day he was to start radiation, his heart fell into an abnormal rhythm. He was surrounded by doctors and nurses when his heart stopped completely. They pumped his chest and fed more drugs into his veins in a futile effort to revive him.

Joanne and Wayne buried their son in the graveyard beside the church in a deluge worthy of Noah. An older woman, who the year earlier had joined the local fundamental church led by Dinah and Paul Whiten, stood by the grieving couple. As they prepared to leave, the woman stepped in front of them and frowned at Martha's father.

"If you had prayed in real faith, your son would not have died," she said to him. "This is your fault."

She then turned and disappeared into the rain, leaving the grieving couple in shock.

The next week, Martha's mother went to her first assembly of the Fellowship of Faith. The congregation met in a renovated barn near the base of Currahee Mountain, where Paul Whiten preached fiery sermons about the dangers of living in a world steeped in sin—a world where demons thrived and drove people to drugs, alcohol, and illicit sex. He preached love of the brethren, submission to church authority, and avoidance of any influences that allowed devils into their homes. And he taught that faith, not medicine, cured people and that all sickness and death were the result of sin. "Kill the sin, drive out the devils, and the perfect body that God Himself gave you will heal."

Martha's mother soaked it all in. She joined the church and changed her name from Joanne to Ruth, for only biblical names were acceptable to the church.

Wayne balked. The few times he went to the church, he felt out of place and uneasy. Paul Whiten's wife, Dinah, appeared to take a special interest in him, sitting with him in church, walking out with him, touching his arm during particularly intense portions of the services. Wayne flinched each time she laid a hand on him and tried to slip out of the building without having to talk to her. But Ruth—for she insisted that everyone call her by her new name—held him back and forced him to endure the conversations and fondling.

Martha's brothers grew to love the church. They worked in the church-owned fields, played football and basketball with the other boys, and fed their lusts by imagining what would happen when they turned eighteen.

Paul and Dinah Whiten visited Brazil several times a year, claiming to have started sister churches in the poorest areas of the country and baptized hundreds into the true faith and away from Catholicism. The congregation greeted these reports with applause and cheers. In establishing the links between the congregations, the Whitens also brought back with them young and seemingly eager brides-to-be, all striking beauties with smooth skin and alluring eyes.

No one married without the consent and approval of the Whitens, and they encouraged the congregation to marry young.

"God set the ages that girls could bear children," Dinah would say to the congregation. "Who are we to delay what He has ordained? To do so goes against the clear will of God and puts a temptation before our children that many of them will not resist."

When a boy turned eighteen, Dinah began looking for a suitable spouse, preferably from within the congregation. If none could be found, she turned to the Brazilian beauties. The boys never complained, though many of the wives could not speak English, and the boys never learned to speak Portuguese.

Martha's brothers talked of little else. They wanted to work in the fields or other church businesses and bring home one of the many girls Dinah paraded around the compound.

Gradually, Paul's sermons began to include more and more details concerning how the congregation should live and manage their personal finances and even their sex lives. Dinah mostly sat in the high-back chairs to Paul's side and enthusiastically nodded along with her husband's admonishments. On occasion, she took the podium herself. The husband-and-wife team told their congregation that they all should sell their homes and possessions, give them to the church, then live together as a single large family, just like the early church of Jerusalem. Their pastors could protect them, drive out the devils that plagued them, and shield them from the evils of the modern world.

One by one, families did just that. Soon they replaced the barn with a large, modern sanctuary. Communal homes cropped up, inhabited by two or more families and all assigned by Dinah and Paul Whiten. Plans were made for a school and farming businesses, all controlled by the Whitens.

One day in early spring, six months after their son died, Wayne and Ruth strolled out of the church. Ruth had linked her arm in

Wayne's in a rare show of public affection. She walked slowly, gently pulling Wayne to her.

"I have something to tell you," she whispered.

He stopped to look at her, tilting his head.

She smiled, another rare thing. Wayne briefly saw the flirty, vivacious mountain girl he had fallen in love with those many years ago. It made doing what he knew he had to do even harder.

"I am pregnant," Ruth said, smiling even more broadly. "Dinah said it would happen, and it did. Isn't this the most wonderful blessing?"

She gazed up at Wayne, trying to read his face. He smiled back at her, and she relaxed.

"We can sell our house and move to the compound," she continued. "Our child will be strong and pure, untainted by the world."

She took his arm, and they continued toward the car. She sensed Wayne was troubled, but he was never good at expressing himself to her. He could talk of cars, crops, and even politics, but when it came to his own feelings, he held back. She would need to coax his thoughts from him.

As Ruth leaned into Wayne's side, she felt him tense. She stopped at the car as other worshippers wove around them to their own vehicles. Facing Wayne with her back to the car, Ruth saw Dinah Whiten watching from the steps of the new sanctuary.

"We will be moving to the compound, won't we, Wayne?" she asked softly.

Wayne shuffled his feet and looked down.

"Won't we?"

"Ruth," he said, "no. We have to leave this place and never return. Listen to me, my love, God is not here. These people are, I don't know, crazy, evil, deluded—I could not tell you. But I can say this for sure: I will never set foot inside this compound again. We are leaving."

His words shocked Ruth. For a moment, she could not speak. She reached up to touch her husband's face but then looked past him to Dinah. In that moment, she made her decision.

CHAPTER FIFTEEN

Month and day unknown
502 years until failure

Among some people, the only sin that cannot be forgiven by either gods or men is to be born a woman. That was not so among the Abittibi.

The people honored Mother almost as if she were the one who had fought Father's battles and won his many prizes and tributes. They brought us food, shared their kills with us, and left us hides to ward off the cold. We knew that as Father's memory faded from the Abittibi, so would the tributes. One day, they would stop, and we would be on our own.

We did not say so openly, but we all knew that our hope lay in Sehoy. If she married well, to a man like Chitto, who respected our family and would protect and provide for us as well as for his wife, we could survive. If not, we might as well follow Father into the Land of Shadows. All of this was made clear when the elders selected our new chief.

My mother aged a lifetime in the days after my father died. She rarely spoke, and I had to prompt her to eat or wash. Most days she sat by the river and chanted wordless songs that sounded as sad as she looked.

The elders elected Dustau to be the new chief, and he immediately declared my mother his third wife. Such was not our custom, but he proclaimed it so in a loud, croaking voice much like that of his namesake frog. Mother did not respond to his words or the gentle way he led her to his hut that day. When she did not come out for two days, I retrieved her and told everyone that she would stay in our hut forever. No one spoke against me, but Dustau frowned at my impudence. On our first night back in our hut alone, he came to the door and demanded she return to him. I ran him off under a rain of blows from my father's spear shaft. After that, he stayed away, but I knew he would not suffer the indignity without retribution.

Life returned to a rhythm of eating, cleaning, gathering, and tending the fires. Mother slowly regained a bit of herself and assisted me in the forest. I was neither happy nor sad during this time. I was just alive, though I relished Sehoy and Chitto's continued courtship as if it were my own.

Curiously, Sequoyah began collecting chunks of soft metal from nearby streams. He used white stones fastened to thick handles to break the rocks containing the metal, then chipped it out into piles. These he put inside small clay pots, which he sealed at the top. He put the pots into a large charcoal fire and used his blowgun to add heat. Sometimes I would help blow on the fire, never talking so as not to interrupt his deep thinking.

It took many trials, but when he finished, he had crafted the metal into the shape of small river stones. Then he would beat it into thin sheets and bands. After he worked the metal, it shone in the sunlight with the color of the rising sun. When left in the rain for a few moons, the metal became dull green. Occasionally, Sequoyah would vigorously rub the sheets of greenish metal with a badger pelt, and for a time it would shine again.

We at first thought he was trying to make weapons from the strange material, but we observed that it was much softer than flint or other stones and would easily bend. People watched him from a distance, and we worried that he was again delving into the dark secrets of the mountains.

I began to accompany him to the river to search for the rocks containing this metal.

"This is too soft to use for anything except trinkets," he said when I brought him yellow metal pieces I had found. "Here is what we need."

He showed me his basket. Inside lay a few handfuls of reddish pebbles. The bits of yellow metal I had brought to him were beautiful, but Sequoyah knew better about such things, so I threw them back into the stream.

Once, Mother came with us. As we approached the Tugaloo, she sat on a mossy log and motioned me to sit with her.

"The man from across the river," Mother said as we sat watching Sequoyah search the shallow waters, "do you know him?"

Her question surprised me as she had so rarely spoken since Father's death.

"Who?" I replied.

"Do not play the fool with me, Atsila," she responded. "The man you stared at while we sang tributes to your dead father. Do you know him?"

I shook my head.

"I know of him," Mother continued. I tried to hide my interest. "His name is Onacona, the nephew of Kanuna, a warrior of great renown. The boy's father died last year of a coughing disease, and his mother now cares for him."

"How old is he?" I asked.

"Why? Does he interest you?" Mother replied. She turned from me and attended to unfinished leatherwork she had carried with her.

"He seems old to be cared for by his mother," I replied.

"Not so old for what God has made him," Mother responded. "Onacona was born blind."

From that day forth, each time I approached the Tugaloo, I would look for Onacona. Soon, this habit would teach me gratitude.

UNDER THE PROTECTION of the First People, our tribe fought few battles in my youth. Most of these were symbolic efforts, more like dances than fighting, where men struck each other with decorative rods or lances and the winners were declared based on style and speed, not blood. To the west, however, lived a few small bands that had broken away from the First People and lived on the harsh slopes of the mountains. These did not farm but instead hunted and gathered what they could. Tales came to us of strange religions and holy men who mutilated themselves and spoke to demons.

In the dead of winter or during a summer dearth, these tribes sent men to raid the First People and the Abittibi. On rare occasions, these men captured one of ours. Sometimes our warriors could track them down and free our people before they disappeared into the impenetrable parts of the mountains. On most occasions, however, we never saw them again except as bodies charred by fire for these tribes' amusement. As much as hunger, my family feared such an attack, for there would be no kinsmen to track us down and bring us home. For this reason, we always foraged to the east, along the banks of the Tugaloo.

One bright spring day, I walked all the way to the river to gather blueberries and collect roots from a site I had kept secret from the other women. While I worked, I caught strains of song from across the river. It was a man's voice, but it sounded as if it came from the gods themselves.

I peeked through the brush and spotted Onacona standing alone by the water. He was naked and washing himself as he sang. He rubbed sand across his body, dipping into the cold, clear water occasionally, all the while making music more beautiful than I thought possible. Long, sleek hair hung across his back, bound together by leather thongs. He was also himself as beautiful as the gods, and watching him, I experienced a warmth in my chest and a desire I had never known.

The river was shallow and quiet in this place, and I carefully placed my basket on the ground and stole forward to listen. As I did, a twig cracked beneath my heel. His singing ceased, and I froze. I dared to look up again at Onacona. He had stopped washing himself and stood in the sun, ankle-deep in the water.

He turned his head this way and that, then called out, "You can speak to me, if you wish. I know you are across the river."

I did not answer.

"We are alone," he said. "There is no need to fear."

After a time, I replied, "I am not afraid."

He turned his beautiful face to me. Long lashes shaded blank eyes.

"Good," he said at length. "Should I be afraid?" The smile on his face and the lilt of his voice spoke of good humor and a suppressed laugh.

"You mock me," I replied sullenly.

"I do not," he replied. "What is your name?"

I stepped to the edge of the water. "I am Atsila," I replied. "You are Onacona."

"Ah, so I am famous on that side of the river?"

He reached for his leather leggings and tunic as he spoke. Part of me wished he would stay as he was, and I was ashamed of the thought.

"Would you sit with me, Atsila? I would like company while I dry."

To this day, I do not know what possessed me to cross the river, but before I thought better of it, I had waded across and found myself sitting beside Onacona on a green log.

"How is it that you can find your way to the river alone?" I asked.

He chuckled. "It is not hard. I count the steps and feel the trees that are familiar to me. I have done so since I could walk. I can also tell when it is dark and light, and the shadows help me."

I nodded, then felt stupid for the gesture.

"How is it that you came to the river today?" he asked. "Is it to pick from the secret spot on that side?"

I gave forth a giggling, childish laugh and immediately felt foolish for it.

We spent most of the afternoon talking of our lives, our families, and how we felt about the gods who had made us as we were. As I prepared to leave, he stretched his hand to my face, and for the first time, I felt a man's skin against mine. The fingers that traced lines across my nose and mouth were gentle and warm. I wanted that touch to last forever.

"You are not like other women," he said.

I drew back from him.

"I know," I said sharply. "You need not tell me I am ugly."

"No," he said with a laugh. "You misunderstand me. The soul I just touched was beautiful beyond words. If others claim you are ugly, they must be jealous."

I searched his face for guile and found none. On impulse, I leaned forward and kissed him. As my deformed face pressed against his, for a brief moment I felt as beautiful as this blind man claimed me to be.

CHAPTER SIXTEEN

Month and day unknown
501 years until failure

I knew joy. I knew the reason young men and women gaze at one another like fools. For the first time in my life, I felt truly loved and at peace with most of my world. Against all hope, I felt beautiful.

Onacona and I met at the secret spot on the river on most days. I call it a secret spot, but enough people knew of the pawpaw and berry patches that grew there that we had to be careful not to be seen. I am not sure why I wanted our love—for that is what it was—to be hidden from our tribe. Perhaps I knew that someday my people would desecrate what I had found.

On nights when the moon was hidden and clouds covered the stars, Onacona would come to me. In such darkness, he was as good or better than any warrior. He could slip into the camp within steps of the guards and find me by the scent of the plants I rubbed on my clothes while making no more sound than a mouse blinking. These were the best of times as we lay on the grass in each other's arms and listened to the night, thrilled by the excitement of our secret love. Always, well before dawn, Onacona would steal away across the Tugaloo to his own hut.

Late one evening after my mother had gone to sleep, I confided in

Sehoy. We giggled as normal girls would and exchanged advice on love in ways we had not done since Father died. Sehoy told me little secrets of her times with Chitto, and we laughed into the night.

The next morning, we awoke to hear Mother arguing outside the hut.

"I can be with you, Dustau," she said angrily. "But she is for another."

"She is for whoever I say." It was the voice of the chief. "I have two wives and still no children. Remember that I had offered to take you before and you refused. Now I will not take a barren old woman like you."

Sehoy and I went out and stood beside Mother as others gathered around. To the side, I saw the old woman, Yonah, showing her toothless grin, and I knew she had put the idea into Dustau's mind.

"Does not the chief give women to be married?" asked Dustau.

A general murmur of agreement rose from the crowd. Dustau turned to face them.

"Do the young know what is best for the tribe, best for their own families?" he bellowed. "I say no. We mate for the good of the tribe, not silly sentiments."

There were more sounds of validation, the loudest from Yonah.

"Since when does the chief select for himself against the wishes of a girl's family?" Mother demanded.

A few women nodded.

"What family?" Dustau shouted back. "I see no family. I see only two foolish girls and an old widow living on gifts of pity."

Mother spat at him. Dustau wiped his face with the back of his hand. Without warning, he slapped Mother hard on the face, and she staggered back. He raised his hand again but hesitated when I picked up a rock the size of my fist and stepped between them. Sehoy moved beside me. From the back of the crowd, Chitto came to stand with us as well. He reached a hand to his love, Sehoy, and they stood as one. Dustau laughed at me; then a hateful scowl stole across his face.

I looked to my left and saw Sequoyah standing at the edge of the crowd. He held a club carved from an oak tree that had been struck by lightning. He believed wood from such a tree carried power. The one time I saw him wield the club in earnest had convinced me he was right.

"A chief has another authority," Dustau growled. "I have the power to banish."

Several of the senior warriors stepped beside him, all armed with clubs of their own.

Pointing at me, he said, "I should have banished this abomination long ago. Out of kindness, I did not. I should have sent her obstinate mother with her, but out of kindness, I did not. You have until tomorrow morning to decide. If Sehoy comes to me willingly, I will let you stay. If she does not, you will all leave. You will take your sorcerer with you," he said, gesturing toward Sequoyah.

Dustau and his warriors left, and gradually the crowd returned to their huts to begin their morning tasks.

Later I went to the Tugaloo and met with Onacona. The story enraged him.

"A chief of the First People would not behave such," he said.

After a moment, he added, "There will be no moon tonight, and I feel the air is dense with water. I think even the stars will be shrouded in clouds."

I knew what he was saying, and the words fell heavily upon my heart. We sat for a long while, and gradually, from the gods, from devils, or from the dark places of our own minds, a plan took shape.

CHAPTER SEVENTEEN

June 12, 1972

Five years and 146 days before failure

Ruth moved herself and her children into the compound and never spoke of Wayne to anyone but God. She miscarried a few weeks later. For the first six months of the children's life without a father, Eve cried herself to sleep each night. As time passed, she spoke less and less of Wayne and then only in whispers to Martha in the dead of night. The boys quickly fell into a routine of school, work, and playground sports. Eventually, Ruth informed them that Wayne had passed away.

Ruth set up a seamstress business in the basement of the house they shared with another family, insisting that Martha work with her. After school, Martha came straight home and descended the creaky steps to the basement where Ruth worked alone. Ruth prayed aloud while driving needles and thread through dresses crafted from designs approved by Dinah Whiten herself. In her prayers, Ruth unleashed a tirade of complaints against neighbors and family, asking that God forgive them for their sinful and selfish ways. Most of all, she prayed that God would forgive Wayne for his offenses, prayed that he would return to his family, and prayed that the devils would leave him. Martha knew the prayers were admonitions voiced for her benefit and not supplications to God.

Ruth rarely left the compound. Dinah Whiten provided them with food and other items. She took the clothes Ruth and Martha made and sold them at the church store or gave them to other church members. Dinah never let anyone in the compound have more than a few dollars at a time, fearing that some would use the cash to buy radios or televisions. "Satan's pathway into our homes," she declared. Dinah, of course, had a television and radio in her home because she was strong enough in her faith to resist such temptations.

The only other relative Martha saw was Ruth's sister, who was married to a theology teacher at Toccoa Falls Bible College. These visits too were often tense and always chaperoned by another church member.

Eve grew straight and tall and more beautiful with each passing month. She had porcelain skin and blond hair that hung in perfect ringlets around her face, even when she played and ran. With her striking blue eyes, she could have stepped from the pages of a fairy tale.

Life was tolerable for the broken family, if not grim. On the surface, everyone seemed loving, and no one complained in the open.

Five years after Ruth moved with her children into the compound, Dinah Whiley discovered the innate sin in holidays, and from that day forward, families were not allowed to celebrate birthdays or holidays of any type. No one swore allegiance to the flag, no one enlisted in the military, and no one took government jobs requiring background checks. Martha and Eve would play quietly on the steps of their shared home as Thanksgiving came and went. Neither of them missed it much. They did not like the dry turkey their mother made and the many relatives who pinched their cheeks and smelled of talcum and tobacco. But as Christmas neared in the second year after the prohibition, Eve broke ranks.

In the middle of a sermon by Dinah Whiten, for Paul was seen less and less, Dinah made a particularly pointed statement about the evils of Christmas and other holidays. She had begun the sermon by saying that anyone who thought differently should speak up and say so—an invitation she often made that was never taken. Unfortunately, on this Sunday, Eve took her seriously.

From the third row, she stood. Dinah stopped talking, and the entire congregation turned to stare. Eve lowered her eyes and started to sit again but then lifted her eyes to stare back at Dinah. She threw back her shoulders, took a deep breath, and broke the cardinal rule of the Fellowship of Faith. She disagreed with Dinah Whiten.

"I do not think it is wrong to celebrate the birth of Jesus, Pastor Dinah. I miss it," she said.

If the congregation had not fallen into a grave-like stillness, they might not have heard her small voice. After a moment of stunned silence, and to Ruth's horror, she continued.

"I like getting presents. I like giving them, too," she said. "I miss the tree, the singing, dressing up in red and green. I miss—"

"You evil child!" Dinah shouted at her.

Eve froze.

"Sit!" Dinah thundered.

Eve dropped to her seat and remained quiet for the rest of the strained service. When the sermon came to a crescendo, the people began "the blast." Nearly five hundred men, women, and children began to shout prayers and praises as loud as they could. This went on for several minutes until Dinah Whiten raised her hand. Silence fell across the congregation like a shroud. Dinah then looked down at Eve and screamed, "Come out of her, you devil!"

Others took up the call, and within seconds, hundreds of voices were pounding Eve with their voices. She began to weep. Soon, she crumpled to the floor as sobs racked her small frame. Martha stood silent with her hands over her ears and watched as her mother joined the congregation to scream at her own daughter.

Eventually Dinah raised her hand, and the congregation fell silent except for the sounds of Eve's crying. Dinah spoke for a short time more, then led them all in a hymn of praise.

When they were done, people filed out, and all of them avoided

Ruth's family. An usher stopped them at the entrance.

"Come with me," he said brusquely.

They followed the man to a door beside the pulpit. After they entered, the man shut the door behind them and led them down a long hallway. None of them had ever been in this part of the building. They proceeded down a set of stairs and another hallway. There were no pictures on the cinder block walls, no windows into the rooms, and only faint lighting from fluorescent fixtures.

The man unlocked and opened a final door.

"Come in here and wait for Pastor Dinah," he said.

Ruth hesitated.

"Send the boys home," she said to the man.

He nodded, and the boys bolted down the hallway. Ruth led Martha and Eve into the room.

Minutes later, three women and four men filed in and surrounded Eve. Martha and Ruth were instructed to sit in the corner and stay out of the way. After a brief prayer, all seven began to shout at Eve.

"Come out, devils!"

"Get out of her, Satan!"

Some screeched or hooted. Occasionally, they would cast accusing looks at Martha. Once, when Martha started to rise, one of them turned and screamed at her to keep her seat.

The blasting went on for hours until Eve collapsed into a trembling heap and began to confess every sin she knew of, whether she had committed it or not. Dinah Whiten finally called a halt.

The pastor leaned over, gently stroked Eve's cheek, and whispered something to her that neither Martha nor Ruth could hear. Dinah smiled at Ruth, then nodded at the others who had assisted in the blasting. They all swiftly exited, leaving Ruth and Martha to carry Eve home.

CHAPTER EIGHTEEN

Month and date unknown
501 years until failure

Onacona came in the blackest part of the night, as I knew he would. Silent as a shadow. Even the dogs did not alert to his presence. He came first to me. I knew my mother and Sehoy could hear us whisper outside the hut. I did not care. After a few moments, Onacona slipped away, the darkness swallowing even the scent of him.

I sat outside the door to our hut and sang to Unetlanvhi. I did not have the voice of Sehoy, but on this night, I did not care. My song would catch the ear of any waking soul in our village, keep them turned toward me and not to the whisper of death descending upon them. I sang praises to my father and mother, thanking Unetlanvhi that I was born to such a family. I sang songs in languages taught to me by Sequoyah—dark songs of evil things and conjurers. I knew that Dustau would hear me and be displeased. I knew he would want to ban all such words.

As I sang, I listened carefully. Time passed, and except for my song, the world was silent and black as the deepest cave. I could not see my own hands or feet. Once, I thought I heard a grunt from far across the camp, but then there was silence. At last, the slightest hint of dawn seeped into the eastern sky, and I fell into an exhausted sleep.

Sehoy shook me awake as gray dawn streamed into the camp. A few guards moved near the forest's edge, barely visible.

"I must go to Dustau," Sehoy said. "He has the right. You and Mother cannot die for me."

I had been sure that Sehoy would sacrifice herself so.

I sat up and pulled her to me. Her soft hair fell against my cheek, and we embraced for a long while. I knew she was stifling a cry of anguish, and I wanted to tell her the truth, but I needed her to believe the lie I would plant in the minds of the Abittibi.

We were still locked in our embrace when a cry went up across the camp.

Other families stumbled out of their huts, seeking the source of the alarm. Soon more began to shout and cry. In some of the voices, I made out my name.

A crowd gathered at the hut of Dustau. Elders clustered together in animated conversation. Waya, the senior-most shaman, joined them, easily discernible by the blue dye he applied to his skin and hair. The sun had risen over the hills before they fell silent. Mother stood with Sehoy and me as we watched them approach our family's hut.

Waya strode forward. It satisfied me to see a hint of fear in his eyes. I looked past him. The warrior and elders behind him kept their distance, and I sensed from their posture and countenances that they too feared something unseen and unspoken.

"Dustau is dead," Waya said. "We heard you singing in the night."

His voice was calm and steady. He could have been describing the rain.

I stood rigid. This moment would determine my fate, the fate of my mother and sister, and, indeed, of all the Abittibi. I could not show even the most subtle flicker of satisfaction. In this moment, my ugliness was my helper, for no one would study my face.

Waya waited for a response I would not give.

"Dustau had no marks on his body, no wounds, no signs of how he died," Waya continued. "We believe it was a ghost killing or one of the water cannibals."

Again, I refused to answer the question he dared not ask.

"Why did you come to tell us this?" Mother asked. I prayed that she would remain silent, knowing she would not.

Waya ignored her and stared at me. Courage built in his face.

"Did you call for them to do your bidding in the night?" Waya asked.

I had prepared for this moment. I stepped within an arm's length of the shaman. He did not show it, but I smelled his nervousness.

"I did no such thing," I said softly. Waya's eyes struggled to look at my ugliness, and any compassion fled in that moment. "Perhaps the water cannibals were displeased by his cruelty, angry over the way he treats us. Who can say? But I did not call them."

Pushing his revulsion aside, Waya studied my face. I stared back with the practiced indifference born of a lifetime of ridicule. Neither of us blinked. I spoke again to Waya, this time in a whisper that none but the two of us could hear.

"There are wicked things in this world, Waya," I said. "Old things branded by ancient evil. These walk in the shape of men. I am not such a one."

I took a flake of sharp stone from the ground and sliced it into my hand. Blood dripped.

"These things would not bleed so," I continued. "You know this."

He watched the blood splatter the grass between us.

"Some are worse than others," Waya replied. "They walk freely in the world of men and do terrible things. But they do not bleed."

I heard someone wheezing and laboring to breathe as they stomped in our direction. Even now, as death crept upon her, the old woman Yonah tried to croak her accusation against me and Mother, her words barely discernible. With each step, she slowed, the drool of a mad animal trailing from her wrinkled and sagging face. The people parted for her.

I was also prepared for this.

"Old woman, you have stirred enough trouble among the Abittibi," I said, pointing my finger at her. "This also is not of my doing," I said, turning back to Waya. "But this woman is a curse on our people."

Yonah stopped and leaned down with her hands on her knees, gasping for air.

"I have not laid a hand on Yonah the hag," I said, now circling her. "You heard me singing all night long and know I did not leave my family fire. But I will accept the justice of the gods for her."

Yonah tried to stand straight but could not. Anger, then fear, then resignation flashed across her face.

"If the gods judge me in the wrong, I will suffer. If not, you will die now!" I shouted.

The old woman tried again to stand straight but instead fell forward. She twitched a few times in the grass, let out one last, long breath, and released her bowels.

I was the only one who knew what was hidden in the small pouch that Sequoyah, now lingering on the edges of the crowd, had tucked into his pants.

The shaman watched all of this in silence. No one made a sound as a few warriors quietly surrounded us with their clubs and spears at the ready. I did not move, did not breathe. After a moment, the shaman spoke.

"Should we kill you and your family?" he asked.

I gathered my courage. "You could try," I replied.

A gasp swept through the people, and even Sehoy turned to me as if I were a stranger.

Just then, a rain crow called from behind me. Waya raised his eyes and followed its looping flight across our camp. It landed on the trunk of a dead sweetgum tree and began to pound its beak into the wood, its great red head shaking in time with the beats of its work. The shaman looked from me to the great bird, then back to me.

"The things we all just saw with our own eyes, did you do them with the power of demons or of gods?" the shaman asked. He spoke loudly so everyone could hear.

"Is there a difference?" I asked just as loudly.

This did not please some of the warriors, and they stepped closer. The shaman gestured, and they stopped their advance. He stood in silence, no hint of his thoughts visible on his painted face. Finally, he spoke and declared our fate.

"This family, the family of Wohali, has always been respected among the Abittibi," he said, facing the crowd. "They have revered the gods, or at least one god," he said, nodding slightly at Mother. "This family we will respect again."

He turned and waved his blue hands over the people as he spoke.

"Dustau was a great warrior, and we will mourn him," he continued. "But he would not have been a great chief. Power without justice is tyranny. To my mind, today we saw the hands of the gods. Is there any among you who disagree?"

None of the Abittibi spoke, but Sequoyah began to sing in a strange tongue. He had laid his war club aside and now held in his hands a mask of thin, polished metal that glowed in the morning light. The face on the mask reminded me dimly of my sister.

Sequoyah danced over to me, then stopped to place the mask over my face. He pulled my hair through the thin leather band that held it in place.

I turned toward the shaman, and for once, he stared back at me with something that was not revulsion.

CHAPTER NINETEEN

1:14 p.m., November 6, 1977
Eleven hours, forty-four minutes after failure

Light from the tunnel had begun to dim when Martha awoke and returned to the throne for one last look at the skeleton. In her dreams, she had felt the murmurings of something familiar. She rounded the pedestal and stood gazing up at the masked skull with the deformed upper jaw. Touching her own face, she realized that in the rush of water, she had lost something so much a part of her that she rarely thought of it.

"The child was born like this because of sin," Dinah Whiten had declared the first time she saw Martha. "The blade of Satan has creased her face."

Martha's mother stifled a sob, believing with all her heart that Dinah spoke the truth. And her conviction grew over the years. It explained so much: Martha's deformity, Wayne's obstinance, their separation.

When Martha turned seven, Ruth asked Dinah to visit her for "counseling." Some of the women had spoken about having Martha's cleft surgically repaired. None of them believed that prayer could heal such a defect. Ruth, of course, would not think of doing such a thing without Dinah's approval.

"Do you think the blade of a surgeon could fix a sin of this magnitude?" Dinah asked.

Ruth searched her mind for the answer Dinah sought.

"Of course not," Dinah continued. "Better to leave this sort of healing to the other side of the grave."

"People stare," Ruth said.

Even at her age, Martha knew what her mother was saying and the unexpressed question it implied. If her face was beyond repair, should she be locked inside, never to see light again? That was what they were debating.

Dinah seemed to be thinking. Her eye strayed to a roll of black netting on Ruth's sewing table, and she raised her eyebrows.

"You are a gifted seamstress," Dinah said. "I trust you can come up with a solution that allows this poor child to join the congregation while sparing us the sight of her."

She picked up the roll of netting, and they understood.

The next Sunday, Martha draped the veil over her face as directed and joined her mother and siblings on the long walk to church. She held her mother's hand on one side and Eve's on the other. People stared, but beneath the veil, Martha felt safe, hidden, and strangely comforted.

From that day forward, she never went outside without the veil. Soon people stopped staring or commenting, and Martha moved freely about the compound. Only at night when she and Eve crawled into their shared bed did she remove the veil, carefully folding it on the nightstand at her side. On those nights, she and Eve would cling to one another as their dreams molded them into whatever their young minds chose.

Martha now felt a jolt of panic when she realized that she had lost her veil in her escape. Had she been wearing it during her flight through the woods? She could not recall. She rummaged through the cloth bag. Nothing.

She tried to reassure herself. *This is a new beginning, a new birth. The world outside of the compound will see me as I am, as God made me.*

Placing a soft kiss on her fingers, Martha gently touched the masked face. Then she turned and went to the narrow tunnel.

A cool breeze caressed her. The tunnel was longer and narrower than she had hoped. Martha had to stoop low, almost crouch, as she moved toward the light. In one spot, rubble was piled nearly to the ceiling, and she clawed at it to dig a way through. Dust from her work choked her and darkened the little light available, and for a second, she feared she could not push past the stones. She envisioned herself dead and desiccated, collapsed beside the enthroned skeleton. She fought the panic and forced herself to breathe slowly and think of anything but the closeness of the space. After a few minutes, her coughing subsided, and she wiggled through. Martha rested on the stone floor as the dust cleared, and she again spotted that feeble light. She crawled to it. Soon, she could stand.

Within two dozen steps, she glimpsed a patch of lead-colored sky through the narrowest section yet. She barely squeezed through, and then, with a rush of elation, she found herself outside, peering over a mossy, car-sized boulder. In the distance and to her right came the constant roar of Toccoa Falls. From her many hikes through the forests with her brothers, she knew she was near the college. She also heard heavy equipment moving, scraping, and stuttering. She glanced at the sky, then at the path forward.

Pushing through brush, Martha started down the hill. She eventually came to a trail that wound across a steep slope, but the trail ended abruptly at a raw cut in the earth where the flood had created a new gorge. The trail continued just a few feet from where she stood.

She was considering whether to risk climbing across the cut or working her way along the slope when she heard a noise behind her. She started to turn, but a strong arm looped around her neck and yanked her backward.

"Family is forever, Martha," the man said, his voice hoarse.

Martha twisted and squirmed, but he held her fast.

"We lost four men looking for you," he hissed. "Two of them were my brothers."

Martha managed to twist her head within the man's viselike grip and saw that his clothing was shredded and soaked with blood.

"Let me go," she pleaded, her weak voice choked by the arm across her throat.

"Never," he replied. "This thing, this flood—all this death is your fault, Martha. You caused this. Devils made you the abomination you are, and we will never let you be free. We will lock you up in a basement, never to see daylight again. Dinah should have sent you to the pits long ago. She was soft. I am not."

He started to drag her up the hill when his foot slipped on the wet leaves. Spinning to catch himself, he lost his hold on Martha, and she pulled away. Both of them slid toward the edge of the fissure. Martha flailed, grabbing desperately for roots or stems. The man caught her ankle as he slid past her to the edge.

Martha clutched a laurel bush, which stopped her fall, but her hands slipped with the man's weight. Luckily, his hold began to slide as well. She clung to the bush with all her strength, almost losing her grip when the cloth bag around her shoulders slipped and she struggled to retain it. She watched with horror as a small object wrapped in wax paper fell from her bag into the void below.

The man dug his fingernails into her flesh. Martha expected him to look afraid, but a muddy, hate-filled face glared back at her. With her free foot, she stomped him hard across his nose, but he did not let go. She kicked him twice more before he plummeted screaming to the rocks below. Martha heard bones crunch when he landed.

She carefully pulled herself up to the break in the trail and peered down the cliff. His upper body lay at an impossible angle from his legs. He twitched once, then lay motionless, still clutching Martha's shoe.

Martha worked around the fissure to follow the trail again. Darkness had settled over the mountains by the time she found a gravel road washed over with mud from the flood. She continued down the road, heading for the sparse lights blinking at her through the trees. Sharp rocks bit into her bare foot, but she hobbled onward, determined not to stop until she reached safety.

Men in large earth-moving machines worked under glaring lights, pushing aside walls and broken houses, searching for survivors. None of them noticed a small figure limping past. Finally, an EMS worker spotted her. She flinched when he draped a blanket over her shoulders and ushered her to an ambulance. She refused to lie on the gurney and insisted they take her to the one house she knew, which fortunately lay outside the path of destruction. He finally coaxed her into sitting beside him in the ambulance and drove her the last half mile.

Warm lights peeked through the windows of the small stone cottage as Martha approached, leaving a trail of blood on the stone path. At her insistence, the ambulance driver remained in the vehicle. She stopped and listened to the voices inside for a minute. She then knocked softly on the unpainted wooden door, and the voices stopped.

A woman around Ruth's age opened the door to gaze upon the ragged, bleeding figure. She studied Martha's face for a moment, then smiled.

"I do declare," she said in an accent so pronounced that the words came out as "Idoo deeclaya." "Is that you, Mowtha?"

Martha nodded. "It's me, Aunt Myrtle."

"Goodness, child. Come in here," Aunt Myrtle said, tugging her into the warm light. Others sat on chairs and a sofa around a small fireplace. The room hummed with unasked questions, and no one moved or spoke as Myrtle guided Martha past them and into an adjacent bedroom.

Martha barely remembered letting Myrtle undress and bathe her. She remembered being fed broth, thin biscuits, and cold water. She then lay back in the soft bed. Myrtle pulled a heavy quilt over her and kissed her brow. Martha was asleep before Myrtle closed the door.

CHAPTER TWENTY

7:35 a.m., November 7, 1977
Six hours and fifteen minutes after failure

When the radio announced news of the dam break and widespread destruction, Louise Beatty hustled Rey into her car and raced back to Toccoa. She was pretty sure that the flood would not reach her father's home or cut him off from help, but she needed to make sure. As she drove, a local radio station gave a confusing and conflicting story of what exactly had happened.

When she had to stop for gas, she used a pay phone to call home. Ridge answered after the first ring.

"I'm fine," he said before she could ask. "Been listening to the news, and it sounds pretty bad down at the college. But I am fine, and the roads here are clear."

"Can you tell what happened?" Louise asked.

"From what I can gather, that old dam above the falls broke in the night," Ridge replied. "How are your people down on the Tugaloo?"

"Different river, different dam," Louise replied. "They should be fine, but since you're okay, I think I'll head that way to check on them."

"Better hurry," Ridge said. "They've been calling here all morning trying to find you. Said you need to come over right away. Something important."

Louise hung up, paid for the gas and a ham sandwich for Rey, then headed toward her dig on the Tugaloo. An hour later and after many complaints from Rey, she pulled into the dig site. Rey hurriedly unbuckled herself and rushed to the toilet in the nearest trailer.

"Everyone here okay?" Louise asked the graduate student who came out to greet her. The rain soaked her clothing, and she began to shiver.

"We're all fine," he replied. "We heard the news and decided to stay put and keep out of everyone's way."

He led her to the tent.

"But I'm glad you're here," he continued. "There's something you have to see."

"What is it?" Louise asked.

He hesitated. "You're going to need to call that sheriff friend of yours. We found two bodies."

"We find human remains all the time. It's our job to investigate, not his."

"You don't understand," he continued. "These bodies have barely started to decompose. They're fresh, or . . . not fresh, but not old either. Pretty sure they were murdered a year or two ago."

"Murdered?" Louise asked.

Rey sloshed through the mud and joined them under the tent.

"Honey, you'll need to sit here while Mommy looks at something," Louise said.

Without a word, Rey sat at a small table strewn with papers and photographs.

The student led Louise to a section under a temporary canopy. She smelled death before she saw it, and when she peered into the excavation site, she took a deep breath despite the stench.

Beneath her, carefully exposed by students she'd taught to remove soil and preserve artifacts, she saw two bodies wearing modern clothing, one male and one female. The withered hand of the man held an object close to his chest. Louise hunkered down and inspected the article.

"A flint knife," the student said. "And look at this." He pointed to a sifting table. "This came up in some dirt we removed before we knew what we'd found."

Louise stepped over to the table and lifted a small, shiny object.

"An earring shaped like Rock Eagle," the student said.

Louise wondered aloud, "What the hell is going on here?"

Back at the tent, they found Rey frowning at the drawings and photographs.

"We've got to go, Rey," Louise said, expecting her daughter to follow her.

Rey did not move but continued to stare at the photographs, which mostly documented the locations of artifacts within the dig site.

When Louise took her daughter's hand to lead her away, Rey pointed to one of the photographs.

"R'k eagle," Rey said.

Louise squinted at the image Rey indicated, of a small petroglyph the students had unearthed earlier. At its center, worn by time but still identifiable, was the same stylized image of a bird of prey.

"R'k eagle," Rey said again.

Louise took the earring and the photograph of the petroglyph and slogged back to their car. With many protests, she bundled Rey into the vehicle and headed into town with her daughter announcing every few minutes that she was hungry.

They pulled into the sheriff's office and a packed parking lot. Inside was chaos. Every phone was ringing or being used. Men in dark suits and a few guardsmen rushed about or pored over maps. Doug Adams spotted Louise and came over.

"Can't talk now," the deputy said. "We're all hands on deck with what's going on at the college."

"I need to talk to the sheriff, and unfortunately, it cannot wait," she said.

"He's out directing rescue operations," Doug replied. "I'm in charge here for now. What's this about?"

Louise told him about the bodies in whispers she hoped Rey could not hear.

"Johan," Doug shouted across the room. "Radio the sheriff and tell him we need him back here. Tell him it's urgent. Tell him it's about . . ." He looked at Rey, who grinned back at him. "Tell him it's about a 187. No, two 187s."

Movement in the room ceased, and everyone gawked at Doug. Murders were rare in Stephens County, but they all knew what those numbers meant.

"It'll take the sheriff a good twenty minutes to get here. Why don't you wait in his office?" Doug suggested.

He led Louise and Rey to the back and settled them in two chairs in front of McClain's desk. A few minutes later, he brought doughnuts for both of them, as well as coffee for Louise and water for Rey. Louise sat and sipped the coffee but dropped the doughnut into the trash can.

Rey chewed her treat as she gazed around the room. Meanwhile, Louise pulled the earring from her jacket pocket and rubbed at the dirt.

"R'k eagle," Rey said.

Louise did not reply.

"R'k eagle," Rey said louder.

"I saw it too," Louise replied absently.

"R'k eagle," Rey said even louder.

Louise finally looked in her daughter's direction and saw that Rey was pointing at a photograph on the desk.

Sheriff McClain entered the office.

"R'k eagle," Rey said again, pointing to the photograph of the sheriff's wife. Rey touched the photograph to indicate the earrings Carol McClain was wearing. Louise stared at the earring in her hand. They were of the same material and style.

"Rock Eagle," Louise said.

"R'k eagle," Rey said with a note of satisfaction as she sat back and resumed eating.

"Tom," Louise said softly. "I need you to come out to our dig site on the Tugaloo."

"Doug already filled me in," he replied. "Said there's a slight chance . . ."

Unable to make himself form the words, he nodded toward the photograph.

Louise held out her hand and showed him the earring just as Doug burst into the room.

"Sheriff, we have a situation," he said. He was breathing fast and kept clutching his holster. Rey eyed him over her doughnut.

"Sheriff?" Doug asked.

The sheriff continued to stare at the earring, then back at the picture.

"Sheriff!" Doug said again.

Tom McClain turned as if just noticing his deputy.

"Sheriff, I know this might be a hard time for you," Doug continued, "but I just got word that President Carter is coming to Toccoa. An advance Secret Service team is already on the ground."

"And why do they need me?" McClain asked with a faraway look.

"Secret Service agents are asking questions about the Fellowship of Faith," Doug said. "Seems it makes them pretty nervous when the president is even close to . . ." He trailed off, then lowered his voice, peeking behind him. "To a cult," he whispered. "After that Squeaky Fromme thing with Ford, I can't much blame them. They say they're going to make sure none of them get anywhere close to the president."

"Those people are pretty harmless," McClain said.

"Seems we'll have to prove that," Doug replied.

"Since when do we have to prove that someone is not going to break the law?" McClain snapped.

"Sheriff, I'm just relaying what I've been told," Doug continued. "Someone at the college told their security that the people in the Fellowship of Faith compound are heavily armed and have made all sorts of threats. This got back to the Secret Service, and they come across to me as having pretty itchy trigger fingers."

"I've never seen guns or heard of any threats from anyone at the compound. If they're planning anything bad, they're keeping it pretty close," McClain said. After a pause, he asked, still staring at the earring, "Just where did they hear about the guns and the threats?"

"You remember Wayne Morris?" Doug asked.

"Of course," the sheriff replied. "Known him for years. His wife lives at the compound, but he never wanted anything to do with it."

"Well, it seems his daughter escaped last night," Doug continued. "Made her way to the college where her aunt lives. She's been talking, making all sorts of claims about the Fellowship. The stuff she's saying could not come at a worse time."

Tom McClain stared at Louise, for a moment uncertain as he struggled to choose between being a good husband and a bad sheriff. Louise sensed his conflict.

"I'll go to the Tugaloo, Sheriff," she said. "I'll call the medical examiner, if I can get her while all of this is going on. You go deal with the other mess. I'll contact you immediately when or if we find out who . . ." She caught herself.

"No sir, you will not," Doug said sternly.

"What did you just say to me?" McClain asked, riled out of his trance.

"Sheriff, you've been trying to find Carol for over three years," Doug continued. "If there's a chance it's her . . ." He trailed off.

McClain looked at Louise, then the photograph, then back at Doug.

"R'k eagle," Rey said, again pointing to the photograph.

CHAPTER TWENTY-ONE

Month and date unknown
501 years until failure

Days passed, and no one challenged Waya's decree. We were left in peace for the first time since the Great Snake had killed Father. Women began to veer closer to our hut as they walked to and from the fields. They stared at me in my metal mask but lowered their eyes when I returned the look. They were afraid, and it pleased me. After a time, they stopped regarding me as an oddity, and the mask became my face.

Days after giving me my mask, Sequoyah handed me a second treasure that, as much as my mask, would dominate my life from that day forward. Using a skill drawn from his travels, he had bound slivers of ash and sourwood into a bow almost as long as I was tall. Thin leather thongs wrapped around the handle.

"Hold like so, my love," Sequoyah said. He put the bow in my hands, and it immediately felt as if it were part of me. He then produced a birch-bark quiver containing at least twelve arrows. I slid one out and turned it in my hand. A strand of metal curled around the end of the shaft, securing a flint tip barely wider than the arrow itself. The metal shone like my mask.

"To make it easy to pull and yet powerful enough to kill, I gave it a long draw," he said.

I pulled the bow and felt its power building.

"Never release the string unless you have an arrow nocked," he instructed me.

We spent the rest of the day shooting at bundles of grass. Despite being only ten paces from the target, I lost two arrows from errant flights. Then one arrow struck the center of the target, and we both cried out in glee.

"Twice each day, you will practice," Sequoyah said. "Twenty arrows each time. Tomorrow, take one step back. The next day, another."

I nodded.

"Then practice shooting while kneeling, then bending over, then running," he continued.

I promised him that I would. And I was true to my word, despite how passing women glared disapproval and a few of the young men openly laughed at me.

"Tomorrow, I will show you how to make arrows," Sequoyah said. "That way, you will never run out."

That night in our hut, my shoulder ached from working the bow. Mother placed on it a hot poultice of poplar leaves. I felt the healing spread, and it helped me sleep.

When Onacona woke me with his warm hand, I winced before rising to lie with him. He was gone before dawn, and I wondered if I had dreamed it.

After that day, Mother and Sequoyah talked constantly, sharing remedies for every conceivable ailment. On occasion, she almost smiled, but the light would flicker out as if any modicum of happiness were a defilement of Father's memory. Sequoyah began to record all he and Mother knew on stretched hides or sheets of bark. The leather door to our hut contained symbols that only he could read. Every tool, wood handle, or piece of flat rock carried messages or symbols.

Sehoy showed no interest in learning either the healing skills or how to sound out the symbols Sequoyah painted. For me, I was consumed. Soon I could read the symbols he painted and the many inscriptions he made and in doing so gathered several lifetimes of knowledge. I knew how to find and shape the metals he gathered. I knew how to prepare and use plants and various animal parts. It was not long before I began to record my own mixtures and my own stories.

I worked with the bow much more than Sequoyah had insisted. Before long, I could hit a spot the size of a man's hand from over fifty paces. I lost no more arrows, and I added a couple each day to a stash I kept in our hut. The twang of my bow and the whisper of the arrows created music that touched a part of me. I heard the arrows in flight in my dreams and in the rustle of a gentle breeze. It was a sound the wind had learned when the world was young. Now I had learned it too.

One day, Sequoyah brought to me an arrow boasting a head slightly broader than the ones he normally made. Along one side, he had chiseled a shallow groove. He was the only one to possess the workmanship it took to make such a weapon without fracturing the thin flint.

"This is a dark way to kill, Atsila, my love," he explained.

Using a chestnut leaf, Sequoyah scooped the smallest amount of a paste he carried in a leather pouch and smeared it across the grooved surface.

"Just a scratch from this arrow will kill the mightiest of beasts or the fiercest warrior," he said, holding it up to the light. "But take care when you handle it, for the poison knows no master."

He tied a strip of muskrat skin around the arrow and placed it in my quiver, then tied the pouch containing the remaining poison to my belt.

"What is it?" I asked him.

"Someday I will show you," he replied. "But not now. For now, I have to make the Abittibi a great people."

Sequoyah began to teach our people how to gather the metal flakes and nuggets from which he had fashioned my mask. He explained how to recognize the valuable copper and ignore the soft yellow metal that proved useless for such things. Long into the night, we heard him at his stone oven, heating and hammering the metal into sheets and small slabs. These he traded for food and other goods he could not find time to gather for himself or for us.

Our people began to wear beads in our hair and woven into our jerkins, and we became a village of constant music as they clinked together. For most of the men, he crafted a flat piece in the shape of a flying eagle. He pierced the eagle, threaded a piece of sinew from a young buck's thigh into it, and then, with great show, placed the shining eagle around their necks as people sang and danced.

Sensing a repeat of the jealousy that had resulted in his banishment from the First People, Sequoyah made special adornments for powerful people and the shamans. For Waya, he made a circle shaped and textured like a snake. Something about the way the shaman smiled when Sequoyah bent the implement around his wrist troubled me. There was darkness behind the smile, and while I did not know it then, I would remember it later when tragedy struck.

Sequoyah found other uses for his metal—needles, gouges, implements for eating. He made heads for the darts children fired from blowguns. These too he taught me to shoot until I could hit a bird or squirrel perched in the highest chestnut tree. For only me, he impregnated some of the darts with the same poison so I could kill larger game with a weapon light enough to carry on a strap on my back and barely notice the weight. When I walked through the forest with the mighty bow in my arm and the blowgun on my back, I felt powerful and invincible.

"No one else has the poisoned arrows or darts," Sequoyah constantly reminded me. "Tell no one about them. No one. Not even Sehoy or your mother."

I pledged to keep this secret.

This was the best season of my otherwise pitiful life. I had the love of a man, which by now I suspected many of the women in camp knew. I had family, people who saw my mask and accepted the person beneath it. I had power, secrets that I could unleash upon our enemies in the dark and now in the light. I felt complete.

Sequoyah's love of the metal he shaped knew no bounds. From it he fashioned great pots that heated faster than fired clay. Soon the pots steamed at everyone's fire, and Sequoyah became as wealthy and powerful as a man in his position could find himself. The injuries of his youth made him useless as a fighter or hunter, and yet the power he had over our lives made him desirable.

Mothers began to urge their daughters to flirt with him or even come to his hut at night. Sequoyah never turned any girl away from his bed mat, and from my family's hut nearby, we often heard them rutting and laughing. A few fights broke out among women vying for his favor. Normally a chief would settle such a conflict, but the elders never replaced Dustau.

At one point, when the quarrels grew out of hand, some of the women went to Waya. Mother, Sequoyah, Sehoy, and I watched the drama from our home fire. The hills carried their voices, and we saw and heard everything.

Waya had stopped painting himself blue after Dustau died. I do not know why. Without it, he looked old and withered, as if the responsibilities of his position had used up his life essence. When he stepped from his hut to confront the gaggle of at least twelve women and girls who came to him, he seemed like one of the walking dead.

Inola, oldest daughter of Yonah, stepped boldly up to the old man, dragging her daughter with her. The girl could not have been more than fourteen seasons old and was round faced and thick of thigh, with broad hips and narrow shoulders—the image of her grandmother in her youth. She was also obviously pregnant.

"My daughter carries Sequoyah's child," Inola stated, forcing the girl to stand beside her. "She is his wife in all but name."

Sequoyah giggled like a girl, and I poked him with my elbow.

Likely the women could hear us as well, and it served no purpose to antagonize them.

Immediately other mothers pulled their daughters forward to confront Waya and began to argue. Someone pushed Inola, and she stumbled into her daughter. Both hit the ground hard but came up clawing.

Waya watched all of this unfold. Behind him, his own wife stirred something in one of Sequoyah's pots. He walked back and accepted a steaming clay bowl from her, then turned and calmly watched the women fight, occasionally sipping from the bowl. Gradually, the women realized that he would not intervene and the fight would have to end or take a serious and potentially deadly turn. One by one, they stopped tussling and turned to him.

"Has Sequoyah agreed to marry any of you?" he asked when they were finally silent.

No one spoke at first.

"But he—"

Inola was silenced by Waya's angry glare.

"You, Sparrow. Do you want to marry any of these girls?" Waya shouted in our direction.

Sequoyah simply shrugged. Had the women possessed bows and arrows, I knew they would have turned them on us at that moment.

Chitto came to squat beside Sehoy as we watched the proceedings. She reached for his hand. During the prior full moon, the shaman had held a celebration of their union as husband and wife. Their first child already wriggled in her other arm. Chitto had built a hut next to ours, and we shared a fire each night. Though they both sat at the same fire as the rest of us, they occupied the small, private world new lovers make for themselves. In her happiness, I found glory.

"If it pleases these fine women, I will take three of their daughters as wives," Sequoyah finally said. I suppressed a laugh, thinking he had made a joke.

"Sequoyah!" Mother warned in a low tone only we could hear.

"You must not toy with these families."

Sequoyah ignored her.

"I will take the first three who bring me a staff of slippery elm," he shouted.

Now I knew he jested. The inner bark of this plant was valuable for many ailments, but mostly to treat breast complaints from nursing women. Over the years, our people harvested it frequently, and it was now hard to find nearby. The closest source I knew of was on the opposite side of the Currahee.

"You would make a game of marrying my daughter and raising your child?" shouted Inola.

Already two of Sequoyah's lovers had raced into the forest.

"I make no game, Inola," Sequoyah replied. "I need a new staff that will warn me of ghosts. These women need a husband. I have room for only three around the fire I share with Ahyoka. It seems a good solution."

At this, I laughed out loud, and Mother swatted my leg. Others also chuckled, and even Waya covered his mouth to hide a smile. Inola rushed with her daughter toward the Currahee. When they were gone, the entire village burst into laughter that echoed from the hills.

One by one, the girls returned with slippery elm limbs. Sequoyah accepted the gifts with much ceremony, singing songs of the girls' beauty and strength. Each song matched the girl perfectly, as if he had prepared long ago for this time. Inola's daughter came last, slowed by the child she carried. In the end, Sequoyah, much to the annoyance of the other young men of the tribe, took her and three others.

Chitto went with four of his age-mates to hunt game for the celebration. We intended a day of feasting for each bride. In an interval much shorter than hunts usually last, they returned with two young does and a rare white buck. Waya declared that finding the white stag was a good omen for the tribe, Sehoy, and the marriages of Sequoyah.

People danced and ate through the night. The next day, the

feasting and dancing resumed until we were all so full we could barely move. On the third day, our excess achieved new levels. I danced as much as my shyness allowed. We sang praises to the hunters, to all the gods we could name, and to our good fortune to have someone as wise and powerful as Sequoyah among us. We sang and ate and danced as our fires cast spirit shapes across the trees.

Not until the wolf light of dawn crept across our camp did we realize our foolishness. Howling like the souls of drowned men, they came. While we lay about, bloated from charred meat and exhausted from three days of near constant dancing, they descended upon us and began the hard work of killing.

CHAPTER TWENTY-TWO

7:46 a.m., November 7, 1977
One day, six hours, and sixteen minutes after failure

Martha felt the bed sag and turned slowly, wincing at the pain of her bruises and strained joints. Habit prompted her to reach for her veil. In the second it took her to realize where she was and that she did not have her covering, she pulled her sheet up to just below her eyes and looked up.

Aunt Myrtle perched on the edge of the bed.

"Lawd, child," she said. "You slept the sleep of the dead. Howdya feel this moanin'?"

Martha rubbed sleep from her eyes and squinted at the room full of adults. She vaguely remembered one or two, but the others were strangers. One wore a tan uniform.

"I'm okay, Aunt Myrtle," she replied. "Who are these people?"

Myrtle pulled Martha's hand into her own.

"These are men from the college, hon," Myrtle replied. "I asked them to come over. They're making a count of all the people who were lost last night, and they may have questions for you. And this here is Deputy Doug Adams. He wants to talk to you. Is that all right?"

"What do they want with me?" Martha asked.

Myrtle did not reply, and the deputy stepped forward. He held his hat in one hand in front of him. The other he kept behind him. He wore a large pistol on his right hip and a radio on his left.

"Let's start with how you got here," he said. "Is that okay?"

Martha nodded. "I ran."

Deputy Adams smiled. "Well, we kind of figured that. But why? Where is your momma? Your brothers and your sister, Eve?"

The deputy noted how her eyes darted around the room. Martha obviously did not like that so many people were listening to her.

"Perhaps you all can wait outside," he said to the rest.

They trooped out the door, leaving only him and Myrtle.

"Where's your family, Martha?" Deputy Adams asked again.

"They're all back at the compound," she replied. "I'm the only one who ran."

"And why was that?" he asked.

When Martha did not immediately answer, Aunt Myrtle said, "Tell the deputy what he needs to know, hon. Yesterday was terrible, just terrible, and we have other souls to attend to."

In the distance, Martha again heard heavy equipment and vehicles. She remembered the chase, the flood, getting caught, and kicking the man in his face right before he plunged to his death. She heard the thud when he hit the rock, and she shuddered.

Doug pulled a straight-backed chair to the bed and sat. He looked like he had not slept in days and bore the weight of a thousand unfinished tasks. Setting his hat on the nightstand, he kept his left hand behind him. Strands of hair spilled over his face while he talked, and he swept them away. When he reached toward his pocket, Martha saw a pack of cigarettes there. Then Doug closed his eyes for a second as if collecting his thoughts.

"Martha," the deputy said, "if you tell me you're okay, your family's okay, and you had some spat with your mom and you just ran away like any other teenager might do, then we'll leave you to work all this out yourselves. But we've heard rumors of what goes on up there. It does not sound good, especially for young girls like yourself. Not for anybody, really. Just tell me. Why did you run?"

"I ran to get help, Deputy," she said, determination rising. "They're taking Eve to Brazil. Momma can't stop them. Eve's only twelve."

"Hold on a bit, now," Doug said. "Who's taking Eve to Brazil?"

"Dinah Whiten is. They're leaving soon. Maybe even today," Martha replied. "Please, you can't let them take her. It's not right. Momma doesn't think so either, but they won't let her leave."

She sat up, not caring that the sheet slipped away from her face. She was about to start her story when the door opened.

At first, she did not recognize him, and she began to pull up the sheet again. Wayne stepped in and knelt at her bed. He reached out and touched her cheek as tears streamed down his face, and she knew him.

"Momma told us you died," Martha choked out.

"Not hardly," Wayne said. He reached for her, and she slid into his embrace. "I'm never leaving you again, and you will never have to go back there."

Martha sobbed into his shoulder for several minutes until the deputy cleared his throat.

"I need to know what happened, Wayne," Doug said.

"She escaped," Wayne replied. "What else do you need to know?"

"I'm afraid I need to know everything," the other man replied.

He brought his hand from behind his back. In it, he held a small, muddy shoe that matched the single one beside Martha's bed.

Martha took a deep breath, and clutching her father's hand, she told her story. When she got to the part where she ran across the failing dam, she stopped.

"You've told some people here that the folks up at the Fellowship of Faith compound have guns. Is that true?" Doug continued.

Martha nodded.

"Have you heard them planning anything, saying that they want to hurt anyone?" Doug asked.

Martha nodded again.

"Anyone specific?" he asked.

Martha looked at Doug, then her father.

"Can you answer the deputy?" Wayne asked as she squeezed his hand.

Martha nodded once more.

"Well," Doug continued. "Did they say they wanted to hurt anyone specific?"

"Everyone," she said in a whisper.

"Everyone?" Doug asked. "They want to hurt all of us?"

She nodded.

"And why?"

"To stop the famine," she said.

"Famine. What famine?" Doug asked.

Staring straight at the deputy, Martha loudly replied, "The famine of righteousness. Pastor Dinah says it goes all the way from here to Washington, DC. Says it will take sacrifice, living sacrifices, to end it."

"When did she say this, Martha?" Doug asked.

"Been saying it for years," Martha replied. "I can't say I really know what it means, but they're serious, Sheriff. Just like they're serious about taking Eve. Please help her."

"Your aunt Myrtle here tells me you ran through the woods and across the Kelly Barnes Dam the night it failed. Is that right?"

Martha nodded.

"She says you told her you were on the dam when it gave way," he continued.

She nodded again.

"How did you keep from drowning?" Doug asked.

"I don't know if what happened that night is real or something I dreamed," she hedged.

"You got here the following afternoon, hon," Aunt Myrtle said. "That's not a dream."

"Just tell us, Martha," Doug said. "We'll help you sort it out."

"I'm not sure how I got there, exactly. But I found a cave."

"There are lots of caves in these mountains, Martha," the deputy said. "Myrtle tells me you found one with a body?"

"A skeleton," Martha replied. "And she's wearing a mask."

"She?" Doug asked.

"Yes," she said. "I am sure it was a girl."

"Is there anything else you need to tell me, Martha?" Doug asked.

"Yes sir," she said. "There is."

CHAPTER TWENTY-THREE

December 19, 1976

Ten months and seventeen days before failure

After her rebellion at the church, Eve was blasted at least weekly, either after the services or at random times. Men came to the house and dragged her to a schoolroom or barn. Sometimes Martha could hear them shouting at her, barely drowning out Eve's screaming and crying. Always, Eve returned with her eyes down and her hands trembling.

After a couple of months, Eve stopped resisting. When they came, she stood, took a deacon's hand, and went with them. Each time, she came back somewhat less of herself than when she left. Martha feared that if this continued, the Eve she knew would be lost.

Fall turned to winter. Pipes froze, windows frosted over, and the sky turned gray. Still, the blasting continued.

One day, Dinah Whiten herself led Eve home after a long blasting ceremony. Eve came in shuffling her feet with her eyes down and her arms limp at her side. Her golden hair had been cut in ragged lines. Martha inwardly raged at the cruelty of taking away such beauty.

"I felt the devils leave her today," Dinah told Momma. "You must read Scripture to her each morning, come to every service, and keep her from any outside influences. Eventually, she may grow strong enough to live on her own. Maybe."

Momma took Eve inside. For three months, Eve stayed indoors except to walk to church services. She never played with Martha, never whispered sister secrets in the night, and rarely ate. Already thin, she shed the soft edges of a young girl's body and became all sharp bones with sunken eyes and protruding ribs. Martha worried over her, encouraged her to eat and sleep, begged her to try.

Martha pleaded with Ruth to take Eve to a doctor.

"She's dying," she entreated. "They have beaten the life out of her."

But Ruth would hear nothing of it. Dinah prohibited such acts of faithlessness. Instead, Ruth brought out the tiger's milk she'd used on them as children and forced Eve to drink the foul mixture. When their mother left, Eve vomited it into the sink.

One day, against all the rules, Martha brought Eve a cat with a coat like fire. Dinah would not have approved, calling all pets frivolous attempts to play God with another living thing. Martha had found the animal hiding under the overhang of a nearby shed, meowing and licking an injured paw. He did not resist when Martha picked him up.

Eve had been sitting alone in the basement where she should have been sewing. Martha bundled the cat within the folds of her apron and carried it down the stairs. Eve did not look up as they approached or even when Martha gently placed the cat on Eve's lap.

"Look what I found, Eve. I know you've always wanted one," Martha said softly.

Eve stared down at the bundle of red fur that had curled against her folded hands. A tear trickled from her eye, then another and another. Soon, tears flooded her face, and she lifted the cat to nuzzle it against her cheek. It was the first time in months Martha had seen her sister show emotion.

"What should we name him?" Martha asked. Eve did not respond.

"Maybe we should call him Fire. Would that be all right with you, Eve?"

Eve continued to hold the cat against her cheek but shook her head. The creature looked up at Martha with eyes that seemed to question what was happening.

"Gideon," Eve said. "We'll call him Gideon."

Gideon swiveled his ears back and forth.

"Gideon," Martha said, and again the cat twitched his ears. "I think he likes that name."

"We can't tell Momma," Eve said. "She would take Gideon away, maybe even let them do awful things to him."

When she clutched the cat closer, he began to squirm, so she sat Gideon on her lap and stroked his back. He closed his eyes and purred.

"How are we to keep a cat in the house without Momma knowing?" Martha replied.

Eve's eyes glazed over, and Martha worried she was losing her again.

"Okay. This may be foolish, but let's try and keep him a secret," Martha said. "He's our cat, and if we want to keep him, no one should stop us."

Martha saw the first glimpse of her sister again in the smile that flitted across Eve's face. Eve reached beneath the folds of Martha's veil and stroked her cheek like she had when they were younger and Dinah Whiten was a distant rumor.

"So, here's what we do," Martha began.

After that day, Eve began to eat and sleep—not normally at first, but better. Gradually, some roundness returned to her body, and her face and hair took on their former beauty. Eve and Martha had a cause. They had someone who needed them. They had a life separate from the craziness of Dinah Whiten and their mother's submission to insanity. They had Gideon.

They cleaned the wound on his paw, and within days, he barely limped at all. As the weeks passed, Gideon's thin frame filled out from the milk and bits of biscuits and ham they snuck to their room. When he was strong enough, they let him out of their bedroom window every morning and watched him stalk through the grass. They kept watch over him until he made it to the gardens. Then they bent to their schoolwork and chores with such enthusiasm that Ruth and their teachers began to notice.

Each evening, the cat would slip through the open window and climb into bed to lie against Eve, sometimes resting his head on her stomach. The girls began to talk again, whisper silly secrets, ask about who they liked and did not like. Martha pretended that she too had a chance at a suitor, and Eve grew more and more her old self.

One morning, some older boys spotted Gideon as he prowled the gardens. They gave chase, and Eve fought to clamber out of the window to save him.

"Watch," Martha said. "Just watch."

Gideon cut back and forth in short dashes as the boys laughed and chased him. Once, one got close enough to try to grab his back, but Gideon rolled over as quick as a blink, slashed the boy's hand with his claws, then rolled back to his feet and ran on. The boy cried out in pain and stood sucking the blood from his fingers while Gideon disappeared into a patch of early corn. They never bothered Gideon again.

Martha and Eve turned back and laughed, took turns pretending to claw each other, and made ferocious cat growls until they heard Momma in the hallway. They dressed quickly and went to the kitchen for breakfast. Every time Momma turned her back to them, they clawed the air and laughed silently.

EVE TURNED TWELVE in late winter on a day filled with hailstorms and winds that shook the house. The boys had left for the barn to move hay to the cattle pens and perform other tasks. After breakfast, the sisters and their mother sat at their chairs in the kitchen, repairing other people's clothes and sipping sassafras tea from roots Martha had found at the forest's edge. The family they shared the home with was visiting someone across the compound.

Momma sat with her needle, some patches, and a few old shirts as Eve and Martha drew pictures with colored pencils, a precious commodity and unusual extravagance that Ruth provided them from the paltry proceeds of her work. The knock at the kitchen door was barely audible over the ruckus of the storm. Martha fastened on her veil while Ruth set aside her work and opened the door. Dinah Whiten and two deacons stood outside. Ruth ushered them in while Eve and Martha scrambled to go to their room.

"Stay, children," Dinah said. Her voice made Martha tremble. "You should hear this."

Martha and Eve stood by the door to their room while Dinah and the two men sat at the table. Dinah frowned when she saw the pictures.

"Not exactly salable art, now, is it?" she said, pushing them to the side. "Do I smell sassafras?"

Ruth poured hot water over some root shavings, then split it into cups and added honey. Martha noticed her mother's hand shaking while she worked.

When the adults were settled and sipping tea, Dinah made small talk, then got to the point of her visit.

"I am going to Brazil in a few weeks," Dinah said. "The Lord has been strong there. Miracles, signs, and wonders such as you cannot fathom. Our work there has so many converts that we need to build more space for them. I want to take your boys with us so they can help with the work and . . . well, you can guess. They can meet some of the girls there that I think would be perfect for them."

Ruth nodded and smiled, but Martha thought the smile was forced. Eve kept her eyes on the floor. Martha slipped her hand into her sister's. She too was trembling.

"We would also like to take Eve," Dinah continued.

Ruth froze for a second, then set her cup on the table.

"Eve?" she asked. "Whatever for? She's just turned twelve and can't hammer worth anything."

Eve tightened her grip on Martha's hand.

"Well, of course she can't," Dinah said. Her voice was as slippery as wet clay. "But you can see that she is beautiful. Not like so many of the other girls around here. Homely doesn't begin to describe most of our girls. I keep preaching on how they need to dress up, do their hair with more care. But it seems that they just get worse."

She glanced at Martha with contempt sheathed in a fake smile.

"Some of them, well, they just can't help what they are," Dinah said. Her smile widened into something resembling a snake's jaw.

Martha touched her veil to make sure it was securely in place.

"But Eve," Dinah continued, "she's something to behold."

She raised her arms toward Eve, who backed away slightly.

"Come here, my beautiful child," Dinah said.

Eve took another step back until she was against the doorframe. Martha felt the sweat forming in her sister's palm.

Ruth looked at Dinah, then at Eve.

"She's shy, Pastor Dinah," Ruth said. "The devils you drove from her did some powerful damage to the poor girl's mind."

"Not shy," Dinah said, her voice now hard. "Willful. I said come here."

Eve held her ground.

"You don't have another devil in you keeping you from obeying me, do you, child?" Dinah said, her voice sickeningly smooth and sweet.

From her head to her toes, Eve started to quiver. Her breath quickened, and she squeezed Martha's hand harder.

"Please, no," she croaked. "I don't have no devil."

Ruth took a breath and started to rise. Dinah stopped her with a hand on her arm.

"No," Dinah said to Ruth. "She must come to me of her own accord."

Eve shook her head slowly. Dinah nodded at one of the men, who stood and left through the kitchen door. When he returned, he held a small crate. Gideon cowered in the back of the cage.

"Do you and your sister think that anything goes on here that escapes me?" Dinah said.

Eve took a step forward, but Martha held her back.

"I will leave this yard cat here with your sister," Dinah continued, "unharmed and free. But you must come to me now. Tell me you can be obedient. Tell me you will resist the devils that have plagued you and your family all of your life. Tell me now."

Gideon hissed and spit. The rain and hail pummeled the house. A radiator popped and wheezed. Eve's breathing slowed, and she released Martha's hand.

With steps as small as an infant's, she tottered toward Pastor Dinah. When she was within arm's reach, Dinah reached out and stroked her golden hair.

"I will do as you say," Eve replied.

"Such a pretty girl," Dinah said. "I have someone picked out for you. He owns a large plantation with horses, cattle, and rubber tree farms."

Ruth inhaled sharply. "Pastor Dinah, she's too young."

Dinah cast Ruth a withering look.

"He's handsome and rich," she continued. "His father died and left him a fortune. A big house. Lots of servants. He even speaks passable English."

"But—" Ruth protested.

"Enough!" Dinah said, pounding her hand on the table and rattling the cups.

Eve ran to Martha and buried her head in her shoulder.

"It will take a while to get Eve a passport, which you will sign for, Ruth," she said. "Then we're off. Just think of the girls they'll send us after that. Just think of the fortunes Eve's husband can provide for the Lord's work. Just think."

Dinah and the other man stood and joined the one holding the cat.

"Just think of what this means to the Kingdom of God," Dinah said. "You are being honored in the tradition of the great kings and queens of old. I envy you."

With that, they left, taking Gideon with them.

CHAPTER TWENTY-FOUR

Exact date and time unknown;
however, investigators believe it was approximately
one month before failure

The boys came home shaking water from their oilskin jackets and brimming with the news. They were going to Brazil on a mission trip. Building houses for God. They had never even been outside the state of Georgia and were full of excitement and plans. When Ruth and the girls showed no interest, they gobbled down some food and retired to their room.

Eve sat silently at the table. Martha joined her and shot accusing looks at their momma.

Surely you cannot let this happen, she said loudly enough in her mind that she was certain Ruth could hear the thought or read it in her face.

Ruth looked back and forth between her two daughters. One so deformed that she would never have hope of a family, the other with a beauty so deep it doomed her to nothing else. She tried to pick up her sewing, but her hands would not cooperate.

"Momma," Martha said.

Ruth shot her a look meant to silence her.

"No," Martha continued. "We have to talk about this. We have to."

Eve looked up, her angelic face ringed in blond curls.

"You can't let them take her," Martha continued. "You can't. She's too young. We'll never see her again if you let them take her. Please, Momma. Please!"

Martha sensed something change in her mother; resolve flashed across Ruth's face. But resolve to do what? Martha could not tell. When she started to speak again, Ruth flicked her eyes toward the boys' room and hushed her daughter with a finger to her lips. Martha nodded in silent agreement. The boys could not be trusted to come to their aid. They had bought into the whole thing—the sequestered lives directed by the Whitens, the early marriages, the communal finances and living. That understanding was almost as hard to bear as the potential to lose Eve. The boys were already lost.

Ruth cleared the table of their sewing materials, then went into her room. A few minutes later, she came out carrying a wallet bulging with cash.

"Been saving this for something special," Ruth said in a subdued voice. "Some came from your father before he left. The rest I got taking jobs for neighbors. It's enough."

"For what, Momma?" Eve asked in barely a whisper.

"Go to your rooms and pack a few things," Ruth said. "Nothing more than you can carry in a flour sack. Nothing that makes noise."

"Momma?" Eve asked.

"No toys, no books. Just clothes and extra shoes," Ruth said. "Then go to bed. Wear your clothes to bed and be ready when I come for you."

"Momma?" Eve asked again.

"Do it, child," Ruth whispered hoarsely.

Martha and Eve did as Ruth instructed. When they climbed into bed, Eve wiggled until Martha's chest was pressed against her, then pulled her sister's arm across her waist. She held her hand, and Martha made out her whispered prayers.

Martha was not sure if she'd slept, but she heard the floorboard creaking when Ruth came to their room. By the time their mother opened the door and turned on the light, both sisters were already sitting up and pulling on their shoes.

Ruth signaled them for silence and led them out to the kitchen. Each step sounded as if giants were sneaking about the house, and they held their breath. When they reached the outside door, the hallway light flicked on. They froze. One of the boys, they could not tell which, peeked around the corner and into the darkened kitchen. They heard him return to his room.

They did not wait to learn of his intent. Instead, Ruth shoved the sisters out the door and into a damp, cold night. Holding hands, they ran across the compound toward the gate, hoping it remained unlocked. Ruth turned just long enough to see the lights in her house flicker on room by room. A dog barked somewhere. They hurried through the darkness across ground they knew as well as they knew their own home.

On a hill overlooking the rest of the compound, Dinah and Paul Whiten's home was silhouetted against a dull sky. As usual, the light of the forbidden television flickered through their front windows.

Ruth and her daughters ran on, hoping the guard at the gate had retreated into his house against the cold. More lights inside Dinah Whiten's home clicked on. Then her porch light flared, so intense that it seemed to swallow all other lights.

The gate lay less than a dozen steps away when they heard someone shout. Ruth pulled her girls the last few feet and out of the gate just as voices began to call her name. The trio dashed down the dirt road. When they heard the rumble of a vehicle starting, Ruth tugged Martha and Eve into the bushes. Wet leaves dragged across their bodies as they tunneled deeper into the brush and away from the road. Shivering, they knelt in tall grass, and two cars and a truck roared past them.

"There's a logging road down this hollow," Ruth whispered, her voice shaking. "We take it all the way to the waterworks."

Just as they started to stand, one of the cars came to a stop a hundred paces from them. They dropped back into crouches and froze.

"We saw you leave, Ruth," Dinah called from the car into the night. "We know you're close. Come back. Family is forever."

The other vehicles halted ahead of Dinah. One of them turned around and rolled slowly down the road. A man leaning out of the back seat shined a flashlight along the edge of the undergrowth.

"They can see our trail in the dew," Ruth said. "If we stay here, they will find us."

She stood and bolted for a dark line of trees, herding her daughters in front of her. If their pursuers saw them, they gave no hint.

Ruth glanced over her shoulder and saw that the car had stopped where they had exited the road. The truck continued toward them. She turned and urged her daughters forward.

"Ruth, please," Dinah called.

Ruth led Eve and Martha farther into the dense forest. Dinah continued to call, and Ruth ran from her, praying to find the old logging road. The family shivered as leaves painted them with cold water from the storm. Eve began to cry.

"Shush," Martha said. "Do you want to give us away?"

Eve stifled her sobs, and they continued. They had no sense of time and were guided only by the slight upward slope of the land. When they came to the logging road, Ruth had them squat while they all listened. The only sounds they detected were a distant train and the rustle of wind through the skeletal branches of old oaks.

They followed the road in what Ruth hoped was a southward direction. Two or three times, she stopped and listened. Nothing.

Once, she thought she heard distant shouting but could not tell from what direction it came, so she continued. Eve and Martha slowed, and Ruth continuously urged them to stay on their feet.

"I am tired and cold, Momma," Eve said. "Can we stop for a while?"

"We can't stop here, my love," Ruth said. It was the first time in years she had referred to either of the girls by their old pet name. "We have to keep going. We can find your aunt Myrtle at the college. She'll put us up. But please, keep moving."

Eventually, they crested a short bluff, and the road made a switchback down the other side. The wind had died, and the forest lay still as a grave. Something rustled in the bushes beside them. They again stopped to listen.

"Family is forever," a voice called.

Ruth turned but saw no one.

"Run, girls!" she shouted just as the lights from a pickup truck parked up the road blazed on.

A man stepped from the bushes and clamped his hands around Martha's waist, hoisting her kicking and screaming into the air. Another grabbed Eve. Ruth dropped her bag and clung to her younger daughter, but a third man grabbed Ruth and forced her into the pickup.

She would not see her daughters until they had returned to the compound. When the gate clanged shut behind them, they seemed to her like the gates of hell.

Dinah had the men put Ruth and the girls in a locked basement room two levels below the sanctuary. There were no windows and only one metal chair. Martha and Eve curled together and tried to stay warm. Ruth could not tell whether they slept or whether hours or days had passed. They were escorted to the nearby bathrooms one at a time. Once, an old woman left them a tray of sweet tea, stale bread, and two apples.

Eventually, Eve and Martha were led upstairs and escorted to their own house. Ruth begged the men to keep them together, but they did not reply.

Martha could not tell what time of day it was—only that darkness had fallen over them. The woman who had left them the food in the sanctuary sat in the kitchen where Ruth should have been. She did not speak but gave them oatmeal, butter, and cranberry juice, then motioned them to go to their room.

Except for using the toilet and eating, they stayed in their room for two days. Eve kept gazing out the window, looking for Gideon or their mother. Whenever the sisters peeked out of their room, the old woman would be sitting at the table.

When Ruth finally returned to the house, still wearing the pleated dress she had worn when they attempted their escape. Now it was wrinkled, stained, and torn in several places, and she had bruises on her neck and one side of her face.

Martha and Eve wrapped themselves around her. She barely acknowledged them except to carefully pry them away, then sat at the kitchen table across from the silent old woman. After a few minutes, the old woman rose and left.

That night, Gideon slipped silently through the girls' window and into their bed.

ON THE AFTERNOON of November 9, Martha told all of this to Deputy Adams.

"So that's why you ran away?" he asked.

Martha nodded.

"And this?" he held up her shoe. "When did you lose this?"

Martha did not answer.

"Tell him, child," Aunt Myrtle prodded. "Don't hold nothing back now. Hear? The deputy's a good man. We go way back. He's here to help you. You got nothing to fear."

Martha leaned into her father.

"A man grabbed me, tried to take me back. He tried to hold on to me but slipped and fell into the ravine."

"This man who grabbed you, do you know his name?" Doug asked.

Martha nodded. "We all called him Deacon Thomas. I don't know if that's his real name or one from the Bible. He does things to people for Dinah. Bad things." She seemed to hesitate.

"What sort of things, Martha?" the deputy asked.

"Other people do most of the blasting," Martha murmured. "That's the time when they scream at you for hours, trying to drive out the devils. But when they leave, he stays."

She looked uncertainly at her father.

"Wayne, I know you just got here, and you have plenty to ask and to say, but would you wait outside for a few minutes?" Doug asked.

Wayne looked at Martha, who nodded her consent. Wayne left, and Aunt Myrtle took his place at Martha's side.

"It's just us now, Martha," Doug said. "What did this Deacon Thomas do?"

Martha buried her head into Aunt Myrtle's shoulder, not meeting the deputy's eyes.

"He hit us," she whispered. "He would make us take off our clothes. He did things to us."

Doug sighed deeply. "Well, he's never going to hurt you again, Martha," he said. "You're safe now. Do you think you can be brave enough to share all of this again later?"

Martha nodded.

"One last question," Doug said. "Did your mother know about what Deacon Thomas did to you?"

"He did it to me and to Eve," Martha said robotically. "She would not say, but I know he did it to Momma. She knew. That's why she took us, tried to run."

"Okay, I've heard enough," the deputy said as he stood.

"They're going to take Eve away, Deputy," Martha said. "They're going to kill Momma. I know it."

The door opened, and Wayne strode back in, having heard everything through the door. He came around opposite Aunt Myrtle and sat on the bed beside Martha.

"You're going to stop them. Right, Doug?" he asked. "If not, I might just need to kill 'em myself."

"Nobody's killing anybody," Doug said. "Enough people died in the last couple of days."

"You can't go, Daddy," Martha said. "They've got guns." She peeked at the deputy, who tilted his head toward her.

"It's the second time you mentioned guns. That's pretty common around here, though," he commented.

"Lots of guns," she continued. "I've heard them say that they don't think the law here has any lay on them."

"What kind of guns?" Doug asked.

Martha shrugged. "Big guns."

"How many?" he asked.

Again, Martha shrugged, but then added, "Can't say. But I know that all the men have them. Pastor Dinah and Pastor Paul have the most."

"I'm getting Eve," Wayne said grimly. "I know the place, and I've got my own gun."

"You'll do no such thing," Doug replied. "I grew up with the Whiten boys. I know them and the compound. I can talk to them, see if we can get this resolved peacefully."

Doug said his goodbyes and went to his cruiser. Knowing that Terrance Head often monitored the radios, he called Sheriff McClain with a discreet synopsis of what he had learned from Martha and his intentions to perform a wellness check on Ruth at the compound. McClain acknowledged the call with an urge to be careful.

HALF AN HOUR later, the sheriff, Rey, and Louise pulled into the Tugaloo dig site. The rain had stopped, but clouds skirted the mountaintops. The medical examiner's car was there with its magnetically secured yellow light flashing.

They plodded through the mud toward the canopy. Louise shooed away several grad students who were watching the examiner at work in the grave.

"Tom," the examiner greeted the sheriff, brushing her gray hair from her face with her forearm as she straightened up. At sixty-two, Dr. Carrie Pruitt was the only medical examiner the county had ever had or needed. She was almost too short to see over the edge of the grave. Dark eyes and a perpetual frown implied she had seen everything. She had not.

"Never seen a stone knife, or at least not one that was used to kill," she said, motioning to the man in the adjacent grave. "That's one for the books."

"The woman?" the sheriff asked.

"Not her, Tom," she replied. "This body's too decomposed to tell much in the field, but I've seen the GBI report on Carol. For one, whoever this is was not dressed like she was when she disappeared. Also, I seem to remember that Carol was about my height. That right?"

"About," McCain replied.

"Well, this young lady is a good six inches taller," Dr. Pruitt continued. "Bodies may shrink after death, but they do not get longer or taller. I'll keep an open mind when we get her to the lab, but I don't think there's any way this is Carol."

McClain took off his hat and leaned forward with his hands on his knees.

"Whoever this woman was, she died from a stab wound to the chest, same as the man," she continued, unsure that he'd heard her.

The students inched closer and started whispering to one another. A withering look from Louise sent them away once again.

"One last thing before you go, Tom," Pruitt said. She hesitated until the sheriff stood and looked her in the eyes. "This body's well less than a year in the ground. I'd say not much more than a couple of months, tops."

"You already know about the potential grave sites we found upriver?" McClain asked.

"Doug told me," she replied. "I asked Roddy about the water levels. Said they should be down later today, tomorrow morning at the latest. I plan to get these two settled, then see if Doug or Leroy can get me over there with a digging crew."

"Thanks," McClain said. "Likely it'll have to be Leroy. Doug and I will be pretty busy up at the falls. Don't spread it around just yet, but President Carter's visiting, and we have Secret Service people already pushing everyone's buttons."

"Got it," Pruitt replied. "I'll keep you informed."

CHAPTER TWENTY-FIVE

Month and date unknown
501 years until failure

Screaming over the thud of their axes breaking bones, the Nermernuh cut through our camp. Only a few of our people managed to cry out before heavy clubs beat them to the ground. Shorter than our men and thick of chest, the attackers wore bearskins over their backs and appeared as beasts and not men.

I screamed for Sehoy and Mother to run and hide while I grabbed my bow. One of the Nermernuh reached for me while I fought to nock an arrow. Chitto felled him with his axe. He warded off two more while I began sending arrows into their shaggy hides. Each time my bow sang, a Nermernuh fell. One, five, then more than ten. Mother and Eve ran to our hut. Mother immediately came out with two more of my quivers brimming with arrows. She carried them to me, and I shot a Nermernuh through the throat as he raised his club to strike her.

All about the camp, people ran and screamed. Some of the men gathered around Waya and slowly drove the attackers toward the forest. I continued to rain arrows upon them, each striking its target. Chitto stayed with me at first, then ran to join Waya. Still I shot my arrows into them, even as they fled. When Mother handed me my third quiver, I barely noted how my arm and shoulder ached.

Waya chased them to the edge of the forest, then called a halt. I knew our warriors could track them and bring a terrible vengeance upon them for this atrocity. But the chase could wait while we attended to our wounded, gathered ourselves, and counted our dead.

I dropped to the ground in exhaustion. I had only six arrows left in my quiver, two of them poison. Mother pulled me to her, and our shoulders touched. Sweat dripped from beneath my mask. About us, our dead mixed with those of the Nermernuh, many sporting my arrows. Some of them moaned and tried to crawl away. Our women pummeled them into silence and bound them. They would make sport of them later.

Something itched in my mind, a twig out of place, a track going the wrong way. I could not put it to words. This attack made little sense. They could not hope to eradicate us. Indeed, their dead outnumbered our own. We were not in their territory, and to my knowledge, we had no Nermernuh captives. Some great need must have driven them to carry out such a costly attack on us.

I stood and peered about me, trying to think what had so tempted the Nermernuh.

Sequoyah! Desperately, I began searching for him. He was not in his hut. I turned over a few of the Nermernuh dead, pulling my arrows from them when I could. He was nowhere to be found.

I called for him. Mother called for him. Soon others took up the cry, and we all searched among the dead as well as the living. Thinking perhaps that he had gone to protect Sehoy, I ran to our hut. I pushed back the leather door. It was empty. Blood was smeared across Sehoy's sleeping fur.

"They took Sehoy and Sequoyah!" I shouted. I ran outside and shouted again. Others came, looked inside our hut, then came back outside, nodding.

In a dark, hidden part of my mind, I admired the Nermernuh for their daring. Sequoyah's wisdom and Sehoy's beauty were our greatest treasures. In one bold move, they had taken both.

Mother helped me gather my arrows. My admiration for Chitto increased when I saw the way he calmly and methodically pieced together what had happened by the faint impressions in the grass.

"They came for Sehoy first," he said. He pressed his hand into indentations that meant nothing to me. "Two men. One much larger."

He followed the trail inside the hut, then in a straight line to a nearby copse of chestnut trees.

"They kept her here," he said. "She is wounded but walking."

Chitto turned and followed another indistinct trail.

"Four others met them here," he said. "They dragged another who could not walk."

"Sequoyah?" I asked.

Chitto nodded.

"They headed north," he continued. "Fast."

Waya listened to all of this. Some of his warriors had already retrieved their weapons and travel pouches.

"We can catch them if we move fast," Chitto said. "Perhaps before they meet up with the others."

"They will already have formed up," Waya said. We all turned to face him. "They head north now, but they will soon turn toward the Chattahoochee. They have done so before."

"Better then," said Chitto. "We know where they are going. We can more easily catch them."

Waya shook his head. "It is no use," he said. "We have tried before. They will have left rafts on the river. They float down faster than we can run and get off on rocks where we cannot track them. Sequoyah and Sehoy are lost."

"We can get them back," Chitto said. "We have done so before."

"We cannot," Waya said. "These are not the Acolapissa or the Houma. These are the Nermernuh."

He pointed to one of the bearskin-clad dead.

"They do not stop to eat or sleep when they travel for war. Their lives mean nothing to them. If commanded to do so, they will slit their own throats or throw themselves off cliffs. We have seen all of this. When you chase them, they will ambush you at places of their own choosing, sacrificing their own warriors to bring about your deaths."

"We cannot abandon them," I said.

"They will take them to a mountain west of the river," Waya continued. "I know of it. All but a narrow slope of the mountain is smooth rock. The Nermernuh make camp atop this mountain. They have burned the forest around the base of the mountain and can see anyone approaching half a day before they arrive. You cannot attack them there. You would all die."

A few of Chitto's friends stepped forward. No more than a handful, all young and inexperienced in war. "We can find this mountain of stone," one of them said. "We can win back Sequoyah and Sehoy."

"You cannot," Waya said.

"Then make songs of us and how we tried," Chitto said.

Waya turned from him, and I saw in his face something dangerous. I did not then understand the significance of that flicker of a smile.

No one challenged me as I stepped forward with my bow and quivers. A few women snickered and pointed to the blowgun. I ignored them.

"Gather as much food as you can carry," Chitto said. "All of you. We leave now."

Mother met me at the door to our hut. She handed me a pack of chestnuts, dried meat, and a water skin. Her look of anguish said more than words. I nodded in answer to the question she could not ask. Even if it cost me my life, I would bring our love home.

CHAPTER TWENTY-SIX

8:38 a.m., November 8, 1975
Two days, seven hours, and eighteen minutes after failure

Deputy Sheriff Doug Adams sat in his car with the lights out, surveilling the barred gate to the compound of the Fellowship of Faith. He could not see beyond the walls of corrugated sheet metal. His own memories of the place warred within him—hatred for what they had done to his family mixed with admiration for what the Whitens had tried to achieve. His immediate family had left the Fellowship eighteen years ago, when he was fifteen, though an aunt and uncle still resided there. He tried to remember who else in the compound would know him.

After a couple of minutes, he started the car and drove the remaining two hundred yards to the gate. He waited, knowing that someone would have seen him approach. A few seconds later, the gate opened, and a lone man stepped through. The man was unarmed.

"Evening, Deputy," the man said. "What can we do for you?"

Doug turned off the engine and climbed out of the car. Something about the way the man stood alarmed him. He was poised like a base runner preparing to bolt to second. The man kept casting nervous looks over his shoulder at the top of the wall.

"I need to see Pastor Whiten," Doug said. "And I need to talk to

Ruth and Eve Morris."

"Why's that?" the man asked.

"Just checking in with them about some reports we've had," he said, trying to sound calm. Inside, his heart raced, and his senses screamed danger. "Nothing big," Doug said. "Just need to clear some things up. I'd appreciate it if you could get them as quickly as possible. They need all the help they can get at the college. With the dam break, we've got dozens dead and missing. I need to get back."

The man nodded, then disappeared inside. Doug stood waiting, wishing he'd brought another pack of cigarettes.

A few minutes later, the man reappeared.

"Pastor Dinah says for you to clear out," the man said. This time, he kept his hands in his jacket pocket, and Doug noticed a bulge on his right side.

"Can't do that," Doug answered. "I need to see the Morrises. I've got a report that Eve and Mrs. Morris were mistreated somehow. I can't leave until I lay eyes on them."

"Pastor Dinah says to leave," the man said.

"I'm staying here," Doug replied firmly. "Got a job to do."

His hand inched closer to his gun as the man took a menacing step forward. Two figures appeared at Doug's periphery, wielding baseball bats and advancing quickly. The deputy swiftly drew his pistol, and the men froze.

"Back off!" Doug shouted. "There's no need to start anything. Just bring the women out."

"I said for you to leave," Dinah Whiten announced, stepping from behind the gate. "You've no authority here. We command you to leave."

Several men appeared at the top of the wall. Doug could not see whether they were armed, but he wouldn't take the chance; he backed toward the open door of his cruiser.

"This will not end well, Dinah," he said. "You're messing with the wrong people on the wrong day."

He slammed his door shut, backed away as fast as possible, then swung the car around and scattered pebbles in his wake as he hit the gas.

"DAMN THESE PEOPLE!" Sheriff McClain said when Doug reported the incident. The sheriff and his other deputies were sitting in his office in town, studying maps of the county.

"We've got President and Mrs. Carter on the way, and now we've got a group of crazy, armed zealots not ten miles from their landing site. GBI and the FBI will be crawling up my ass."

As he said this, two men wearing dark sunglasses and navy-blue suits strode into the office.

"Yes sir, Sheriff," one of them said, pulling off his sunglasses. His face was weathered and tan, with a permanent frown across his brow. "We'll be crawling anywhere we need to go."

CHAPTER TWENTY-SEVEN

6:14 a.m., November 9, 1977

Two days, four hours, and fifty-five minutes after failure

Sheriff McClain stood in a large Army tent, inspecting the map. The tent was pitched on a flat piece of high ground overlooking the lower section of the college. Around him, several men of the National Guard glanced nervously at one another. Two field agents from the Georgia Bureau of Investigation stood shoulder to shoulder with McClain, listening to the Secret Service agent.

"POTUS is determined to visit the college campus and survey the damage for himself," the taller of them, Agent Hart, said. He had to shout to be heard over the cars, trucks, and heavy equipment moving around them. He wore a short black jacket with a five-pointed star over his collarbone and had salt-and-pepper hair and an air of authority that forestalled interruptions.

"We have several details arriving with him and the First Lady. Our job is to contain the people in this compound," he said. "We are not to engage. Is that clear?"

"You've got a lot of firepower for someone who does not want to engage," the sheriff stated.

"Most of this was on standby as normal SOP when POTUS is entering an unsecured area," Agent Hart replied. "We're just here to make sure these people are contained. When the president leaves, we will go with him, and they are all yours. Until then, I have command."

Sheriff McClain frowned at this. He then pointed to the map.

"These are old, Agent," he said.

"Show me," Agent Hart replied.

Radios crackled, and a helicopter flew close overhead, rattling the tent. McClain indicated a nearly square area of the map labeled FOF COMPOUND.

"For one, the compound is much larger than this shows. It now covers around twenty acres. It has mostly sheet metal walls, but toward the west is almost all chain link. Some areas have a few unrepaired gaps. There are at least six gates, not the two you have here."

Agent Hart took a mechanical pencil from his pocket and handed it to McClain. "Sketch it in."

The sheriff called over Deputy Adams, and within a couple of minutes, they had updated the map with what they both could remember. They drew in trails and logging roads as well as fields.

"We can do a flyover and check it out," Hart said.

"I wouldn't do that," Doug said. "These people are on edge. They hate the government and especially Jimmy Carter. They still recall his stint as governor, and they say he's a heretic. Assuming they have the guns our witness claims, if they see a government helicopter overhead, I can guarantee they will take a shot at it."

"Have they ever threatened the president?" Hart asked.

"Threatened him?" the deputy asked. "You mean, threatened to kill him?"

Sheriff McClain shot a warning look at the deputy that did not go unnoticed by Agent Hart.

"Deputy?" Hart asked. His voice dripped with suppressed violence. "Have they ever threatened the president or his family? As you know, that would be a federal violation, and the rules would change."

Doug hesitated, then shook his head. "Not a real threat," he said. "More stuff about him being a devil in disguise, part of a shadow government. That sort of thing. No threats."

The sheriff felt the agent relax a bit, and they all took deep breaths.

"Are there other vantage points from where we can see the whole compound?" Hart asked.

"I can send someone here and here," McClain said, pointing to one site to the northeast of the main gate and another on a nearby bluff. "They'll see almost everything along the perimeter. There's no way to see inside."

"I will position snipers—" Hart started.

"You will not," the sheriff interrupted.

The agent glared at the sheriff but allowed him to speak.

"These people may not think like us, but they are citizens of Stephens County, and I will not have you setting them up like a turkey shoot."

"We have our rules of engagement, Sheriff," Hart said. "We don't do turkey shoots."

"And we have rules," McClain answered. "One of them is that we don't shoot our neighbors. I will take one of my own deputies, binoculars, a radio, and my own rifle."

"Your own rifle?" Hart said, raising his brow.

"From there, I can take a beer off a man's head anywhere on the front gate," McClain said, pointing to a spot on the map. "I shoot competitively and have placed in all the state matches for rifle and pistol. Unlike you, I live here. Anything goes down, and it's my job on the line. I can't just escape to DC."

Hart eyed the sheriff for a moment.

"Fine," he said. "But we're sending one of our men with you. And I want roadblocks on all roads accessing the compound. No one goes in or out during the president's visit."

"But some of these people have jobs in Toccoa," Doug said. "How will they get to work?"

"They won't," Hart countered. "We'll detain them as they leave, but out of sight of the compound. If there's a threat, I want it to stay where we can contain it. I don't want any of them moving around while we're guarding the president."

"That won't go well with them," Doug replied.

"Not my problem," Hart said.

"It *is* my problem, though," Sheriff McClain said. "You expect me to arrest people who have done nothing illegal except listen to a fundamentalist preacher? What should I charge them with?"

"Again, not my problem, Sheriff," Hart replied. "Would you rather I have the National Guard stop them?"

"No," McClain replied. "That would be worse. I can station people at the checkpoints that at least some of them will recognize. We'll handle it. But I want command of the operations around the compound."

Hart smiled. "Fine," he replied. McClain got the impression that the agent had conceded nothing.

THANKS TO A high-pressure system that pushed the clouds to the south, Sheriff McClain, Doug, and a field agent of the Secret Service named Alex Edmunds moved into position on a night that was clear and cold. Frost crunched beneath their feet as they reached a grassy knoll about 150 yards from the main gate to the compound. All three carried radios, binoculars, and sidearms. Over his shoulder, McClain carried a Remington 7mm Magnum Model 700 bolt-action rifle with a large black scope and attached tripod. He unfolded the tripod and set the rifle on the ground.

McClain and the deputy pulled foam pads from their packs and sat on them. Agent Edmunds sat directly on the ground, and the melted frost soaked his pants in seconds.

"One in position," Doug whispered into the radio. It crackled loudly as he fumbled for the volume knob.

They heard the other two observers reply, then confirmed that the two roadblocks were in place and waiting.

"Okay, people," McClain. "Stay alert and stay put. Remember, we're here to contain them, not confront them."

After that, there was silence. Though the night was moonless, the stars shone brightly enough to throw shadows across the landscape. The men wrapped themselves in their down jackets and settled in to wait. An hour later, the first hint of dawn slunk across the rolling hills to the east. The world seemed colorless, as if drawn in black and white.

"They call this the wolf light," Deputy Adams commented.

"Who calls it that?" Edmunds asked.

"The Native Americans," Doug replied. "Bright enough that a wolf can hunt by sight, but still dark enough that humans cannot get around or defend themselves."

"How do you know what they call anything?" Edmunds asked curiously.

"He's half Indigenous himself," Sheriff McClain replied. "Trust me. He knows."

"Wolf's light," Edmund repeated. "Good one."

"Movement at the gate," a voice hissed over the radio.

"Roger that," Doug replied. "We have eyes on them."

The gate to the compound swung open. A man wearing combat fatigues and a floppy hat held it open while two cars eased through. The first car stopped while someone inside exchanged a few words with the man holding the gate, then proceeded slowly past the knoll where Sheriff McCain, Deputy Adams, and Agent Edmunds sat. Frost covered the side window, and they could not see who or how many people were inside.

"The first car is headed your way, John," Sheriff McClain said into the radio. "We can't tell how many passengers. Remember, these are not criminals. You cannot allow them to go back to the compound, but you have to be easy with them. Got it?"

"We've got it, Sheriff," a voice over the radio replied. "We see 'em coming."

The other car sat at the gate, smoke drifting from its exhaust. The driver rolled down the window to speak. Immediately three sets of binoculars focused on the car.

"I don't recognize the driver," Doug said. "But look at the front seat, passenger side. That's Pastor Dinah."

"You sure?" Agent Edmunds asked.

"I've known her for a better part of my life," the deputy replied. "That's her."

"Failsafe, are you on the air?" Agent Edmunds said into his radio.

"Who is Failsafe?" the sheriff asked.

"We're here," a voice came over the agent's radio. The voice did not come over either McClain's or his deputy's radio.

"Why are you on a different frequency?" the sheriff demanded.

"Blue Ford, at the gate. Front seat passenger side," Edmunds said.

"Got it," replied the voice on the radio.

"Who is Failsafe?" Sheriff McClain demanded again. "You need to bring me up to speed."

"My boss found out that the ATF has a file on these people," Edmunds said. "Seems there are some unserved warrants out for several individuals inside, including Dinah and Paul Whiten."

"And you're just telling me now?" the sheriff asked.

"Not my call, Sheriff," Edmunds replied.

"So, who is Failsafe?" McClain asked again.

"An observation team. They're nearby," Edmunds replied.

"An *armed* observation team?" McClain asked.

Agent Edmunds raised his binoculars again, but the sheriff yanked them down.

"Is this other team armed?" he asked.

Edmunds nodded. "They're armed."

"Shit!" Sheriff McClain exclaimed. "Where are they, exactly?"

"I can't say exactly," Edmunds replied. "They are a highly trained sniper team. Their only instructions were to get into position to watch the gate and await further orders. They will not fire unless lives are threatened. But when Agent Hart learns that at least one person with a warrant on them is confirmed inside, we will be sending in our own troop."

"Damn!" the sheriff replied. "This will not do. It will not do at all."

He stood, handed his rifle to his deputy, and started down the hill.

"Where are you going?" Edmunds called after him.

"I'm going to try and stop a war," McClain replied.

CHAPTER TWENTY-EIGHT

Month and date unknown
501 years until failure

Chitto set a brutal pace. I was determined to keep up with the men as we raced through the hills and skirted the mountains to our north. Waya had refused to send anyone else on what he deemed to be a futile effort to bring Sequoyah and Sehoy home. This rebuff ate at my mind like a colony of ants. As I loped behind Chitto, another thought formed—one that, once allowed to enter my mind, could not be refused.

The Nermernuh had descended on our camp with a force unlike the small raiding parties they usually formed. They also timed the attack perfectly for when we had no guards and the people were sluggish from dancing and feasting. Some of us had even taken potions that trick the mind into seeing visions of lost loved ones.

The Nermernuh looked so different from us that they could not normally have infiltrated our camp without notice. They even smelled different, like bears or badgers. And while rumors and stories spread across the nations like fires, to my knowledge, the Nermernuh never interacted peacefully with any tribe, so it seemed unlikely that they could have learned of Sehoy's beauty or of Sequoyah's skills from other bands. These thoughts burned in my heart.

Six of Chitto's closest friends and age-mates joined us. They wore rawhide breechcloths with leggings that came up to their knees, and their chests were bare despite the cold of the high mountains. All carried clubs and lances strapped to their backs. Two had bows. I had seen them shoot and knew that I was superior to them in distance and accuracy.

I carried no club, only a knife, my bow, quivers, and a blowgun. I reasoned that if caught in close quarters, I would have no chance against any Nermernuh. My best hope lay in arrows and darts and in trusting my companions to shield me from close attack.

Chitto drove us directly toward the stone mountain Waya had described to us. He said it would take us four days at best pace to reach the Nermernuh stronghold. I shuddered to think what they would do to Sehoy during these days and nights. I knew she would be taken, likely by all of them. It was their way. I also knew that Sequoyah would be tortured, bound, beaten, and burned. Perhaps Sehoy as well, especially if she failed to please them. These thoughts buzzed about my head and made me drive my body past where it should have broken.

We did not rest the first night but slowed our pace to avoid injuries on the unfamiliar trails. We passed one small band of the First People, perhaps twelve warriors. They carried the carcass of a buffalo calf strapped to poles. None of us spoke or gestured to them as they headed for the Tugaloo, and we pressed on.

At nightfall on the second day, we reached the Chattahoochee, a clear river much larger than the Tugaloo. Chitto called for us to stop and camp for the night. My joints screamed protests as I unstrapped my weapons and laid them carefully against a nearby log. Chitto allowed a small fire, and we warmed ourselves against it. One of the warriors began a song, a new song, that must have formed in his mind as we traveled. The firelight danced across his face as he sang softly. The other warriors gazed into the fire.

I cannot recall all the words and at that moment wished I had Sequoyah's writing tools to save it to skin and stone. He sang of

Sehoy's beauty, Sequoyah's wisdom, and the love warriors had for each other. Then he sang of a great war woman clad in a shining mask, as beautiful as her sister as she rained death upon our enemies. I cried into the darkness and wished for the comfort of Onacona's touch or the warmth of my sister's embrace.

Then, one by one, we all laid our heads on the damp earth and slept.

Chitto roused us before dawn. He covered the coals from the previous night's fire, and we strapped our weapons to our backs and continued. His pace was slower at first, allowing our bones and joints to loosen. Then, as the sun broke across the distant hills, he started the trail-eating lope of hunters.

A well-worn path followed the Chattahoochee, but still we had to cross many tributaries that fed the great river. We slowed to a walk only while eating our cold provisions. Otherwise, we pressed as fast as our legs would take us.

The sun had reached its highest peak when the gods interceded—for our good or just to toy with us, I cannot say. At a place where a river from the northern mountains spilled into the Chattahoochee, we found four rafts of ash logs strapped together with strong vines. Two of them would hold our entire party.

We left a crude stone knife we had taken from the Nermernuh dead at the river's edge as if inadvertently dropped and covered all our tracks except for mine, hoping that my smaller footprint would look more like a Nermernuh's.

I lay flat against the logs while warriors at the front and back of the raft used long poles to guide us into the current. Cold water from the Chattahoochee soaked me through the raft, but I did not care. The river was taking me to my sister and the man who for most of my life had loved me as a brother might. We rested as we floated, covering ground much faster than we could have on foot. Slowly, as the trees traced shadows across my face, I began to paint a picture in my mind of how we got here. I had a strong sense that we were being pushed to our doom. The rocking of the boat and the sun's warmth soon lulled me into a troubled sleep. In my dreams, I discovered a terrible truth. I knew how and by whom we had been betrayed.

At one point, Chitto brought the two rafts together so we could talk without shouting. His face showed the strain of the last two days, but he radiated a reassuring calm.

"The Chattahoochee has many rapids north of us," he said. "If the Nermernuh went from the Currahee directly to the river, it is possible that we are ahead of them. There is no way to know. I think we should continue on the river, find the mountain of stone, and lay an ambush. If they are behind us, we can catch them before they make it to their stronghold. If they are ahead, we can scout their camp and know where Sequoyah and Sehoy are."

The other warriors, for now I considered myself one of them, grunted in reply. We continued downriver, keeping a watchful eye to our rear.

On two occasions, we spotted strange men and women staring at us from the shore. They wore peculiar painted symbols on their faces and bodies and smooth twigs woven into their hair. They were not, mercifully, the Nermernuh. The strangers offered no greeting, and we pretended we did not see them.

We all took turns using the poles to guide the rafts, the river bending here and there but always returning to take us ever south. We slept, ate from our meager stocks, drank from the river, and waited as the Chattahoochee took us toward whatever fate the gods had waiting for us.

ON THE MORNING of our second day on the river, Chitto stood and gazed long into the morning fog. I could tell that he was thinking his way to the mountain, recalling all he had heard of the path we would take. As we approached a fork where another river merged with the Chattahoochee, he told us to move to the western shore. We pulled the rafts deep into the bushes and brushed away our tracks.

We then pushed through the brush and up a steep slope. When we reached the top, we moved to an open spot just as the fog began to clear. There in the distance rose the stone mountain, bald and streaked with age. Around the base, numerous fires smoldered, creating a shroud of smoke that hid all approaches.

Chitto told one of the men to stay on the slope within sight of the river. He would wait for most of the day, watching to establish whether the Nermernuh raiders were behind us. If he saw no one, he would follow the markers we left for him and join us at the mountain's base. If he saw the raiding party approaching, he was to race to us so we could prepare an ambush.

We set off again, refreshed and strong, ready for what awaited us. Or so we thought.

Past more thick vegetation, we came to a thin trail that appeared to be rarely used. We followed it around hills and ravines. Through breaks in the trees, we saw the mountain growing larger. My unease grew as well.

Night fell as we entered hell.

The forest stopped abruptly more than twice a bowshot from the stone mountain. Coals glowed from a hundred burning logs and stumps. A single trail wove through this wasteland, visible in the dim light as a shard of red clay against the blackened earth. In the distance, Nermernuh warriors slunk toward the mountain, their posture speaking of great fear. Fear of what, we did not know. One small band dragged a woman by her hair as she screeched and begged. The little clothing she wore was ragged and torn but still carried the marking of the First People.

While we waited, the warrior we had left at the river returned to us. He had seen no one, and we all believed that the Nermernuh had Sequoyah and Sehoy on the mountain. When after a time no more Nermernuh appeared, we ran silently forward, stopping wherever a boulder or fallen tree gave us cover. We approached the mountain from the west, where a few trees marked the most gradual slope upward. We saw no Nermernuh until we were within a stone's throw of the first crag. Chitto raised a hand, and our group halted under the cover of an outcrop large enough to hide us.

Chitto signaled that he had seen a man, likely a guard, perched on a log by the trail. One of our warriors pulled his bow from his back and was preparing to nock an arrow when Chitto raised a hand to stop him. He pointed to me. I nodded.

I removed my blowgun and quivers, then took the bow from around my neck. Carefully stretching the bow to awaken the wood, I selected an arrow, one without the poison. We were at least fifty paces from the guard. The distance was child's play for my bow.

On Chitto's signal, I stepped onto the path and saw a flicker of movement in the weak light of a shaven moon. I took another step onto the trail. Again, movement. This time, the Nermernuh guard made a fatal mistake. He emerged from the shadows, and my arrow disappeared into his chest with little more than a whisper. He turned, took one step, and fell on his face with a gurgle.

We ran to where the guard lay, half expecting others to be with him to raise the alarm. We saw nothing.

A far-off night bird called. The faintest of sounds filtered through the sparse trees. Fires we had not before noticed dotted the crest of the mountain, forming a line that left the trees and crossed over the mountain to its peak. At the top, a circle of fires gave the mountain the appearance of an enormous eye peering upward into the heavens.

We dragged the Nermernuh guard into the bushes, and I reclaimed my arrow and took his bearskin covering. Two more guards fell to my arrows before we made it to the first fire. Children and old women sat on stones, clawing and chewing the bones of an animal I did not recognize. We scanned the area, and Chitto decided to evade the fires by moving along the bushes beyond their light.

At the next fire sat more women and children. Some of these women appeared to be Sehoy's age. We saw no more men until we reached the next fire. There, six or so had gathered around the woman of the First People we had seen before. She was now naked and being violated by a young man while the others laughed and cheered for him. We were still slipping by when the man rose from her to be replaced by another.

We worked our way silently to the top of the mountain. So confident were the Nermernuh of their numbers and their stronghold that they had no other guards and no one to raise the alarm. Once, a child who could barely walk stumbled toward us while we crouched nearby. He looked intently into the bushes and directly at me. A woman, his mother I suppose, came to lead him back to the fire.

We reached the circle we had seen from the field below and stopped at a copse of cedar trees. Men and women danced into and out of the circle, chanting and banging sticks and drums of stretched skins. From inside the few crude shelters, we heard men and women rutting. Then, I heard a scream.

Chitto drew up his head and listened. He too recognized the voice. My admiration for him was renewed as his mind corralled his heart and he suppressed the urge to rush the camp to free his lost love. We listened and heard the scream again; it came from the other side of the circle. We had no way to get there without exposing ourselves to the light. I placed my bow on the ground at Chitto's feet and shifted my blowgun to hang along my spine. Strapping my bundle of darts to my thigh, I then donned the bearskin. Chitto restrained me as I stood.

Me, he signed with his hands.

Too tall, I replied.

He looked around at the others. They were also much taller than the Nermernuh.

Wait here, I signed to him. He reluctantly nodded.

I smudged my face and hands with dirt and pulled my hair into a knot to fit inside the bearskin headdress. Then I hesitated. In the dim light, with the others staring at me, I took off my mask. I felt naked in the cool night air as I handed the mask to Chitto, pulled the bearskin over my head, and stepped into the light. Sehoy screamed again.

No one challenged me as I stalked steadily toward the thatched grass hut. Light from a small fire filtered through the grass wall. A man sat outside the hut, wearing only a breastplate of rib bones. His bearskin lay on the ground beside him. He called once to the man inside and laughed at whatever he heard in reply. I loosened the knot holding my blowgun in place, then slipped it free. I looked around. No one watched me as I slid my hand into the pouch of darts. By feel, I could tell which ones carried the poison. I carefully extracted a dart and removed its sheath.

I was less than twenty paces from the hut when the man stood, leaned over, and slipped inside. I heard voices, a whimper, a laugh. While I stood watching, another man stepped from the hut to crouch outside. Sehoy screamed once more as I lifted the blowgun to my mouth and blew.

The man swatted the air as if warding off an insect, stood unsteadily, then fell to his knees. I slit his throat before the poison had finished its job.

Inside the hut, I heard my sister whimpering and a slap. I knelt by the door and eased it open just a crack. A man sat astride Sehoy. Her hands were tied above her head and fixed to a post. While I watched, the man pulled a burning twig from the fire and waved it over Sehoy's face. Without warning, he plunged the twig onto her right breast, and she shrieked.

Her agony was still echoing across the camp when I killed the man with a dart to his neck. He fell silently across my sister.

As I slid the woven-grass door forward, I heard a growl to my right and barely had time to turn and face the Nermernuh woman who launched herself at me. To my shame, I had not seen her hiding in the shadows. She encircled me with powerful arms and bit my shoulder. She was still tearing flesh from me when I drove my knife under her ribs and into her heart. She rolled away and onto the fire, drenching the hut with smoky blackness.

I felt my way toward Sehoy and rolled the dead Nermernuh off her before cutting the thongs that held her to the post.

"My love," I whispered. "I am here. We have come for you."

Sehoy sobbed as we embraced.

"We must go now," I whispered.

She resisted when I tried to pull from her grip.

"Chitto awaits," I said, and she relaxed somewhat.

We peered outside and saw no one nearby. Dancing and singing continued, but we heard no alarm, no sign that we had been discovered.

Sehoy took the bearskin from the slain Nermernuh inside the tent, pulled it on, and followed me to where Chitto and the other warriors waited. The two lovers embraced for longer than I would have wanted. I replaced my mask and felt more at ease.

"Sequoyah?" I finally asked in a whisper.

Sehoy pointed farther up the mountain, at a group of Nermernuh clustered around the largest fire. Despite her protests, Chitto had a warrior escort her off the mountain with instructions to meet us across the ravaged expanse. When they had safely slipped away into the night, we ventured closer to the commotion.

Sequoyah had been tied upright to a dead pine. They had stripped him, and one particularly large and fierce-looking Nermernuh wore his breechcloth. They laughed and pointed as children ran up to Sequoyah with rods and lashed him across the chest and legs. An old woman reached into a fire and pulled out a burning stick. She chuckled as she shuffled toward him. Sequoyah eyed the woman, then spit at her, and she shrieked and thrust the flaming stick into his groin. Sequoyah's scream split the night. My heart broke for him.

At least sixty Nermernuh surrounded him. We had no hope of escaping with Sequoyah. Still, we sat and schemed how it could be done.

The man wearing Sequoyah's breechcloth settled the issue for us.

He approached our friend, carrying a large, crude stone axe. He said something to his captive, and Sequoyah replied in a language I had never heard him use. Whatever he said enraged the Nermernuh, who swung the great axe down and severed most of Sequoyah's left foot. Blood spurted across the ground, and Sequoyah slumped in his binds. The Nermernuh laughed and hooted their approval.

To our horror, the big Nermernuh plucked up the severed foot and chomped into its flesh. It was then that I noticed a copper band around his wrist. I had seen this thing before, twisted into a spiral resembling snakes mating.

Chitto pulled me back into the brush. He slowly shook his head.

Cannot, he signed to me.

Try, I signed back.

No, he replied. *Cannot walk, cannot run. Death only.*

My heart bled. We returned to the shadows and began our long trek back. When we reached the second fire, we stopped behind a jumble of boulders at the base of a stone pillar. A white pine grew alongside.

Free him, I signed.

Cannot, Chitto replied.

Not bring him, I signed back. *Free him.*

I touched my quiver. Chitto nodded his assent, and I began to climb the pine. When I could do so, I edged out on a limb and carefully stepped onto a foothold on the stone tower. I continued climbing until I found a place where I could stand unobstructed.

In the distance, Sequoyah was still being tortured by the Nermernuh. Dawn was crawling upon us, and I was almost out of time. I pulled from my quiver the straightest arrow I had ever made, child of a sourwood struck by lightning and burnished in flames of the sacred red oak and hickory. I nocked the arrow just as the sun slipped from the underworld and struck me in the face. A soft sparkle reflected onto Sequoyah's face, and he looked up at me. My heart thudded in my chest, screaming for me not to do this terrible thing.

Then Sequoyah nodded. Over the heads of those intent on causing him unknowable pain, he gave me permission.

I let the arrow fly. It arced upward through sunlight as pure as when the world was young, then plunged into the darkness to reemerge in firelight. A woman rose up in front of Sequoyah, and for a moment I thought she would take the arrow. She bent to do something cruel to their captive as the arrow flew a handsbreadth above her head and into his heart.

The singing stopped.

I scrambled down the stone tower to rejoin my friends. We ran as angry voices rippled down the mountain, passing fire after fire and not stopping to wonder if we were seen. As we neared the last two fires, a group of Nermernuh men leaped into our path. Chitto and his men cut them down without breaking stride. My bow took another who stood holding a rope near the fire. At the other end of the rope knelt the woman of the First People. I pulled the rope from her neck and motioned her to come with us. She quickly gathered what clothing still lay around the fire, stopped to kick and spit at the man I had shot, then ran to join us.

A few more Nermernuh stood in our way, but they moved in a confused and aimless manner, and we charged through them easily. Slipping down the trail without further challenge, we entered the wasteland, where we met up with Sehoy and the warrior accompanying her.

"If we make the forest, we can outrun them," called Chitto. "Run!"

I was surprised how fast the woman of the First People could move. She had no covering for her feet or any other part of her body, and she ran while clutching her leather jerkin and a few other strips of clothing. When we had reached the shadows of the forest, she stopped and donned her garments. The mountain crawled with Nermernuh. In the morning light, we saw them forming into bands as people shouted and drums beat. Already, a few of the faster men were pelting down the single trail off the mountain.

Eight Nermernuh poured through the gap in the trees where we had killed the first guard. I nocked an arrow and sent it soaring as they reached the badlands. It struck the one in front, who careened into those behind. They turned and retreated out of range as we fled into the forest.

We found the trail to the Chattahoochee and used no stealth, just speed, as we scrabbled through brush and limbs, always watching for the Nermernuh pursuers. The rafts would be no good to us against the current, so we found a rocky place upstream and crossed. Chitto inspected the banks and used a pine branch to sweep away signs of our passing. We then shoved through vegetation until we emerged into a stand of chestnut trees. Here, the underbrush thinned, and we could run freely.

Chitto soon slowed to a loping stride, but we did not stop until the sun was directly overhead and peeking through the chestnut trees. Sehoy struggled to keep up, and I stayed with her. We ate what little food we carried when the group paused to rest. I shared mine with Sehoy and the woman of the First People.

"I am called Chenoa," she told me as we ate.

"A good name, White Dove," I replied.

I tried to talk more to her, but she had slipped into that place within herself where people heal. I knew the place well. Sehoy sat close to her, their sides touching. She pulled White Dove to her, and they both cried silently in shared grief at what had been done to them. The men sat a respectful distance from us and pretended not to see or hear us. I could tell that Chitto wanted to come to Sehoy, but he knew that in these things, women can help women best.

The warriors chafed at the wait, but Chitto allowed time for Sehoy and White Dove to bathe in a clear stream. I used sand and fennel to scrub them as they sat holding hands in the water. When they had dried and dressed, only their bruises and memories remained of their ordeal.

Chitto kept us moving north through the trees and along ridges where we could see in all directions. Several times, he sent warriors to backtrack us, watching for pursuers. There were none.

On the third day of our trek home, we came to a small village. We crouched behind trees and saw no one moving. No dogs, no people. Nothing.

After a time, Chitto ventured down, leaving us among the trees. He approached slowly with his club at the ready. Pushing open the doors to several huts, he found no one and motioned us to join him.

I knelt to feel for warmth in one of the firepits.

"Whoever this was," I said, "they left here not three days ago. I still feel coals burning beneath these ashes."

We spread out to check the other huts. Some had broken doors. I found a few clubs. One of our warriors called out, and we ran to join him. I wished we had not.

"Nermernuh," Chitto spat.

We stood staring up into a stand of around thirty new pines, where bodies had been strung like meat for drying. Women, children, men. All had been terribly mutilated, most of them lacking arms or legs. Fires had been built beneath the trees, and the branches were scorched and burned, denuded of all green. We saw the gnawed human limbs scattered across the ground, remnants of a feast of demons.

I vomited.

White Dove turned and walked away.

"We will hunt these Nermernuh like wolves," Chitto swore. "We will not stop until they are removed from the earth."

We followed a well-worn trail from the village and headed north. We did not speak, each of us wanting to forget what the past few days had shown us.

On the morning of the fifth day following our raid on the stone mountain, the trail led us into a valley. In the distance, we saw the peak of the Currahee. Home.

Chitto slowed. Something worked in his mind. I wondered if he had the same thoughts as me. When we rested at midday, I sat near him.

"You saw the metal bracelet the Nermernuh wore?" I asked.

"Twisted snakes and an eagle."

He nodded.

"You have seen it before?"

Again, he nodded.

"The Nermernuh did not find us by chance," I stated.

"I know," he said.

CHAPTER TWENTY-NINE

11:42 a.m., November 9, 1977

Three days, ten hours, and twenty-two minutes after failure

Sheriff McClain approached the gate, careful to keep his hands far from the pistol strapped to his waist. The man standing by Dinah Whiten's car saw him approach and took a few steps in his direction. Another man appeared at the top of the sheet metal wall to the sheriff's right. McClain hadn't been aware that they had platforms overlooking the gate. He held both hands in front of him and stopped about ten paces from the car.

"Sheriff," the man said. His fatigues were ragged and streaked with oil, and thin, stringy hair fell from beneath his camouflage hat.

"G'morning. Is that you, Ryan?" the sheriff asked.

"The name's Jacob now." Jacob peered suspiciously down the road behind the sheriff.

"I haven't seen you since your mom died," McClain said. "A fine lady. Your dad, too. I heard you moved up here. Things going okay?"

"What are you doing out here on foot?" Jacob demanded, still eying the road and woods.

"I mean to talk to Pastor Dinah," Sheriff McClain replied.

Jacob glanced back at the car. The passenger door opened.

"I think for now it's best if you stay in the car, Mrs. Whiten," the sheriff said.

The door slammed shut. The angle of the sun cast a glare across the windshield, and the sheriff could barely see inside. Above him on the wall, another man appeared and glared down at him. This one carried a pump shotgun. He kept the gun pointed into the air, but his finger rested on the trigger.

"Son, I think you'd better put that gun out of sight," McClain said. "We don't want anyone misinterpreting anyone else's intentions, now, do we?"

The man lowered the shotgun but stayed where he was. The other man at the wall turned and spoke to others below him. Three more popped up along the wall on the other side of the gate. As far as the sheriff could tell, they were not armed.

"Why do you want to talk to Pastor Dinah, Sheriff?" Jacob asked.

"I think that's between her and me," he replied. "Can I come inside?"

Jacob glanced inside the car before answering, "Not with that gun of yours, you can't."

"Well, I think it best if we have this discussion inside," McClain said. "And I'm not giving up my sidearm."

He took a step forward. The man with the shotgun raised his weapon and pumped a shell into the chamber.

"Don't!" the sheriff shouted. The warning was barely out of his mouth before the man slumped forward. The crack of the gunshot reached McClain's ears a split second later. Jacob bolted inside, and Dinah Whiten's driver threw the car in reverse and skidded into the compound. As the gate closed with a clang, another shot pierced the windshield on the passenger side. The sheriff could not see whether Dinah was hit. He turned to run to cover, and a shotgun blast hit him, pain searing his back. He heard another shot and saw the grass bend as pellets flew past him.

When he reached a deadfall of logs, he rolled over and lay flat.

Pulling out his radio, he shouted, "Cease fire! Cease fire!"

Other voices blared over the radio, overlapping his.

"Officer down. Officer down. Request immediate backup and EMS," he heard.

McClain rolled to his side and felt along the back of his legs and jacket. Dozens of holes pierced his pants and leaked small drops of blood.

"Bird shot!" he yelled into the radio. "They hit me with bird shot. I'm fine. Call off the EMS. And cease fire immediately!"

He heard another rifle shot echo but could not tell where it originated.

"I say again," he hollered over the radio, "cease fire! Do not engage with anyone at the compound. Do not return fire. No one tried to kill me. Cease fire!"

"Sheriff McClain?" Deputy Adams's voice came over the radio. "You okay?"

"I am fine," McClain replied. "Are you not listening? They peppered my backside with bird shot. That's all. I didn't see any other weapons."

"These guys are pretty hyped up, Sheriff," Doug said. "They've called in more firepower. Won't listen to me. Any chance you can get back up here—like, now?"

"Do you still have eyes on the wall?" the sheriff asked.

"I do," Doug replied. "I don't see anyone. Our guys on the other observation site by the back fence say there's a lot of commotion in the compound. People running around, herding children into buildings and such. Up here, we can't see over the walls, so I've no idea what else is happening."

"Anyone reporting more guns?" McClain asked.

"Nothing except for the one that shot at you," Doug replied. "Should I meet you back at the truck?"

"Stay there until I get to you," the sheriff said. "Keep your eyes on the gate. If you see any movement, radio back to me immediately.

Got it?"

McClain ran to the hideout spot, half expecting to hear shots following him. Doug and Agent Edmunds stood as he approached. Sheriff McClain marched straight to the agent until their noses almost touched.

"What the hell is wrong with you?" he shouted. "You just killed a citizen of my county."

"From where I sat, he was an imminent threat to the life of another law enforcement office," Edmunds replied. His voice was steady and confident. "In fact, someone from that wall took at least two shots at you. We likely should have fired earlier, and you are lucky to be alive."

McClain took a deep breath and stepped back. He picked up his binoculars and took his rifle from Deputy Adams.

"Now how are you going to execute that warrant?" McClain said. "They've gone to ground, we'd say. Holed up behind that fence."

"They're contained," Edmunds said.

McClain stomped down the hill toward his truck, calling back over his shoulder, "There's near three hundred people behind those walls. You spilled their blood, took the first shots. They've got food, fuel, water. Everything they need to hide out for months. You damn fool. You just started something that I'll have to finish, and it will not end well."

They made it back to the road as two cruisers skidded to a halt near the sheriff's pickup truck. A deputy climbed out of each. They looked about nervously.

"Doug, you go with Randy here," Sheriff McClain said. "Circle back around the rock quarry and come in from the other side. Stop as far from the gate as you can but where you can still see it. Got it?"

Doug and Randy nodded.

"Seth, you ease up on this side," McClain said. "Keep an eye on the gate. If anyone shoots toward you, back up. Do not engage. Got that? Do not engage. One shooting is enough."

When the two patrol cars had left, McClain slung his rifle on the rack behind his seat and hopped into the driver's side. Agent Edmunds climbed in beside him.

Neither spoke as McClain drove back to the base at the college, working around mud and debris from the flood on their way to the command tent. Outside, more Secret Service agents mulled about. McClain saw several severe-looking men wearing US Marshal badges. All carried holstered pistols, and a few had M16 assault rifles over their shoulders. Overhead, a helicopter circled.

Sheriff McClain entered the tent and into a world of chaos. Everyone was talking. Guardsmen wearing headsets spoke into radios set up on folding tables along one side of the tent. The paper map Sheriff McClain and Deputy Adams had corrected the day before was now mounted on a board atop a tripod. Pins dotted the map. Agent Hart stood at the map, speaking with a guardsman in fatigues bearing a silver eagle on each lapel.

"John," McClain said to the colonel, glaring at Hart as he spoke.

"Tom," the colonel replied.

"So," Hart said, "you know each other. Good."

"Cut the crap!" McClain barked. "John, did he tell you that his agents shot some people at the Whiten compound?"

Colonel John Watts nodded. "From what I'm told, Tom, they may have saved your life."

"They hit me with bird shot," McClain retorted. "They had no intention of killing me, and they only shot at me after this bozo's goon killed one of their own. Now they're holed up inside that compound of theirs, and we may never get them out."

"We'll get them out," Hart said.

Sheriff McClain squinted past the agent and saw three more trucks rumbling down the road. Two of them had flatbeds carrying armored vehicles of a type the sheriff did not recognize. What he saw on the other sent a chill down his spine.

"You've brought a Bradley?" he said, rounding on Hart. "You can't be serious. This is not Vietnam, and these are not terrorists."

"Governor Busbee ordered me to provide the agents here with whatever they requested, Tom," he replied. "This is what they requested."

"Armored vehicles and enough firepower to blow away half of Toccoa?" Sheriff McClain shouted.

Voices lowered, and eyes turned their way.

"Listen, Tom," the colonel said, "I'm not happy about this either, but I'm following orders."

He pulled the sheriff to the side.

"We're having our JAG officer render an opinion as to whether or not this is legal," he said. "He's going up the chain of command while we're asking Justice about it. I'm moving as slow as I can without violating a direct order. But it may be a couple of days before I can get a clear opinion from the JAG. In the meantime, go along, see if you can help us keep a lid on this."

McClain turned to glare at Hart again, who by that time had picked up a headset and was barking orders. Before the sheriff could get his attention, he took off his headset and shouted for attention.

"Listen up, people," he said. "POTUS is inbound. ETA twenty-five minutes."

Sheriff McClain returned to his truck and brought out the radio. "Doug, do you copy?"

"Copy, Sheriff," a voice crackled in reply.

"Any activity at the compound?" he asked.

"Nothing from the compound," Doug replied. "But there's a helluvalot of Army trucks pulling up. They're closer than we are. If they have rifles inside the compound, someone's liable to get killed out here. What's going on?"

"Just stay put and keep me informed," Sheriff McClain replied.

Colonel Watts came out to stand beside him.

"This is crazy, John," Sheriff McClain said.

The colonel nodded. "Yep. Batshit crazy."

A fighter jet flew overhead, followed by another two.

"Just an escort for the president's plane," Watts said.

As they watched the sky, a large helicopter passed over them. Its base was glossy green, while the top of the aircraft had been painted white with an American flag near the front.

"Marine One," Watts said. "He's here."

Agent Hart brushed past them and jumped into a hard-topped jeep, then sped off with three black cars in tow.

"You probably should stay nearby, Tom," Colonel Watts said. "Word I get is that President Carter is here just to show support for the townspeople and the college. He doesn't know about the Whitens, and the Secret Service is not going to tell him."

"Ride with me, John," McClain said.

The colonel retrieved a radio from the command tent before climbing into the car with the sheriff. They drove the half mile to the college's entrance. Soldiers at a roadblock stopped them, peered in to see the colonel, then waved them through.

From a distance, McClain and Watts watched Marine One land on an athletic field. Both men stayed in the truck while the blades wound down and President Carter and Mrs. Carter disembarked. At the base of the steps, the president turned and assisted the First Lady to the ground. Secret Service agents surrounded them, and they were whisked away to view the devastation of the flood.

The sheriff's radio sputtered to life.

"You'd better get up here, Sheriff," Doug said. "They've got a whole army here. They just brought in some sort of tank or something."

"Anything from the compound?" McClain asked.

"Lots of movement now, Sheriff," Doug replied. "People along the wall. Jimmy says the back fence is crawling with men."

"Guns?"

"Not that I can see from here, Sheriff," the deputy replied. "But Jimmy says that a few people up front may be carrying. He can't tell what."

"On my way," McClain said.

CHAPTER THIRTY

Month and date unknown
501 years until failure

We strode into our village, passing guards who nodded at us in respect. Our people busied themselves in the fields and huts as if the world had continued normally while we were gone. Knowing that our fields had been planted, nuts harvested from the forests, and game hunted while we drove ourselves on the quest for family and friends disheartened me. Foolishly, I thought that life had stopped anywhere except within the range of my bow.

Chitto and Sehoy walked together again. She leaned on him, and he kept his arm draped over her shoulder. I saw them again retreat into the world of lovers. It made me ache for Onacona's touch.

Mother was sitting by our fire when she saw us. She ran past me to embrace Sehoy, and I felt a pang of jealousy. It did not last long. Mother brought me to her, and I felt her warmth spread through me, a warmth that she alone seemed to make. I cried, and she cried. Sehoy left Chitto and joined us. We were together. I had brought my sister home.

Across the village, we heard other greetings as the warriors returned to their own huts. Soon a chant went up, drawing us to the center of the village and near the huts of Waya's family. The shaman stepped out. His face revealed much. Surprise, concern, confusion. Then I saw in his face confirmation of what I had suspected. I saw fear.

"You have come back," Waya said.

Chitto nodded. Sehoy returned to his side and clung to him like a child. Heedless of my position, I slipped my bow from my back and stood with the other warriors.

"We had thought you were lost," Waya stated.

"I want no banter from you, shaman," I said. "Let us not waste each other's time. We know what you did."

As one, the people of the Abittibi turned to Waya.

"If you have an accusation against me, speak," he replied. "But I will remind you that I was your father's shaman and his father's before him. I have led the people's spirit life for longer than your mother has lived. But if you must, speak now."

A murmur rippled through the people.

"We saw the twisted snake bracelet," I said, turning to the crowd. "Made by Sequoyah himself. It was worn by one of the Nermernuh."

People cast angry looks at Waya, but I noticed a circle of warriors forming around us. They moved quietly and wore a circle of blue paint on their chests.

"Where is Sequoyah?" Waya asked. Sequoyah's wives stood beside him, and when they took up the question, more of the crowd's anger seemed aimed at us.

I did a quick count of the silent warriors who encircled us. For every one of us, they had at least five. White Dove backed slowly away, then turned to disappear into the forest.

"Where is my son-in-law, Sequoyah?" shouted Inola.

"He is dead," Chitto said.

"How is it that you bring back your own wife, your sister, and yet leave behind Sequoyah, the man who brought wealth and prestige to our tribe, the man who healed us, taught us things that no one had dreamed we could do?" Waya said. "What happened to him?"

"We could not save him," Chitto said. "It was not possible."

"So, you left him to die with the Nermernuh?" Waya demanded. "At the hands of the Nermernuh, his death would last for days. I even heard rumors that they are cannibals." A cry went up from the women. Waya waited for it to die down, then continued. "How did you leave him?"

"He was tied to a tree and tortured," Chitto replied. "We saw it."

"How did you leave him?" Waya asked again.

"They cut off his foot," Chitto said.

More of the people cried out. Now most glared at the rescue party in anger.

"And that is how you left him?" Waya asked.

"I killed him," I said.

Shouts erupted across the camp. Mother came to stand by my side. Sequoyah's wives lunged for me but were restrained by Chitto's warriors.

Waya raised his hand, and gradually the people quieted.

"Since Dustau died, we have had no chief," he said. "We have no council for moments such as this."

No one else spoke. In the distance, I heard blue jays scream to one another. Fatigue draped me, threatened to drag my body to the ground. This was not the time to bring justice to Waya, who, in our absence, seemed to have solidified his support among the Abittibi. It is an easy thing to do when the people are afraid. Our courage had gained little favor.

"Would you have me as chief?" Waya said, raising his hands as if to embrace the crowd.

A roar of assent enveloped him. He turned slowly, no doubt taking note of who shouted approval and who remained silent.

"Does anyone oppose me?" he asked.

Words burned in my mind, but I remained silent. Already, an idea began to take shape. A thought so cruel and outrageous that I feared dwelling on it. It was, however, a thought that would not be denied.

CHAPTER THIRTY-ONE

Month and date unknown
501 years until failure

The next day, a gentle rain sprinkled the Currahee, and the trees wept. As the sun broke through the clouds, I slipped out and headed to my spot at the Tugaloo, hoping to find my love. I needed his hand on my face, needed to hear the many names he used for me that made me feel like a cherished child.

I came upon him bathing and singing in the spot where I had first met him. Sidling up to the water's edge, I watched him for a while—watched the water make intricate designs down his back, saw the way his smooth hair draped across his shoulders. When he turned to face me, I let out the smallest of gasps.

Onacona tilted his head slightly but continued to scrub himself with the fine sand. He showed no sign that the frigid water bothered him. Onacona shook his head, and shards of morning light burst from him. Then he went to sit on a log warmed by sunlight.

"I would rather you join me, my love," he said, laughing. "There are stories spreading across our tribe. I would hear them from your lips."

I giggled, as I had years before. I waded across and fell into his arms. When we had satisfied our lusts, we lay on a warm mat of moss. I had taken off my mask, and he traced lines around my nose with warm fingers that smelled of fennel. I told him everything.

When I shared our suspicions about Waya's betrayal, he hissed in disapproval.

"The Nermernuh came from the west," he said. "We heard that they had been hunted there, their tribe splintered and driven in all directions. Some came to a peaceful people who lived on the stone mountain. By treachery, the Nermernuh gained access to the fortress and killed those who had befriended them. These people, if they are people, make nothing of their own. No art or song. No dance or even weapons. They steal and loot. Always retreating to the stone mountain."

Much of this I had known.

"While you were gone, Waya came to our elders," Onacona continued. "He claimed that you had called the Nermernuh to the Currahee. He claimed that you are a witch and that you would use your powers to lay waste to all of your people, then to ours."

Again, anger burned in me, and my plan took on firmer flesh.

"He claimed that you consorted with demons," Onacona said. "He said that you were with child. The child of a demon."

He gently placed his hand on my stomach. At that moment, we both knew.

"Did your elders believe him?" I asked.

"Some did. Some did not," he replied. "My people still fear the ghosts of the Currahee. No one wanted to interfere with them. They were still undecided until White Dove returned to us. She told us all of your bravery on the stone mountain. She told us of how the woman behind the mask became a great warrior. She convinced the elders that you could be trusted.

"In her time with the Nermernuh, she learned that it was Waya who had betrayed you, led the Nermernuh to your camp, advised them of when they should attack. He had grown weary of Sequoyah's power and influence and lusted to have back his old powers. Many of the First People wanted to attack the Abittibi, drive your people from the land. But still, the fear of the ghosts restrains them."

A question from my childhood arose.

"I have seen no ghosts in my whole life of living in the shadow of the Currahee," I said. "Why do the First People think such things?"

"Long before we ever heard of the Abittibi, a small band of an ancient people lived where you live," he replied. "My grandfather still speaks of them, retells their story so that the memory of them will not die. He says that if we forget these people of the mountain, great calamity will befall the First People.

"He says that there is a race of people somewhere in the east that musters great armies of warriors. They wait. When the time comes, we will be driven from our lands, hunted, and killed. Our children will be stolen from us. We will wander, fighting endless wars that we cannot win, hoping to keep memories of us alive. Grandfather says there is power in remembering those who would be forgotten, and he tells stories of the people of the Currahee so that this power will remain with the First People and hold back the calamity from the east."

"What does he say of these people of the Currahee?" I asked. "Are they ghosts?"

"Perhaps now they are ghosts," he replied. "At one time, they were a gentle people who lived peaceful lives. They farmed and rarely hunted. They were small, much smaller than any of us, and we would seem as giants to them. They called themselves the Tsvdigewi. Grandfather could not say if they were humans or not. 'That is for the gods,' he would say. These Tsvdigewi preferred to be invisible but would take the form of a small person when the need arose. Not everyone could see them. He said that twins, especially girl twins, were most adept at seeing the Tsvdigewi, even when they were invisible to others. I do not believe this part of the story, but Grandfather likes to tell it so.

"Three clans of the Tsvdigewi lived in the lands to the west. The Rock Clan was most likely to become offended at the least indiscretion. They were vengeful and not liked by the other Tsvdigewi. The Laurel Clan, a stern group, was very serious and preferred to be left alone. The Dogwood Clan was full of jokes and most likely to interact with humans. This was the clan that came to the Currahee.

"They carried ancient knowledge of healing potions and how to appease the gods of the mountains. They painted themselves with elaborate shapes. I think Sequoyah stumbled upon a few of their survivors in his many travels, those who had left the mountain before the tragedy."

I propped up on my elbow and gazed down at Onacona. His beautiful face glowed in the morning light.

"Grandfather tells of how these people migrated great distances, crossed immense stretches of water to come to the Currahee," he continued. "When they got here, they found that the land was already occupied by an even more ancient people. This band, however, was dying. No one knows why, but Grandfather says they were betrayed by neighboring tribes, who were tricked into believing this ancient people had set dark magic upon them. The Tsvdigewi treated the illnesses of the few survivors. Some of them lived and stayed with the Tsvdigewi.

"The survivors told stories of even more people who had lived by the Currahee in ages past. They told the Tsvdigewi that some of these earlier people were so old that they must have been formed from the earth itself. The Tsvdigewi remembered these earlier people and gave thanks to them in ceremony, song, and dance. These were the great Mound Builders whose monuments you still see.

"Grandfather told us that the Tsvdigewi lived in peace, never passing the Tugaloo and never again turning east. They were here when the First People came to this region. Our ancestors would see them across the Tugaloo, watch them dance about the forest, and hear their songs float through the woods. He says that the songs sometimes warned the First People of an approaching enemy or dangerous weather. The songs also told us to stay out of their land.

"One day, a young warrior of the First People gave in to his curiosity and ventured into the land of the Tsvdigewi. He walked in the endless shadows of great chestnut trees on soft ground that silenced his footfalls. Eventually, he met a Tsvdigewi girl. She was so beautiful that the warrior immediately fell in love with her. When she would not go with him, he grabbed her before she could turn invisible. He carried the struggling girl back to his camp, but when he placed her on the ground, she appeared as a child made of wood. The warrior kept her in his hut, hoping that she would again take the form of the beautiful girl he loved. When she did not, his anger grew, and he tossed the wooden form into his fire. She immediately became a girl again, but she burned to death before he could drag her out.

"The Tsvdigewi learned of the young warrior's treachery. They had no tools of war but began to throw evil dreams at the First People. Then they sent plagues. The First People responded by invading across the Tugaloo. Led by those adept at seeing the Tsvdigewi, they hunted and killed them. They tracked the last of the Tsvdigewi to a cliff atop the Currahee. He told his pursuers that his people would forever haunt the land on which they now stood. They would have no peace until they had appeased the ghosts of the Tsvdigewi they had killed. Only blood of their own innocents would do. With that, the Tsvdigewi threw himself from the cliff and plummeted to his death.

"The First People returned to their camp but made no dances of victory. The next day, their children began to grow sick and die. This continued until a shaman of the First People claimed that in a dream, a Tsvdigewi ghost told him how to stop the plague. They were to do as the last living Tsvdigewi had demanded. At every full moon for an entire year, they would choose a child of the purest and most noble families. A girl-child of beauty and perfection without blemish. They would take that child to the top of the Currahee and throw her from the mountain. Only then would the plague stop. If they did not comply, the Tsvdigewi told him, the First People would be exterminated. This was the blood price the Tsvdigewi demanded.

"After much discussion and many tears, the First People complied. On the night the first child was sacrificed, the plague stopped. In fear, the First People sacrificed one child at each full moon, just as the shaman had been admonished to do. The plague never returned, but the First People remained afraid of the Currahee. Then came the Abittibi."

"Echoes," I said. Onacona turned to me.

"We are echoes of these people," I said. "Fated to come here. Fated to remember them. To become them. We are echoes of the voices of gods, stories that they tell over and over in our lives as they watch us."

Onacona turned to me, and we embraced. With my head buried in his shoulder, I told him my plan, or at least a part of it.

CHAPTER THIRTY-TWO

1:55 p.m., November 9, 1977
Three days, twelve hours, and thirty-five minutes after failure

Sheriff McClain pulled up next to Deputy Adams's car amid a sea of green vehicles. Guardsmen held positions behind every tree, log, and stump within sight, armed with AR-15s, grenade launchers, and a few sniper rifles. They had already set up a mess tent in a field around the bend of the road, and men were lined up for chow.

"First things first, I guess," McClain said, eyeing the mess tent. He turned to Doug and asked, "Who's in charge here?"

"Sheriff, I wish I could tell you," the deputy replied. He stood observing the activity around them. "I keep asking, but no one seems to know. They just showed up."

McClain adjusted the frequency of his radio, then spoke: "This is Sheriff McClain. Get Colonel Watts on."

"Command here," someone replied. "The colonel is not in here."

"Then find him," McClain demanded. After a second, he added, "Who is the highest-ranking officer you can lay eyes on right now?"

A few seconds later the radioman replied, "Major Jessop."

"Then let me talk to the major," McClain said. A few more seconds elapsed.

"Jessop here," came the reply.

"Major, this is Sheriff Tom McClain," he said. "I'm at the compound of the Fellowship of Faith. I've got maybe a hundred or more of your men here, heavily armed. Pull them back, now. This is not helpful."

Another delay.

"Sheriff, I don't have that authority," the major replied.

"Then find someone who does," McClain shouted into the radio. A few nearby soldiers glanced his way.

"To my memory, Sheriff," Doug mentioned, "there's only one phone on the whole compound, and that belongs to Paul and Dinah Whiten. She never allowed anyone else to get one."

McClain switched frequencies again.

"Julie, this is the sheriff," he said. "Copy?"

"Copy, Sheriff," came a woman's voice over the radio.

"Look up the phone number for Paul or Dinah Whiten," he instructed. "If you can't find that, check under the name of the Fellowship of Faith."

Almost before he stopped speaking, Julie replied, "Got it, Sheriff."

"Okay. Patch me through this radio to that phone."

A few seconds later, the sheriff and his deputy heard a phone ringing over the radio. They waited until they heard someone pick it up, but no one said anything. After a few seconds, McClain introduced himself.

"This is Sheriff Tom McClain," he said. "I am on my radio outside of your compound. Who is on the line?"

Through the hiss of the radio, they heard muffled voices.

"This is Dinah Whiten, Sheriff," Dinah said. "We've met, I believe."

"Yes ma'am, we have."

"Why are all these people outside of our walls? And why did you shoot our Glenn?"

"Ma'am, I sincerely apologize for that. It was not me or my men. A federal agent shot Glenn. He believed that my life was threatened."

"Remember, Sheriff, I was there," Dinah replied.

"What is his condition?" McClain asked.

"He's alive."

"Could we get him some help? Take him to the hospital?" McClain asked.

"No need for that, Sheriff," she replied. "We just want you to leave us in peace."

"I can't do that, Pastor," he replied. "I would like to talk, just talk for a while."

The radio crackled for a few seconds.

"We offered to let you in, Sheriff," Dinah said. "All you had to do was take off your gun. Was that asking too much?"

"No," McClain said. "It was not, and I should have taken your offer. Can I take it now?"

Doug shook his head vigorously.

"Of course, Sheriff," Dinah replied. "Leave your gun behind, and I will have someone meet you at the gate."

CHAPTER THIRTY-THREE

4:43 p.m., November 9, 1977

Three days, fifteen hours, and twenty-three minutes after failure

Jacob escorted the sheriff to Dinah and Paul Whiten's home. The wood-frame house sat on a slight rise and had a wraparound porch and a steeply pitched slate roof. People milled about the building, eyeing their visitor with suspicion.

McClain started up the steps, but Jacob stopped him.

"Your radio, Sheriff," he said.

"Why?"

"I'm just following orders, same as you," Jacob said.

Sheriff McClain unhooked the radio from his belt and handed it over before following Jacob up the steps. The Fellowship member held the door, and McClain entered first. Inside, at least a dozen individuals stood behind Dinah Whiten. They were hard-looking men in denim work clothes and flannel shirts. One carried a bush axe. In the corner, being tended to by a young woman who knelt before him, sat the man who had been shot on the wall. The woman was busy wrapping his shoulder while he winced in pain.

Dinah Whiten stepped forward in a black wool dress with a red collar. Her copper-colored hair had been teased into a windproof helmet.

"Sheriff McClain, you've got some explaining to do," she said.

McClain removed his hat and stood with it in both hands.

"Yes ma'am," he said. "We do. May we speak in private?"

"We may not, Sheriff," she replied. "My deacons represent our church. We all live here, in peace. When the government shows up and shoots one of us, what are we to think?"

She gestured to include the men, all of whom eyed the sheriff angrily.

"Okay, so here's the situation," McClain said. "You know about the flood?"

"We do. God has used floods before to wash great sin from a people."

"Be that as it may, President Carter is here to show support for the town and the college," he continued. "As usual, the Secret Service comes before and during any presidential visit. While preparing for this one, they came across a federal warrant for your arrest, Pastor Dinah. I haven't seen the warrant—something about weapons charges, or, hell, I can't tell you because I don't know."

"Sheriff!" Dinah said. "Language, please."

"Sorry, Pastor," the sheriff replied. "They thought it best to corral all of you here until the president leaves. They're not willing to take chances that any of your people would threaten him."

"We've threatened no one," Dinah said in an icy voice.

"I'm not saying you have," McClain continued. "They've got their jobs, and I've got mine. We were watching the gate this morning. While I was talking to Ryan—sorry, Jacob—here, they thought someone was about to shoot me. They shot first. It was a mistake."

"A mistake that almost killed this boy," Dinah replied.

"A mistake," McClain repeated. "Nothing more. I'm here to make sure that no one else gets hurt."

One of the deacons stepped forward. He was powerfully built and towered over McClain.

"Best thing you can do is to leave us alone," he said, his voice a deep growl full of strength and violence.

"That's exactly what we plan," McClain replied. "Right after the president leaves, we'll get these guys out of here, and we can talk about that warrant. Could be it's a mistake."

"It's no mistake, Sheriff," Dinah replied. "They've been after me for years. Charges of tax evasion, violating labor laws, even claims we've encouraged underage sex. It's always something. They'll never leave us alone. And now you've come with your army, your guns. All in the name of the heretic Carter."

She turned to face the deacons.

"I say let them come," she declared, spreading her arms. "I say let them face the legions of angels that will descend upon them to protect us. I say let them come, and let us see who worships the true God. Let them come!"

The deacons shouted, Jacob shouted, the wounded man shouted, "Let them come!"

When the noise died, McClain said, "It doesn't have to be this way, Pastor. We can work this out."

Dinah turned back toward the sheriff.

"Oh, but it does, Sheriff. It does. The shadow of this moment fell across our paths on the day we laid the first brick here. We've prepared ourselves for this the way King David prepared. We've girded our souls. Now we will see the glory and the power of God driven through the heart of the beast."

"I'm not sure what any of that means," McClain said. "I just want peace in our county."

"Your peace, on your terms, Sheriff," Dinah said.

"Okay," he replied. "My peace. But we can work out the terms. Why don't you and Paul—"

"Paul's been silenced," Dinah snapped.

McClain frowned. "Silenced?"

"God struck him dumb sometime back," she said. "He's here, but he does not walk or talk. We're at peace with it."

"Could I see him?" McClain asked.

"No."

He fiddled with his hat.

"Listen, we've got to—"

"*We* don't have to do anything," Dinah said. "You, however, need to leave us. We have a lot to do, and it seems your people are giving us precious little time to do it."

"Let's go, Sheriff," Jacob said.

McClain hesitated, tried to think of what to say, what to offer, but nothing came to mind. He followed Jacob out and down the hill. When he got to the gate, he stopped, and Jacob handed him his radio and gun.

"Jacob, you need to tell everyone to stay away from the wall. Hear me? Stay away from the wall," he said.

Jacob squinted at him. Deep wrinkles formed around his eyes.

"Me and your folks go way back," the sheriff continued. "I need time. The president will only be here today. Tell your people . . ."

Another man strode briskly toward them.

"It's against the rules for me to talk to an outsider without someone from the church as a witness," Jacob said as the other man came to stand beside him. "Say your peace."

"I'm just saying, keep everyone off the walls," McClain continued. "Just for today. Stay inside. Whatever you do, don't bring out any weapons."

"Could have killed you, you know?" the other man said. "Had slugs and buckshot in my pocket. Could have changed it out and killed you."

"I appreciate your restraint. And you are?"

"I am none of your concern, Sheriff," he replied.

"Just one day," McClain said. "Just give me a day to see if I can get everyone to stand down. One damn day."

Another man opened the gate, and the sheriff returned to Deputy Adams's patrol car.

"Still no idea who's in charge on the scene here?" he asked Doug as they drove back to the cluster of National Guard vehicles.

"A herd of cats that smell mice," the deputy replied. "Best I can figure, they got called into this position by someone in Atlanta that nobody can name. No written orders. No clear objective. Just surround the place and wait. Their ROE are pretty vague."

"What do you mean?" McClain said.

"One of those boys told me it's weapons free if anyone in the compound even looks at 'em wrong," Doug replied. "Well, not exactly like that, but they're pretty primed to shoot those big guns at someone."

"And the Bradley?"

"They were on maneuvers somewhere close to Hiwassee," Doug said. "Got word to bring it here. The other armored vehicles too."

"Shit! What in the hell were they thinking?"

McClain surveyed the area, noted the positions of the troops, trucks, and the armor.

"Let's get back to the college," he said. He switched to his own vehicle and followed Doug past the troops and vehicles. Minutes later, they came to a roadblock near the entrance to the college. Both patrol cars changed lanes to pass a line of vehicles and were waved through.

McClain left Doug and hurried to the command tent, which seemed even more crowded. He finally spotted Agent Hart in a corner, smoking a cigarette. He had his foot propped up on a plywood box and was chatting with a female guardsman, who sat with her radio headset around her neck.

Hart stood as McClain approached.

"There's a damn army out by the compound, Agent," McClain said loudly. The din lessened slightly. "Armor? Really, you need armor to contain a few crazy people hiding behind a tin wall with nothing but a few bird-hunting guns?"

"I didn't call for 'em, Sheriff," Hart replied. "Your own governor sent them. The attorney general himself authorized all of it."

"You can't tell me that anyone in Atlanta knows the situation on the ground here," McClain said. "Pull them back."

"Can't do that, Sheriff," Hart said. "So many federal agencies now involved, even I don't know who's in charge. Justice, federal marshals, the Guard. Hell, even the Marine Corps has a presence here. This thing escalated the minute the president decided to visit. Best thing to do is to wait it out. Don't make any moves, and let him go back to DC. Then we can de-escalate. Until POTUS is off the ground, the troops will stay put."

They argued for almost half an hour until McClain stormed out of the tent. Doug stood at the patrol car, smoking.

"Where to, Sheriff?" the deputy asked.

McClain mulled his options.

"I want to talk to that Martha girl myself," he said.

CHAPTER THIRTY-FOUR

Month and date unknown
501 years until failure

Mother, Chitto, Sehoy, and I built huts closer to the base of the Currahee but still within sight of the other Abittibi. A few of Chitto's friends also constructed huts nearby. We lived, farmed, and hunted for ourselves. We were with the Abittibi but not of them.

At first, I joined Chitto's hunting parties. Soon I grew larger, and everyone could see that I was with child. When I could no longer keep up with the men, I stopped my hunts.

Waya tried several times to rally the Abittibi to drive us away. The people feared us more than they feared Waya. They would insult us when we drew too near, and occasionally some of the women would even throw stones at us. But they did not attack us directly. I saw Waya eyeing us, plotting. I knew that he controlled the hearts of the Abittibi, even if he could not command them to move against us.

My loathing for him and the other Abittibi festered. I occasionally wavered in my resolve to take revenge, only to be brought back to hatred. Then, one day, some of Chitto's men caught a Nermernuh spy sneaking away from the Currahee toward the Chattahoochee, carrying another of Waya's copper bracelets. Our warriors killed him on the spot and brought the trinket to me. I knew then that I must carry out my plan or wait for Waya to have us killed.

We suffered through a particularly harsh winter that year. Shivering in the hut as the wind howled outside, I gave birth to Onacona's son. Mother attended me while Sehoy washed the child, then bundled him tightly in beaver furs. He cried, his fierce voice rising above the winds. When I took him to my breast, I should have ended my madness and allowed Waya's evil to win. I should have let my life remain as it was, but the memory of Sequoyah's death and Waya's betrayal burned in me.

Even before my son was born, Mother warned me that my festering hatred would contaminate my milk and become a slow poison. I cannot say if this was true, but the first time I gazed at him, I knew he could not stay with us. Either my bitterness or Waya's scheming would kill him.

I sent word by one of Chitto's warriors to Onacona to tell him of his son. The warrior returned with a gift. When I unwrapped the bark covering, I found a carving of a woman. The details were remarkable. She carried a bow and blowgun and was poised as if watching for enemies in the distance. As I peered closer, I gave a startled cry. The woman wore a mask over the bottom half of her face.

I held the wooden figure out to our son. After a time, he focused on it and reached for it with unsteady hands.

The warrior who brought me the carving said, "Onacona said that the boy's name should be Sequoyah."

By spring, Sequoyah had grown strong and could crawl as fast as a serpent. Sehoy gave birth to another child. This one was short and darker than her first. No one would voice what we all suspected of his Nermernuh blood.

Against Mother's advice, I started to wean Sequoyah. I also began to take him to the Tugaloo to spend time with his father.

"You could come live with me among the First People," Onacona said on one such day.

"I cannot live with the First People," I replied. I refused to discuss the matter further.

On the day Sequoyah took his first steps, I again took him to meet Onacona and, after much argument, convinced Onacona to take him to live with his family. It was the hardest thing I ever did, and I resolved that day to covet power over love. Soon I would add to my soul's transgressions sins so terrible that they could not be forgiven, and I meant for our son to know nothing of them.

Mother wailed for days when I returned without Sequoyah. She resolved to go to the First People and demand the return of her grandson. I finally dissuaded her, lying that I did not want a son. We sulked about the camp for the better part of the summer while I plotted. It was during this time that I returned to the cave Mya had shown me and in which I now make these symbols. Here, I began to lose myself in telling these stories. But on the darkest nights, Onacona came to me. In our passions, I smelled our son on him and wept bitterly.

ON A NIGHT when the wind would hide the sounds of my movements, I went to the hut of Waya. I saw the light of his fire flickering through the cracks. All of Sequoyah's wives had become his wives. They had built new huts in a half circle around his, but on this night, no one moved.

I sat quietly by his door and waited. From afar, I had counted the people going in and out and knew that only two people slept inside. Creeping into the smoky darkness, I crawled to where Waya kept the remaining copper implements Sequoyah had made for him and those he had stolen when Sequoyah was killed. I took one, a thin band barely wider than a finger that would wrap around one's wrist. I then took several arrows, a spearhead bearing Waya's emblems, and a pair of his moccasins.

The night was still young when I donned Waya's moccasins, sprinted to the Tugaloo, and, for the first time in my life, crossed the river and into the lands of the First People.

I took a trail that had been described to me, one that followed the river downstream, and slowed as I entered a large village of perhaps two hundred huts. Sentry fires burned on the other side of the village, but it was as Onacona had told me: they expected no attack from the side occupied by the Abittibi. I made sure to leave tracks, easily found in the daylight, as I stopped at several family cook sites. From my pouch, I pinched powders and pastes and slipped them into the pots. Some of the First People would sicken immediately. Others would not feel effects until days passed. None, I believed, would die.

I then stole several small furs and a carved totem no larger than my hand. I dropped one of Waya's arrows in a section of tall grass where it would be found, but not immediately.

I returned to our camp as the eastern sky gradually lightened. Tossing Waya's moccasins in the coals of our fire, I piled on more wood until the leather had turned to ash.

When I entered our hut, I settled onto my furs, but sleep did not come.

Onacona came to me the third night after I had visited his camp. At his request, I woke the others, and we sat by our fire to hear him. Through Onacona's voice, I discovered my plan was working.

"The First People will come soon," Onacona said. "People in our camp are growing ill each day. They believe the Abittibi are responsible."

"How can they think such a thing?" Sehoy asked. She held her youngest child to her breast as she spoke.

"They think your shaman has come to them in the form of a ghost and brought sickness to them," he replied. "It is decided. White Dove and I have pleaded for you to be spared."

He waved his hand to indicate our small group.

"The elders have agreed that they will not hunt you," Onacona said. "But if you are here when they cross the Tugaloo, they will kill you."

Chitto placed a protective arm over Sehoy. "Where can we go?" he asked. "If we go south, the Nermernuh would find us. If we go north, we risk encounters with the Iroquois Nations. We are too few to survive."

A couple of Chitto's warriors offered suggestions, none of which gained approval. Finally, I spoke.

"I know where we can go," I said. "The First People will not occupy this land. They only want to drive out the Abittibi. Let them."

I told them of the cave. After much discussion, we began to pack. We slipped out of the village well before dawn the next day. On our way to the cave, the gods favored us. A lone yearling buffalo stood in our path. He was far from any herd, and it was a wonder that the wolves had not already killed him. He did not seem afraid but rather waited expectantly.

I shot him through his heart. He took a few steps toward us, shaking his head as if in wonder at what was happening to him. Then he dropped dead.

We set upon the buffalo and quickly cut him into sections that could be carried on our travois. Dragging the refuse to a stump hole, we covered it with leaves and branches. We could only hope the rain would wash the blood away and hide it and our tracks.

At midday, the sun hit the ravine that hid the entrance to the cavern, and we entered the shadows with all we possessed. We began to stack firewood, knowing that we could not venture out until the First People had left the land. That night, we roasted and ate as much of the buffalo meat as we could stomach, then smoked the rest. Before dawn, we extinguished the fire and entered the cave. Outside, it began to rain.

Chitto sent a single warrior to watch from a nearby ridge and report movement from the Tugaloo. On the second dawn, he ran back.

"They have come!" he exclaimed.

We huddled in our cave, not daring to imagine the wrath the First People would bring upon the Abittibi. All of us had proven our bravery many times over, but in that cave, we began to doubt ourselves. We sneaked looks at one another, seeking hints of what the others were thinking. No one spoke for a long while. We waited two more days before Chitto went out. He snuck to our village and came upon total devastation. He reported back to us, and we all returned with him to the village.

Men, women, and children lay strewn around the camp. Most had been bludgeoned to death. A few sprouted broken arrows from their backs and chests. I recognized where intact arrows had been extracted for reuse. All the huts had been burned and still smoldered. The First People were thorough and efficient in their killing. There were no signs that anyone had been tortured or taken prisoner. They had simply been killed as we would kill vermin in our maize pots.

Except for our small band, the Abittibi no longer existed. While I had my own purposes, why the gods used me to destroy them is a question they alone can answer. Was it just? It comes close enough for me.

DURING THE WINTER after the attack from the First People, as we attempted to resume living in the location of our old village, Mother began to cough. I used all the medicines I could recall from her and Sequoyah's teachings. I gave her hot brews of various barks, put poultices on her chest, and took her to the Tugaloo for a dip in its cold waters. Nothing worked. She coughed all night long, exhausting herself in trying to expel the clumps of poison in her chest. I sat with her and listened as she breathed her last. When she died, we realized the tragic loneliness of life on the mountain without a village. We carried her to the Tugaloo, tied her to a raft, and set her free to drift to the edge of the world.

Sehoy died in childbirth the following spring. Shortly after, I began painting my story and the story of the Abittibi. The loyalty that Chitto brought to Sehoy he now gave to me. He would not hear of leaving me to go live with the First People, even if they would take him. The warriors loyal to Chitto stayed with him for a season more. They then slipped away, one by one, until only the two of us remained to inhabit the haunted land.

On rare days, I would leave the cave and slip down to the Tugaloo and look for Onacona. On one occasion, I saw him playing with a boy child. The sight tore at my heart, but I could not go to him, could not bring my sin to my son's life.

I do not hope for redemption in the telling of this story, for I am too stained for such a thing. Perhaps the wise men you bring here can tell you whether my actions were just. As for me, I will wait in this cave as death stalks me. My final request of Chitto was that when it comes, he affix me to the stone slabs in this cave, where I will wait until I am discovered by men, demons, or the gods, if there is a difference.

CHAPTER THIRTY-FIVE

4:56 p.m., November 9, 1977
Three days, fifteen hours, and thirty-six minutes after failure

No one could say how it started. Farmers and hunters from miles away heard gunshots, explosions, the crunch of metal being crushed. As distant as Toccoa, people in town to shop or enjoy the Christmas decorations stopped on the streets to listen. Hundreds of people saw and heard destruction being rained down on the compound, but no one would ever know how it started. They only knew how it ended.

The first volleys came while the usually quiet and peaceful town was still reeling from the death and destruction wrought by the dam collapse. Reporters had been swarming the town, trampling fields, and interviewing stunned farmers and business owners who knew little about what had caused the dam to break. They would know even less about events surrounding the impending assault on the compound.

President and Mrs. Carter finished their tour of the damaged campus, waved to the crowds, and expressed sympathy and support for the families of the thirty-nine people who had died in the flood. For a day, Toccoa Falls Bible College reluctantly basked in the nation's consciousness. Then the Carters left with promises of aid to the survivors and a pledge to form an investigative body to study what had happened. Across the South, people began to look at their ponds and lakes with apprehension.

The president's visit distracted reporters from the drama occurring a few miles away. Corporal Brian Gastley of the Georgia National Guard swore later that he began taking fire from the compound around 4:52 p.m. He shot back. A few of his friends told investigators that the corporal was anxious to fire his newly acquired assault rifle and simply fired a few shots into the air. His buddy, Corporal Steve Coker, joined him and emptied his rifle, which he forgot was set on automatic. Unfortunately, he kept his finger on the trigger while the rifle sprayed across the landscape. Others joined him, taking aim at the compound.

Their commanding officer screamed for his men to cease fire. Instead, the squad of twelve began firing, reloading, then firing again at the thin metal wall. Inside, bullets careened off brick buildings and shattered windows. Women and children screamed and ran for cover. A man holding a shotgun rose atop the wall by the gate and was immediately killed. His body fell inside, and his gun went off. Across the compound, a teacher and the group of preschoolers she was herding toward a brick building for safety were sprayed with lead pellets the size of BBs. Legs puffed with baby fat dribbled blood along the packed dirt walkway.

Some children sat and cried, while others ran with their teacher to the building. Once those were inside, she rushed to retrieve the stragglers. A bullet hit the center of her chest. She swayed, confused at what was happening to her, and placed a hand on her chest. She pulled it away and stared at it before another bullet sliced through her neck and she slumped in a pool of blood.

In less than a minute from the first shot, the people of the compound had fled into the alleged safety of their homes, the school, and the church. Spurts of shooting continued for another minute or two. One stray bullet pierced the thin, unpainted wooden walls of a house where Mrs. Abigale Thompson huddled with her four children on her bed. The bullet shattered her glasses, then veered off to hit a framed picture of Paul and Dinah Whiten. She rushed the children through her kitchen and down to the cellar. She and the children would remain hidden for two days, living off canned pickles and beets. When her husband searched for them during the assault, he failed to look in the basement. Assuming that they had fled to a neighbor's house or the church, he went to the school to wait out a seeming apocalyptic siege.

Positioned on the hill, Dinah and Paul Whiten's home sat in direct line of sight of the soldiers outside. Despite this, not a single of the hundreds of rounds expended struck the house. A few survivors later claimed to have seen angels with flaming swords protecting the house and that Dinah Whiten stood on her porch, calmly watching the bloody scene below her. Those inside the house, however, saw her hide under her kitchen table.

Six minutes into the barrage, the shooting suddenly stopped. Dinah stayed hunkered down for a few minutes, then crept to the window.

Below, the compound appeared empty. She eyed the heavy brass bell hanging from a wooden beam in her front yard. She had rung the bell only twice since building this house and compound—both times to announce a direct revelation from God.

Steeling herself, she stood upright and strode confidently outside to the bell. She grasped the rope and gazed across the compound walls to those arrayed against her. She saw the trucks, the groups of soldiers bristling with guns, the Bradley armored vehicle. Her eye was drawn to the southwest, where the Currahee had begun to cast shadows across the foothills. Over the years, the mountain had shown her myriad shapes sketched in the streaked granite bluffs and the pines that clung to cracks in the mountain's face. It struck Dinah as strange that on this day, the mountain seemed at peace.

Dinah brought her eyes back to the compound as lights inside the church flickered to life. She tugged the bell's rope, and clear, beautiful peals echoed across the hills. She turned and walked slowly up to her porch and into the house.

AS DUSK FELL, Dinah sat in her living room surrounded by her twelve deacons. They had pulled chairs from the kitchen and dining room. After a moment of silence, Dinah stood and began to pace.

"I have had the Word of the Lord about this," she said. "Pray with me."

As one, they leaned their heads between their knees and broke out in strange sounds and words, interrupted occasionally by expressions in English, all speaking of deep devotion and despair. They beseeched God to reveal to them and their leader the path of righteousness so that they might gladly take it. Some beat their chests and stomped their feet.

While this continued, Paul Whiten cracked his bedroom door open and peered outside. Dinah saw him and shook her head, but he placed one shaky, slippered foot slowly in front of the other and slunk into the room in his striped pajamas and a thick black robe. His gray-blue eyes darted around the room. One by one, the deacons saw him, stopped praying, and stood.

Dinah went to him, and he shrugged her away, raising a thin hand streaked with broken veins.

Just then, music broke the silence. Not church music. This was blaring, screeching guitar music, pleasant only to the most ardent rock and roll fan. Windows rattled.

Dinah and the deacons ran onto the porch. The awful ruckus came from somewhere beyond the wall and poured right through the sheet metal. It was so loud that they had to yell to be heard.

"They are blasting us with Satan's voice," Dinah shouted to the deacons. "Trying to corrupt us."

They came back into the house to find that Paul Whiten had retreated to his bedroom.

SITTING IN AUNT Myrtle's house in front of Martha, the sheriff heard the guns, followed by the music. He sent Doug to investigate before turning back to Martha.

"Are you sure, Martha?" McClain asked her again.

"Tom, she's already answered you a dozen times," Myrtle said. "You gonna get her sister and momma out of that place?"

"Yes, Myrtle, I am."

He stood, took his hat from the bedstand, and headed outside. Doug met him by the patrol car.

"You're not gonna believe this one, Sheriff," Doug said.

McClain frowned at him.

"It's the Guard," Doug said. "I got Sam on the radio. He's outside the compound right now. Says it's the National Guard blaring that awful music. Right at the Fellowship of Faith compound. Worse, he said the noise we heard earlier was a raging gunbattle. They've stopped shooting for now, but it won't take much for it to start up again."

Deputy Adams drove McClain up the winding roads as darkness fell. They came to a convoy of green Army trucks headed in the same direction. They could not see inside the canvas coverings. At McClain's instruction, Doug turned on his flashing red light and passed the convoy on a yellow line.

A couple of miles from the compound, a guardsman with a rifle slung over his shoulder waved for them to stop. Ahead, more men blocked the road with jeeps and trucks.

"Mind turning off your light?" the man asked, and Doug complied.

Leaning across his deputy, McClain said, "I am Sheriff Tom McClain. This whole area is in my jurisdiction. You're in my jurisdiction. I need to get through."

The man stepped away, spoke into a walkie-talkie, then waved him through. As they started to move, the music abruptly stopped.

Doug and McClain passed other guardsmen lounging along the road or sitting in the backs of trucks. All carried rifles. A helicopter with flashing lights on its undercarriage flew overhead. They watched it land in a pasture next to a cluster of trucks and a large black trailer. Lights on poles lit a circle around the trailer. What looked like the same command tent from the college now sat at the edge of the light.

"These guys work fast," Doug said as he parked.

The sheriff and his deputy went unchallenged to the tent, where they found Agent Hart chatting with the same female guardsman. She sat on a box and smiled at whatever he was saying to her.

"Thought you guys were clearing out," McClain said flatly as he and Doug approached.

Hart turned to him. With his cigarette bobbing between his lips, he replied, "So did I, Sheriff."

"Listen, Agent Hart, I am tired. My men are tired. My town is tired. We've got dozens of people dead and injured from the flood. I have no idea how many your people killed or wounded inside the compound. This is not necessary. Pull your men out. We can handle the folks inside that little compound. There is no hurry. They're not going anywhere, and neither are we."

Hart nodded. "I feel for you, Sheriff. But I take orders from people who also take orders. We've got a bunch of bureaucrats in Washington talking to another bunch of bureaucrats in Atlanta. They talk to my boss's boss. He talks to me. And on it goes."

"So, what are these bosses of yours saying?" McClain asked.

"They're telling me to keep a lid on this thing. No news in. No news out. We give them one day to surrender peacefully."

The guitar music again blared from hidden speakers angled at the compound. A short hill blunted the noise in the direction of the tent.

"And that?" Doug said, gesturing outside.

"We have found that perpetrators are more likely to surrender or make mistakes when they are sleep deprived," Hart said. "A day or so of this, and they'll give it up."

"And when they don't?" McClain demanded.

"You don't sound too hopeful that they can be persuaded," the agent replied.

"They won't come out," Doug said. "I know these people. I have relatives inside that place. An aunt and an uncle, couple of cousins. It would go against everything they believe to surrender to the government. They'll never come out. Not one of 'em."

"Never?" Hart asked.

"Never," replied Doug.

The agent pursed his lips and frowned.

"Then I'm not wasting any more time. We go in at dawn," Hart said. "Excuse me, Sheriff. I've got plans to make, and one of them is to find a bunk for a few hours." He smiled at the female guardsman as he spoke. She did not smile back.

When McClain began to protest loudly, Hart motioned across the tent, and a couple of burly MPs escorted them outside. The MPs took their radios from their belts and the microphone from the truck. They left them their sidearms.

Doug and McClain sat on the hood of the patrol car and shared a cigarette.

"Hard to believe this is happening in America," Doug said. "Land of the free, my ass."

"We're still free," McClain said darkly.

The music grated on his nerves. He could only imagine how disturbing it was to those inside the compound.

"I'm thinking that we can work our way around by Davis Creek, then down the trail to where we busted up that old still last year. Should get us close enough to sneak up and maybe even inside the compound," the sheriff said as he flicked the cigarette to the ground.

"We'll have to leave the car at the first checkpoint, then sneak through the woods back to the road," Doug said.

"It's what I figured," McClain said.

"It'll take most of the night," Doug said.

"I figured," McClain replied. "You in?"

"Damn straight," the deputy said, hopping into the car.

CHAPTER THIRTY-SIX

5:02 a.m., November 10, 1977

Four days, three hours, forty-two minutes after failure

SHERIFF McCLAIN AND his deputy caught a break when on the way to Davis Creek they were stopped by a jeep pulled across the narrow dirt road. A guardsman sat inside with his feet propped on the dash and headphones on. He looked at the uniforms and badges and frowned.

"The action's that way, Sheriff," he said, pointing back to the compound and the blaring music.

McClain hesitated before answering, "We have business this way."

"You won't get through in that," the guardsman said. "We all have orders to stop all civilian traffic."

"So, is a sheriff considered to be a civilian?" McClain asked.

"Couldn't tell you," the guardsman replied. He thought for a minute, then asked, "Want a ride? I'm just sitting around doin' nothin'. They said we can't bivouac, can't sleep. Just sit. Glad to have something to do, especially if it gets me away from that awful racket."

"Need to check with someone?" Doug asked. The guardsman shook his head.

"Don't know who," he replied. "Can't even say for sure who's running this rodeo. Climb on in."

The jeep tires kicked up a cloud of dust as the vehicle raced down the bumpy dirt road. Men at the roadside checkpoints raised their hands in greeting, but the driver didn't slow down. Suddenly, they approached a rickety wooden bridge with no railing. The jeep jerked and swayed as it crossed, and both passengers held their breath until they were safely on the other side.

"This'll do," McClain shouted over the noise of the jeep.

They slid to a stop, and the sheriff and deputy jumped out.

"Can't thank you enough for the lift," McClain said. "Saved us a couple hours walking."

"Glad to, Sheriff," the man answered. "You don't remember me, do you?"

McClain looked carefully. In the dim light, he could barely make out the guardsman's silhouette, much less any features.

"Sorry, I don't," he replied.

"Didn't think so. You coached me in Little League football, the Big A Elementary School Eagles. Name's Jonesy Haygood. I live in Marietta now. Got a wife and a couple of kids. I never forgot how you formed our team by taking the scrubs the other teams wouldn't. Meant a lot to me. Never got around to thanking you."

"Well, you're welcome," McClain replied. "Didn't your dad work in the furniture store downtown?"

"He did," Jonesy answered.

"I remember," McClain said. "Can I ask a favor?"

"Of course."

"Me and Doug here, we've got to get into that compound and see if we can get everyone to stand down," McClain said. "Not sure either side really wants to. If we can't stop this idiocy, maybe we can get a few people out. There's a trail following this creek that should take us almost to the back of the compound."

"I know it," Jonesy replied. "Used to fish for suckers there."

"If I can't get Pastor Dinah to surrender peacefully—"

"She won't," Doug interjected.

"If I can't," McClain continued, "then I plan to get as many of them as will follow me to sneak out the back and come out here."

"Won't work, Sheriff," Jonesy said. "There's a patrol camped in the woods. They're watching that back fence."

"It might if we can get your help," McClain said.

After a moment, Jonesy replied, "I'll do what I can, Sheriff."

"So will we."

"Why don't you take this?" the guardsman said, holding out a walkie-talkie. "I'll be on channel six if you need me or need to change the plan."

"Won't they miss it?" Doug asked.

"Hell, they were in such a hurry to get us off training maneuvers and here that they didn't even take names or do proper checkout when they gave us all this stuff. No one even knows I have a couple extras. Thought I'd sneak one home when all this's done. You can have it."

MINUTES LATER, MCCLAIN and Doug slid off the road and groped their way to the trail. The deputy reached for the flashlight at his belt, but McClain stopped him.

"Just stay on the trail," the sheriff said. "If you light that thing up, they'll spot us a mile away."

They heard Jonesy turn the jeep around and speed back toward base.

"Stay behind me," McClain said. "From here until I say so, no talking. Step lightly. Do not, under any circumstances, pull your weapon. Got it?"

In the darkness, McClain could not see, but he knew that Doug nodded in reply.

They worked their way down the trail, stopping every few

minutes to listen. Nothing. The night turned colder. Both wore only their thin uniform jackets. They had only the vaguest notion of where they were but were reassured by the fact that the blaring music grew gradually louder.

Above the music, they heard voices coming from ahead and to their right. They slowed and stole upon four guardsmen sitting on logs in a circle. All four wore headlamps and were focused inward, laughing and cursing as money changed hands and they dealt cards. The sheriff and deputy waited for a few minutes to make sure the guardsmen had not posted a watch, then went on. Doug tripped over a vine, rattling the trees around him. The laughing and talking stopped for a minute, then resumed.

The music grew uncomfortably loud. When McCain and Doug came to a bend in the creek, the path sheered to their left and parallel to a six-foot hog wire fence. First, they had to scale a steep bank of kudzu to reach the fence. At the top of the bank, they scanned for Fellowship of Faith guards and found none.

McClain and Adams easily climbed the fence before noting the unlocked gate a few yards away. Light poured from every window in every building. Floodlights buzzed above, and the interlopers felt exposed.

"At least they haven't cut off power," Doug whispered.

McClain signaled him for silence, then led him to the next building. People were shouting inside. He and Doug retreated behind a pumphouse.

McClain leaned in and whispered, "Could we convince your aunt and uncle to assist us? Maybe they could even get out themselves." The loud music and fatigue were taking a toll on him.

"They've never shown any signs to me they'd leave the Whitens," Doug said. "But they might be willing to talk. I know where they live, or where they used to. It's just across the yard there." He pointed to a small wooden house.

The two skirted the brighter areas of the yard and slunk along the side of the house. They could not hear anyone inside, but shadows moved across the windows. They went to the back porch and eased up the steps. Doug knocked twice, but no one answered. He opened the door a crack.

"Uncle Don? Aunt Sue?" Doug called as loud as he dared.

Fearing that light from the open door would expose them, he and McCain slipped inside.

"Uncle Don?" Doug called again. This time they heard footsteps and floorboards creaking.

A short, bald man wearing overalls and a blue flannel shirt stepped into the kitchen. He had the weathered look of someone who had spent his whole life working in the sun. He frowned when he saw his visitors. Behind him followed an even shorter woman with braided gray hair and wearing a blue-spotted dress with long sleeves and a white collar.

"Doug?" she said. "What on earth are you doing here?"

"We need to talk, Aunt Sue," Doug said. "You know the sheriff here, don't you?"

McClain reached a hand out. Don hesitated, then shook it briefly.

"Sheriff," Don said, retrieving his hand. "What're you boys doing in here? This is no place for outsiders. 'Specially not now."

"We know, Uncle Don," Doug said.

"Do you know what's going on outside your walls, Don?" McClain asked.

"I know enough," Don answered.

"Not sure you do," McClain replied. "Let me tell you."

Over the next few minutes, Sheriff McClain sat in Don and Sue's kitchen and described the forces arrayed outside and the federal officers' intentions.

"All this true, Doug?" Sue asked.

The deputy nodded.

"Whatcha need from us, Sheriff?" Don asked, sounding far more reasonable than any other Fellowship member the sheriff had encountered in the past few days.

"Would you be willing to gather as many women and children as you can get without alerting Dinah Whiten?" McClain asked. "We need you to bring them to the north fence."

Doug's aunt and uncle looked long at one another before Sue nodded.

"But we're not going to help you kill anyone, Sheriff," she added.

"I'm not asking you to," McClain replied. "I just need to know where I can find Ruth Morris and her daughter Eve. I want to get them myself. I made a promise."

Don and Sue exchanged another look. Finally, Sue replied, "Pretty sure they're being held in the basement of Pastor Whiten's house, Sheriff. Gonna be pretty hard to get 'em out. Lots of deacons up there."

"Will the doors be locked?" he asked.

"Just fastened shut from the outside," she replied. "You won't need a key or anything."

"Anyone at her house armed?" McClain asked.

"Not that I know," Sue said.

Sheriff McClain thanked them.

"One more thing, Sheriff," Sue said reluctantly. "I took food to them a couple of times over the past few days."

"Aunt Sue?" Doug asked.

"I think Eve's okay," she continued. "At least, her body is. But her mother is in bad shape. Not sure what they're doing to her, but it's bad. She had some trouble walking when I saw her this morning. Poor thing's all bruised. Lip's cut. I told Don about it this morning. It's one of the reasons we were planning to leave ourselves. We don't want any part of this thing anymore. Enough's enough."

The four agreed to meet at the back fence just after sunrise. Doug removed his uniform jacket and pulled on an old hunting coat before he slipped into the darkness with his aunt and uncle. Sheriff McClain stood in the shadows and stared up the hill at Pastor Dinah's house. In the end, he decided his best chance of going undetected was to hide in plain sight. He turned his thin sheriff's jacket inside out to hide the emblems, took a deep breath, and marched confidently up the flagstone walkway.

It took him less than two minutes to reach the short white picket fence surrounding the house. He opened the gate and strode up to the house. When no one challenged him, he bolted to the shadowed side of the building, listening with his back to the wall. Inside, people were shouting, singing, and stamping their feet. He neither knew nor cared what they did as long as they stayed away from his destination.

Sue had told him where to find the outside door to Pastor Dinah's basement, and he reached it without incident. The rusty hinges seemed to scream when he eased it open, but the noise upstairs continued unabated. He held his hand over the lens of his flashlight, then clicked it on, letting a small sliver of light escape between his fingers as he scanned the room. He saw a set of steps leading up, old machine parts, and stacks of books and boxes. Under the stairs was the door, just as Sue had told him. He went to it, unbolted a latch, then opened it.

McClain cringed back at the odor of sweat and urine. He played his flashlight across the room. A cot in one corner held a figure dressed in sackcloth and curled into a ball.

"Ruth?" he whispered. "I'm Sheriff McClain. I'm here to help you."

The figure on the cot shifted, the barest of movements.

"Can you hear me?" McClain asked.

The woman moaned.

McClain scanned the rest of the room. Crouched in one corner, holding a ragged stuffed rabbit, Eve stared back.

"Eve, honey," McClain said softly. "I came to get you and your momma out of here."

When he took a step forward, Eve screeched and retreated farther into the corner.

"Please be quiet, honey," the sheriff said. "It'll be okay. I promise."

The door at the top of the stairs creaked open. McClain clicked off his light just as someone turned on the overhead light outside the basement door. The person took a step down the stairs, stopped for a few seconds, then resumed their descent. The sheriff unsnapped his holster and drew his pistol.

The figure on the cot moaned again, and the person on the stairs stopped and waited another second before continuing.

"You down here, Bob?" a man called. "If you've come in here again to mess with the prisoner, I swear I'm gonna tell. You can't—"

The man swung open the door and stared into the barrel of the sheriff's .357 service revolver.

"Inside," McClain ordered.

The man held up his hands and stepped into the room.

"That you, Sheriff?"

"Turn around and put your hands behind your back," McClain ordered. The man lowered his hands and turned.

"No need for that, Sheriff," the man said. "You know me. I used to stack hay for your father. I'm Randy. Randy Taylor."

"Quiet," McClain said. He holstered his gun before placing handcuffs on Randy. "Do you expect anyone else to come down here?"

"Absolutely, Sheriff," Randy replied. "They check four times an hour."

"He's lying," Eve said from the corner. "They only come when they want to hurt Momma. They won't come for a long time. He's here just to hurt her too."

"You shut up, demon child," Randy hissed.

"No more of that," McClain said, pushing Randy to his knees and moving cautiously toward the figure on the cot. "Ruth," he said. "I'm here to get you home, back to Wayne and Martha."

Ruth turned slightly and uncurled. She blinked up at the sheriff in the light pouring from the open door. She swallowed hard.

"Martha?" she rasped.

"That's right, Ruth," McClain said. "Let's get you out of here.

They're waiting for you. They're waiting for you at your sister Myrtle's house. You remember Myrtle, don't you?"

Ruth nodded.

"Can you walk?" McClain asked.

She nodded again.

"Come on, then," McClain said. "Let me help you."

Ruth swung her legs gingerly over the side of the cot and let the sheriff help her to her feet. Eve went to her mother and took her hand, and Ruth stood on wobbly legs, wincing with her first step.

"We have to hurry as much as you can, Ruth," McClain urged.

Just as they reached the door, Randy howled, "Down here! Outsiders are down here in the basement."

The noise upstairs ceased.

Rushing the ladies through the door, the sheriff slammed it shut, muffling Randy's caterwauling. Then McClain dragged Ruth to the outside door by her arm, pushing her into the darkness, followed by Eve. Behind him, the upstairs door opened. Men shouted down to Randy.

"They're trying to get away!" Randy shouted. "Stop them!"

Sheriff McClain drew his gun again. At the top of the stairs, two men peered down at him, uncertain. McClain shook his head in warning, then backed into the cold night to join Ruth and Eve.

He hustled the two as fast as Ruth could walk as more shouts erupted. He kept turning and scanning for signs of pursuit and found none.

The three of them had made it to the first house at the base of the hill and turned north toward the perimeter when something hit the sheriff in the back, and he fell forward, dragging Ruth with him. He saw the attacker just in time to roll to the side as a wooden two-by-four crashed into the ground beside his head. He pulled his weapon and fired at the dark shape. The man fell onto him, then rolled off, twitching a couple of times before lying still.

McClain heard shouting near the front gate. Scrambling to his feet, he pulled Ruth up and towed her and Eve to the back fence.

They ignored the patches of light and ran as fast as Ruth could muster. Neither she nor Eve wore shoes.

They rounded the last set of buildings and nearly crashed into Doug. Around him, at least two dozen people huddled nervously. A few children cried.

"Go now!" McClain said. "Take Ruth and Eve. I can hold them back for a while."

"Don't think so, Sheriff," Doug said. "Uncle Don and Sue know these woods better'n me. They'll get these people to the road."

"This is not the time, Doug," McClain fired back.

"This is just the time," Don interjected. "Me and Doug are staying with you. Sue'll take 'em out."

"No time to argue," the sheriff sighed. Flashlights bounced through the darkness as men hollered to one another.

"Will they be armed?" he asked Don.

"Don't think so, but I can't be sure," Don replied.

"Then don't shoot anyone," McClain said. "I think we can scare 'em off. Doug, hide over there. When you hear me fire, shoot a couple of times in the air, shout like you're talking to a big posse, then shoot a few more times."

Sue started to lead Ruth away, but the injured woman resisted and, in a voice hoarse from days of screaming, called the sheriff near.

"Go on now, Ruth," the sheriff said. "You and Eve'll be safe soon."

Ruth motioned him closer until they almost touched, then gingerly placed her hand on the sheriff's shoulder.

"She's here, Tom," Ruth whispered. He could barely make out her words against the blaring music.

"Who's here?" McClain asked.

"Carol," Ruth replied. "Carol's here."

In the dim light, Sheriff McClain saw Sue drop her gaze.

"My wife? She's really here?" he asked.

Sue nodded. "She dyed her hair and goes by a different name now."

"Where?" McClain asked.

Sue shook her head.

"Where is my wife?" McClain demanded.

"I don't know," Sue replied.

Angry shouts and gunfire erupted in the distance, and Sue and the group took off toward the north fence, leaving McClain with Don and Doug. The trio saw a mass of people moving rapidly in their direction, some carrying flashlights.

"Stay behind me, Don," McClain said.

With Doug crouched behind a stack of fence posts thirty yards to his left, McClain shouted, "Sheriff's office! Stop where you are. Turn around and go home."

No one answered, and the flashlights kept coming.

McClain aimed his gun in the air and fired two shots. Doug fired two more, shouted a few obscenities, then fired again.

As one, the flashlights went out. McClain waited for a good minute. When he discerned the shapes of men fleeing back to the lit areas closer to the gate, he called Doug to him, and they followed the other escapees. They climbed the fence and clambered down the hill to the trail to find that Sue and her group had made little progress. Doug ran to the front and urged them on.

More of the children were crying. McClain heard the staccato of far-off automatic weapons fire. The music suddenly stopped, and in its place, diesel engines roared to life.

They kept running along the trail until headlamps abruptly bathed them in white light. Doug came to a halt, and the group piled up against him. McClain heard angry voices ahead as he worked his way to the front.

"I have orders," a voice behind one of the lights called out. "No one in. No one out."

"Who is this?" McClain shouted.

"Sergeant Jason Hamrick. National Guard, 3rd Battalion, 121st Infantry Regiment, out of Cumming."

"Damn, Jason," Doug said. "It's me. Doug Adams. We went to

football camp together."

"Doug?" Jason replied. "It makes no difference. Everyone in the compound is supposed to stay there."

"Son, we've got to get these people to safety," McClain said. "Listen to what's going on back there. You really want to send these unarmed, innocent civilians back into that?"

Jason was silent. Doug and McClain heard murmuring.

"No sir," Jason finally said. "We do not. This whole thing is a cluster if I ever saw one. Follow me."

By the light of the headlamps, they saw the guardsmen turn to lead them up the trail. McClain pulled Doug aside.

"Take the radio," he said, thrusting the walkie-talkie into Doug's hands. "When you're close to the bridge, call Jonesy on channel six. Tell him to bring the trucks. He'll know where to go, so don't say it over the radio. Assume that a hostile is listening."

"You got it, Sheriff," Doug replied. McClain felt Doug staring at him.

"You're going back, aren't you?" the deputy asked.

"If she's there, I have to find her. Besides, there's got to be someone on-site to stop this thing."

McClain hurried back down the trail while Doug herded the crowd after Jason and his squad.

The sheriff pushed through the back gate as more gunfire erupted. He simultaneously heard the diesel engine of what he assumed was the Bradley, but as dawn bathed the compound in a reddish light, he saw his mistake. Instead of a Bradley or a conventional tank, the Guard had deployed a Combat Engineering Vehicle, or CEV. The sound of the engine slowed for a few seconds, followed by a loud *boom*. McClain ran as fast as he could.

He dashed from house to house, then crouched behind construction materials. When the wind changed, he was immediately engulfed in tear gas. He took off his jacket and turned it right side out, revealing his badge and the other emblems, then pulled his T-shirt up to his nose. It did little to protect him from the gas. As McClain watched through eyes blurred with tears, the CEV pulled up to the school building and used the snout of what looked to be a cannon barrel to punch through the cinder block wall.

Fellowship members threw open windows as smoke and more gas poured through the first floor. Then, to the sheriff's horror, the CEV pushed farther into the building, the walls collapsing around it. A minute later, flames began to flicker inside.

The corporal handling the mounted weapon on the back of a jeep as it roared through the compound would later say that he was there to intimidate and not kill. However, as he fired the .50-caliber machine gun, cutting through walls and windows, the sheriff saw the corporal smile.

McClain scanned desperately for any sign of command, anyone who could call off this carnage. Men and women lay about the compound, their bodies shattered and pierced with bullet holes. He registered the briefest relief that he saw no children—until a side door at the school opened. A girl no older than eight rushed outside, flames climbing the back of her dress.

McClain ran to her, all the while watching the machine gun and the CEV. When he reached her, he wrapped her in his arms and rolled with her on the ground. The girl struggled against McClain's embrace. When her dress had stopped smoking, McClain sat with her on the ground, listening to her labored breathing between deep sobs.

"Where do you live?" McClain asked her. She pointed to a small wooden house now engulfed in flames.

Just then, the jeep carrying the machine gun roared around the corner and skidded to a halt. The man in back leveled the gun at them.

"I am Sheriff McClain," McClain announced. "This girl's hurt. She needs attention. Take her to the hospital or an aid station."

He prayed that his voice carried more authority than he felt. The gunner pointed the gun in the air, and the driver, a private, stared back at the sheriff.

"What's to think about, guys?" McClain shouted. "Take her now."

The driver patted the passenger seat. "Want to ride in a real Army jeep?" he asked her.

The sobbing girl slowly shook her head, then reached over and clutched McClain's hand. He knelt beside her.

"You need to go with them, darling," he said. "It's not safe here."

"Pastor Dinah says it's not safe outside either," she replied.

"Well, maybe she's right most of the time," McClain replied. "But right now, she's not here, and I really need you to go."

From behind the sanctuary, an explosion shook the compound, and they all ducked.

The girl threw her arms around the sheriff. He felt her soft, silky hair and her warm cheek against his and renewed his resolve.

Reluctantly, the girl released her grip and walked with the sheriff to the jeep. McClain made a show of noting the name tags sewn into the guardsmen's uniforms. When the girl was settled into the seat, he brushed a sprig of grass from her face.

"Are there other people in the school?" he asked.

She nodded.

"How many?"

"A lot," she replied. "All of the grades, I think. We were walking in a line real fast, going to the basement. There was so much smoke. I couldn't see anything. I let go of Carey's hand just for a second, but I couldn't find her again. I am sorry. I got scared and ran in the wrong direction."

"You did great, hon," McClain said. "Go!"

The jeep roared away as he bolted toward the school. He grabbed the doorknob but jerked back in pain, his palm already blistering. Pulling his sleeve over his hand, he opened the door, only for smoke and flames to pour outside, searing his face. He closed the door and ran around the CEV to the next entrance. This doorknob seemed warm but not scalding.

McClain cautiously opened the door to a smoke-filled hallway. Miraculously, the lights still worked, and he spotted a stairway to the basement.

"Anyone here?" he shouted, doubting he could be heard above the machinery and the crackle of the flames. He took a deep breath, pulled the T-shirt over his nose again, and ran inside.

He stumbled half-blind to the stairwell. As he rushed down the stairs, the air grew slightly clearer, but he coughed hard when he finally took a breath.

"Sheriff Tom McClain!" he called. "If anyone's here, we've got to get you out."

Above the din of the fire, the sheriff thought he heard children crying. He ran toward the source and threw open a metal door. Inside, at least thirty children and half a dozen women huddled against the back wall.

"Listen, I'm Sheriff McClain. Please, come with me now. This place can't hold up much longer."

No one moved. Overhead, something crashed to the floor, shaking the ceiling and walls.

"Please," McClain shouted. "If you don't come out, I don't come out, and I really don't want to die in here today."

One by one, the women stood and took a child's hand. In turn, the children stood and took another hand. Seconds later, as one human chain, they hustled up the stairwell. An impenetrable conflagration confronted them at the top, and McClain turned them around.

"Is there another way out?" he coughed when they had reached the bottom of the stairs again. For a moment, no one responded.

"This way, Sheriff," a young lady with dark eyes said. She had a deep accent that McClain could not place. "No one wants to say because we are forbidden from going there."

She walked as briskly as she could with the children in tow until she came to another metal door with a small wired-glass window. It did not respond when she tried to open it. McClain tried also, but it was locked.

"This it?" he asked. All the adults nodded.

McClain kicked the door a few times and almost broke his foot in the process. The door did not budge, and the window was nowhere near large enough for him to fit through. He turned to the children.

"Okay, listen," McClain said. "I'm going to shoot this window out. It'll be very loud, so go over there and cover your ears."

Once the children had obeyed, McClain drew his service revolver and took aim. In the confines of the hallway with its cinder block walls, the shot sounded like a cannon. Children screamed. He had to shoot the window three more times before he was able to use the butt of his gun to push the broken glass outward.

"We need someone on the other side to open this door," he said.

"I can do it," the dark-haired lady said.

"No, you can't," McClain replied. He looked at the children.

The women held a brief discussion, and in seconds, one of them came forward with a young boy of perhaps six years. He clutched his teacher's hand and stared at his shoes. He had short, curly hair and amber-colored eyes.

"This is Tony," the lady said. "He's very strong, very brave, and very smart."

Tony looked up, and pride flashed across his face before he stared back at his shoes. The sheriff knelt eye level with the little boy.

"Tony," McClain said. "I'm a real live sheriff, and I need your help. Think you can squeeze through that window?"

Tony looked up again, thought for a second, then nodded. "But we're not supposed to go in there," he said, again dropping his gaze to his shoes. Behind them, a section of the ceiling collapsed.

"Son, this is a special time," McClain said. "I need you to climb through that window and open the door from the other side. It's special sheriff stuff. Got it?"

The slightest hint of a frown creased the boy's brow when he lifted his eyes this time.

"Got it," Tony said.

McClain laid his jacket across the shards of glass clinging to the bottom of the window frame, then hefted the boy through. In seconds, Tony found the other doorknob, and the door clicked open. The hallway beyond was dark, and none of the switches worked, so McClain turned on his flashlight as the others followed him inside.

They passed several doors on either side of the hallway. McClain called for anyone inside to follow him but got no reply. The doors to some of the rooms were open. When he angled his light inside, he saw tables with straps and other types of restraints.

"Anyone here?" he called. "You need to leave now."

Already, smoke had formed a cloudy layer above them. A muffled cry emerged from one of the doors.

When the sheriff opened it, a man rushed at him. In the dark, with only the flashlight to illuminate the attacker, he appeared monstrously large. He said nothing but shoved the sheriff to the ground and sat astride his chest. McClain's arms were pinned to his side, giving him no access to his sidearm. The man began to pummel him, alternating with each fist. Stars darted across the sheriff's vision, and he worried that he was losing consciousness.

Suddenly, the dark-haired woman who had led them here jumped on the huge man's back and began to claw at his eyes. The man roared and tried to rise, but two other women joined the fray. By the time McClain had made it to his feet and retrieved his flashlight, the man had been subdued and was rolling on the floor, holding what was left of his face.

"Deacon!" the first woman said as she spat on him.

He tried to stand, but McClain slammed the butt of his gun against his temple, and the deacon fell to the floor.

More smoke and flames came from all around them. McClain turned back to the room and spotted a woman restrained to a padded table by her wrists and ankles. She was gagged.

McClain stepped toward her but was stopped by one of the teachers.

"We know what she's been through, Sheriff," she said. "Let us."

The women surrounded the frightened young lady and gently removed her gag and restraints. She stood shakily with a woman on each arm.

"Time to go, ladies," McClain said. He turned just as the deacon rushed him again. This time, he brought his revolver out and fired twice. The man toppled to the side as children shrieked.

The sheriff hustled the group up the stairway at the end of the hall. They burst through the outside door and into the open under a clear dawn sky.

McClain rushed them out the gate just as Doug and Jonesy drove up in an M35 deuce-and-a-half. The teachers climbed in the back, and the sheriff handed up the children. He passed Tony up last, and the little boy held on to his arm a second longer.

"Tom!" Doug called from the back of the truck. "Look."

The deputy pointed across the compound to a woman with flowing black hair that billowed in a sudden gust of wind.

McClain gasped when he saw her.

Standing on her side porch, Dinah Whiten called, "Miriam!"

The woman turned toward Dinah's voice.

"Carol?" the sheriff called, and the woman spun his way. "Carol, it's me. Tom."

"Miriam, come to me," Dinah called again. The woman looked back and forth for what seemed an eternity to McClain. Then she ran to her husband, and he bolted her way. They met in an embrace that threatened to squeeze the breath from them both.

More gunfire cut across the compound, and McClain pulled Carol to the truck.

"I am sorry, Tom," she choked out. "I didn't know . . . I thought—"

"There's time for this later," McClain said. He embraced her once again, then helped her into the truck.

"Get them out of here," he shouted.

"I think this is everybody, Sheriff," Doug said. "Hop in."

McClain shook his head. "Not everybody."

The big truck roared away as McClain worked back toward Pastor Dinah's house. Only a few guardsmen remained, and the compound lay in shambles under a shroud of smoke. As he stumbled up the hill, he realized how tired he was and how desperately he wanted to leave this place with Carol. But, he reminded himself, he was still the sheriff of Stephens County, Georgia.

When he reached the house, he stepped up onto the wraparound porch. A few shots rang out, and a window shattered. He ducked before continuing around the porch to the side opposite the gate.

Pastor Dinah stood staring into the face of the Currahee. She still wore the black wool dress with its blood-red collar.

"You need to come with me, Pastor Dinah," McClain said as calmly as he could manage.

She turned slightly but kept her back to him and her hands out of sight.

"It was always something," she said. "Taxes, payroll laws, truancy. They never would just leave us alone."

"It's done now, Mrs. Whiten," he replied.

"It's not done, Sheriff," she said so softly he barely heard her.

"How about we get Mr. Whiten and leave now," McClain said.

"Paul's gone," she replied.

The sheriff went into the house and through the open bedroom door. He found Paul Whiten lying peacefully with his hands folded over his chest. An empty medicine bottle sat on his bedstand.

McClain returned to the porch to find Dinah staring down the hill at her ruined compound. In her right hand, she held a revolver pointed toward the ground.

"Best you put that down, Dinah," McClain said. He brought his hand to his holster, trying to remember how many of the six rounds he had already fired.

The sun broke across the horizon. Down the hill, a young

guardsman glanced up as the light fell across Dinah's face. From where he stood, he could not see the sheriff behind her, but he saw the gun in Dinah's hand. He set his M16 on full auto and brought the iron peep sight to bear on her. His movement caught McClain's eye.

"No!" the sheriff shouted, lunging for her. They both tumbled off the porch as all twenty rounds from the M16 splintered wood around them.

"Sheriff Tom McClain here!" he shouted, then stood so that his sheriff's uniform was easily seen. The young man did not respond, instead simply turning and trotting away. McClain frowned down at Dinah. Blood poured from her mouth and melded with the crimson collar. He could not see a bullet hole.

McClain sat in the grass as the morning sun angled down the hill and across the compound. Dinah still breathed, but only just. He was torn between futilely searching for medical help or waiting with her as she died. He decided to stay.

Dinah slid her hand across the grass to his, and he took it. Her skin was cold. A minute later, she breathed her last and lay still.

CHAPTER THIRTY-SEVEN

November 11, 1977
Four days after failure

On their return, McClain swore Doug to secrecy regarding Carol, but things being as they are in a small town, the Stephens County district attorney visited the next day. The sheriff and a local criminal defense attorney met him at the door to McClain's house. Two hours later, the attorney left them with assurances that assuming no evidence turned up to contradict what she had told him, Carol would not be prosecuted for any crimes.

Two days later, Terrance Head knocked on their door, looking for a story. Against McClain's strong objections, Carol gave him one.

Carol was drawn into Dinah Whiten's cult one fateful evening when she found herself caught up in the fervor and passion of their religious gatherings. At first, she bought into the teachings with her whole heart, and the Fellowship seemed to fill a void she did not know existed. As she became more immersed in their teachings and rituals, doubts and conflicting thoughts arose within her. She couldn't deny the sense of belonging and purpose she felt among her fellow members, but she also couldn't ignore the unsettling rumors and whispers about the group.

On the night she committed herself to them, Dinah and a deacon helped Carol stage her disappearance. She moved to the compound, took on a biblical name, and dyed her hair black. Dinah preached that God demanded perfect obedience, and when that lacked, He demanded a blood sacrifice, as in the Old Testament. At first the call to sacrifice seemed symbolic, but as Carol was brought into the inner circle, she realized that Dinah meant it literally.

"I saw them kill people," Carol said, weeping.

"Terrance," McClain said, "Carol and I have talked about this. I want it made clear that she did not herself kill anyone. She's a victim too."

Terrance seemed almost too stunned to reply, but he nodded as Carol continued.

"Dinah claimed to be descendant of a lost tribe of Native Americans," Carol said. "When she read of how Israel's King David gave seven men to be hanged before the Lord in order to end a famine, she believed she had found her calling. She believed we should make a similar atonement for what happened to the Indians. She told me so herself."

"Atonement? How?" Terrance asked.

The sheriff reached for his wife and shook his head in warning.

"That part of the story will have to wait," McClain said.

"Okay," Terrance continued. "Did you ever try to escape, contact Tom, or alert authorities that Dinah and her followers could be dangerous?"

"I was hardly ever left alone," Carol replied. "I did not get a chance. I was actually able to slip out to a local church service just the other day, but I was punished when I returned."

McClain relaxed a bit, and Carol continued.

"Most of the members of the Fellowship of Faith are solid, well-meaning people," she said. "Very few knew about the other stuff Dinah and the deacons did. They just took care of their families, worked, worshipped, and seemed to love one another. It all seemed so perfect. I belonged, I thought, to something greater than any of us. Of course,

I missed Tom and my children, but when you're convinced that God Almighty wants something from you, you give it. In my case, it was complete devotion to the Fellowship and to Dinah's teachings."

"That's enough for now, Terrance," McClain said, rising. "We'll consider another interview in a few days if you can agree to sit on the story for now."

"Of course," Terrance said. "But could I ask just one more question before I leave?"

Carol nodded.

"What about the slaves?" he asked.

When Carol responded with a puzzled frown, he continued.

"Dinah said that the country has a blood guilt for how we treated the Indians. How about the slaves? How about the millions of African Americans who were brought here in chains, many to their deaths. Did she ever talk about making atonement for them?"

"Not to my knowledge, Terrance," Carol said softly. "But you have to understand something. There were no Black people in the Fellowship of Faith."

With that, Terrance made the usual dubious promises to be fair and impartial, then left.

RUTH SPENT TWO nights recuperating at the hospital while Martha and Eve reunited with Wayne at Aunt Myrtle's cottage on the Toccoa Falls Bible College campus. Heavy equipment still roved the grounds, removing downed trees and power lines. Aunt Myrtle's husband was one of the college chaplains who had been busily planning services for the thirty-nine known victims of the flood, all while dodging reporters.

Sheriff McClain stopped by early the morning after Ruth returned from the hospital. Myrtle led him to the formal living room, and they sat on uncomfortable, thinly padded chairs and sipped tea and talked about the unusual weather. Myrtle already knew what was coming and was not surprised when Hilary Greene, an FBI investigator, also dropped by. She was an attractive agent with white-blond hair and piercing blue eyes. They sat around the fireplace while Myrtle served more tea and biscuits the size of silver dollars.

Without a word and with only a nod of acknowledgment toward the sheriff, the Morris family joined them, and all four sat scrunched together on a flowery sofa that squeaked every time one of them squirmed. After introductions all around, Greene began.

"I want to say right off the bat that at the present time, no one is in trouble here," Agent Greene said.

"Nobody thought we were," Wayne muttered. Ruth gently touched his arm.

"But it seems there was some serious misinformation given to the law enforcement officers," she continued. "Information that led to a lot of people getting killed and hurt. Property damaged."

She paused for a response. Eve clutched Martha's arm.

"Best get to it," Wayne said.

"First of all, Martha, we had a hard time reconstructing the route you took when you escaped the compound," Agent Greene said. "So, the sheriff and I retraced your steps as best we could. With all the rain, it was not easy, but you have some pretty gifted trackers here."

"We didn't doubt how you got away, Martha," Sheriff McClain interjected. "We just couldn't figure out how you crossed the river. We wanted to make sure that none of the other men who followed you from the compound were stuck or dead up there. We nearly lost your trail in some rocks on the other side of the dam. Doug Adams sorted it out. We found the cave, Martha. It's real."

"It is? I didn't dream it?" Martha asked.

"It's real. From the other side of the river, we saw only an opening in the bank, but there's definitely a cave. I think when the dam gave way, you were swept into it. We haven't figured out how to get in ourselves without climbing up a pretty steep and unstable cliff, but we can deal with that later," McClain said. "There's something more important we have to discuss."

"You see, Martha," Agent Greene continued, "we discovered this at the same scene where Sheriff McClain found your shoe after the flood."

She held up a leather-bound book wrapped in wax paper.

"Do you recognize it?" Greene asked.

Martha nodded.

"I realize that this was private," the agent continued. "A girl's diary should be hers alone to share or keep secret. But what happened at the compound is serious stuff. So last night, I read it. Front to back."

Martha blushed beneath her veil.

"I'm not worried about the normal stuff—what girl likes what boy, that sort of thing. What struck me was that in two and a half years of entries, you never made mention in your diary of seeing a single gun on the compound. Not one."

The agent waited.

"There were guns on that compound, Agent Greene," the sheriff said. "I saw 'em."

"You saw two shotguns loaded with bird shot and a single .38 revolver owned and held by Dinah Whiten," Agent Greene responded, then turned to Martha. "That's a far cry from what you told the deputy and what he relayed to our officers. Care to explain?"

Martha pulled away from Eve. "They had guns."

Agent Greene pulled a notebook from her purse and flipped through the pages.

"The notes I got from Agent Hart is that you, Martha, told the deputy that they all had guns and that Pastor Dinah had the most. Did you say that, Martha?"

"What're you getting at, Agent?" Wayne asked.

"What I'm getting at, Mr. Morris, is that we have twenty-six people dead at the compound. Twelve of them are children. We used the power of the state and federal authorities to launch what may well have been an illegal attack on civilians, based, it appears, solely on the word of this young lady. So, I ask you again, Martha. Did you say that the people of the Fellowship of Faith were all armed?"

This time, Martha nodded.

"Why would you say such a thing?" Ruth asked.

"I thought it was the only way to save you and Eve, Momma. I did it for you and her."

Tears dripped from beneath Martha's veil and onto her chest.

"Also," Agent Greene continued, "you never wrote anything in your diary about being inappropriately touched or seeing anything of that sort done to your sister."

She waited for a response as Martha began to sob.

"In my experience, that is the sort of thing that would be mentioned in a girl's diary," Greene continued. "There should be at least an obscured reference to it somewhere. There was not."

"So, what's next?" McClain asked.

Agent Greene stood and folded her notebook.

"Lying to authorities is a felony offense. But I don't think anyone in DC or Atlanta is interested in publicizing this mess," she said. "If you can keep a lid on it on your side, we can keep a lid on it on ours. Not even the president knows what happened here."

"We can keep a lid on it," McClain replied.

"One last thing," Greene said. "Mrs. Walters, do you think you can take these two young ladies out? I think they've heard enough."

When Myrtle had taken Eve and Martha to the other room, the agent continued.

"Water levels of the Tugaloo have dropped just enough to expose Eel Island again. We were able get Dr. Beatty and one of our forensic teams to the site you described to us, Sheriff. Just as you suspected, we found two more bodies. Same MO as the ones at the other dig site—killed with a newly formed flint knife. We've interviewed a few of Dinah Whiten's followers, and they tell us there are more. We don't know how many."

"My God!" Ruth said. "I had no idea."

"Neither did most of the other Fellowship members," Greene

continued. "We're still conducting interviews and searching for more bodies. There will likely be a few plea deals to avoid prosecution, but all done discreetly. Martha's lies contributed to a lot of death and destruction, and I cannot condone it, but in my experience, sooner or later we would have had to go into that compound anyway, and it would not have been peaceful. Between us, Martha helped stop a serial killer, a fact that should afford you a significant measure of comfort. She is a brave and resourceful young lady. For you and your family, Mr. and Mrs. Morris, you can consider this long ordeal behind you and move on with your lives."

Without another word, Agent Greene handed the diary to Ruth and left.

WHEN WORD OF the cave Martha had discovered the night of the dam failure made its way to Louise Beatty, the archaeologist immediately dropped all work on the Tugaloo dig and rushed to beg an audience with Martha. With Sheriff McClain and Aunt Myrtle in attendance, Martha agreed.

After Martha's brief description of what she had found there, Louise wanted to see for herself. Martha balked at taking anyone to the cave.

"It was all done by a girl like me," she said.

"What do you mean, 'like you'?" Louise asked.

Martha pointed to her veil.

"You mean a girl with a cleft palate?" Louise asked. "How would you know she had a cleft palate?"

"She's still there," Martha replied.

After more coaxing and with difficulty, Martha retraced her steps to the hidden cave entrance. Dr. Beatty's team carried lights and cameras, trowels and chisels. With these, they carefully expanded the opening through the rockfall Martha had squeezed through.

When they stepped out into the main cavern, there was a collective gasp. For several minutes, they shined their lights across the walls and ceilings, all covered with minute, finely painted images. Warmth radiated from the walls.

"There must be some sort of geothermal activity under the cave," Louise commented. "It would act as a natural dehydrator. That probably explains how all of this is so well preserved."

She and her students continued carefully, making notes as they moved.

"Copper," one of the researchers exclaimed as he brushed the dust off a small bowl. "They had copper. This has to be pre-Columbian, and they had metallurgy!"

"There are thousands, no, tens of thousands of images on these walls," Louise exclaimed.

"She's over here," Martha called out.

They walked cautiously toward her, careful not to disturb the tools and weapons. Finally, they stood around the throne.

"See." Martha pointed. "Like me."

Covered in centuries of green tarnish, Atsila's copper mask still held the shape of her beautiful sister's face. Beneath the mask, they saw the cleft that split her upper teeth. She sat upright on a bench of granite with her arms resting on short stone slabs. The bow and quiver in her lap had long since disintegrated into dust, and only the flint and metal arrowheads remained. In her left hand she held a child's skull, while her right hand clutched a bone pen.

"This'll take years. Decades maybe," Louise said. "Here's where I'll spend the rest of my career. Martha, this is amazing."

"Do you think you can give her rest?" Martha said.

Louise frowned.

"Rest?"

"Yes ma'am," Martha said. "Rest."

"Do you think she's tired, honey?" one of the other researchers asked, his voice dripping with condescension.

"She's dead," Martha retorted sharply. "She's not tired. But she's not at rest either. Can you give her that?"

Louise thought for a minute, then nodded.

"Eventually, yes," Louise said. "We'll try to find out what tribal affiliations she had, what living relatives. That sort of thing. Then we let them tell us what to do. Most of the time, they take the remains off, bury them, and never tell anyone where. I'm not sure what they'll do here."

She turned her light toward Atsila's face. Beside her, Martha let out a soft sob, and Louise draped her arm around her.

"Do you want to come back here sometime?" Louise asked. "It'd be okay if you did. We owe you a great deal."

"I would like to, very much," Martha replied. "But I'll be busy for a while. Tomorrow, I'm going to the doctor in Gainesville."

"That's right, I heard," Louise said. "Going to a plastic surgeon."

"Aunt Myrtle says 'Law, chile. High time you burned that veil,'" Martha said.

Their laughter echoed through the cave.

CHAPTER THIRTY-EIGHT

11:15 a.m., April 10, 1992

Fourteen years, five months, four days, nine hours, and fifty-five minutes after failure

A soft, misty breeze whispered up from the hills and ruffled Martha's hair as she and Wayne sat atop the rounded granite face of Currahee Mountain. The damp air carried the scent of pine and earth. A patchwork of green fields and clusters of trees stretched eastward to the horizon. The sky was the color of lead. Maples, oaks, and sweetgum trees sprouted green tips, hinting at the coming spring. To the north stretched a gash in the earth made by a rock quarry. One pit had filled with water and in the subdued light sparkled like dusty emeralds.

"Thinking about Mom?" Martha asked.

"Yes," Wayne replied. "Scattering her ashes from this very spot was exactly what she would have wanted. It's what I want too, when the time comes."

"Geez, you can be a bit morbid," Martha said.

Wayne laughed.

"You know, Atsila sat on this exact spot," Martha said.

"I read your book," Wayne replied.

"The dirt road up here follows the trail she would have taken,"

Martha continued.

"All in the book," Wayne replied. They both chuckled.

Martha slid closer to Wayne and rested her head on his shoulder.

"I sure wish you'd reconsider and move down to Athens with me," Martha said. "Eve's not so far away. Her kids would love being closer to Grandpa."

"I appreciate what you're saying," Wayne replied. "I can't explain it, but I feel like I need to stay close to right here. Besides, you're starting your new university job, and you've got this guy nosing around. You don't need me in the way."

Martha swallowed her reply.

"I don't have the words to describe it, but there is something about this mountain," Wayne continued. "There is a grace here that I can feel as sure as I feel the wind on my face. We saw it in Atsila's story. Evil deeds followed by heroism. Vengeance followed by redemption."

"Grace? Not a word I would have chosen, but it fits," Martha said.

Wayne nodded and took a deep breath.

"People here have long but selective memories," he continued. "It's much easier to recall an offense than it is to remember kindness. We remember Jesse Walton's death at the hands of the Native Americans. Hell, we even have a memorial to him at Traveler's Rest. But we forget the decades of peace that preceded it. We remember atrocities on both sides of the Indian Wars, the Revolutionary War, the War between the States, your own story. The list goes on and on. That much blood needs a special sort of healing that I sense here. The ebb and flow of history has left a hard mark on this place, but so has the rhythm of grace."

Martha squeezed Wayne's arm. "That's more words than I think I ever heard you say at one time," she said.

"I think we'd better be going down," Wayne replied.

He stood and extended his hand. They turned the car around under the radio tower, then descended the gravel road. As was his habit, Wayne saluted when they passed the brass plaque indicating where Camp Toccoa once stood.

"My dad was in the 101st Airborne, the *Band of Brothers*. They trained right here," Wayne said.

"I read the book," Martha replied. They both laughed again.

Wayne turned the car onto Highway 123, past the Georgia State Patrol Station and the Currahee Vineyard and Winery. They crossed railroad tracks several times before reaching downtown Toccoa. They had no trouble finding a parking place.

"Are you nervous?" Wayne asked.

"No. Well, yes. I suppose a little," Martha replied.

She linked her arm with her father's, and they meandered down West Doyle Street, past the classic Stephens County Courthouse with its Ionic pillars, clock tower, and redbrick walls. The clock bell struck three times. A brisk wind blew from the northeast, remnant of an unusually long winter. Blue sky peeking through breaks in the clouds cast shadows across the courthouse lawn.

"Sure wish your mom could be here," Wayne said. "She'd be proud."

Martha pulled a bit closer to him.

"What am I saying?" Wayne continued. "She *is* proud."

They kept walking almost due west until they reached North Alexander Street, where they turned left and were immediately confronted by a large crowd seeking the best spots to watch the proceedings.

Eve, pregnant again, spotted her sister and ran to them. Martha released Wayne's arm and rushed to meet her. They embraced as the crowd parted for them.

"Let me look at you," Eve said, brushing hair from Martha's face. "I can't get used to not being the most beautiful daughter in the Morris family."

Martha smiled. Her upper lip had a nearly imperceptible dent under the well-blended makeup that hid the surgical scar descending from her nasal passage.

"Don't worry," she said. "You've still got that spot."

"Not from what I hear. Is it, Daddy?" Eve said as Wayne came to join them.

"Boys, boys, boys," he said. "All they do is clog up my phone lines and drive across my flower beds thinking she still lives at home with me. If she doesn't pick one soon, I think I'll have to move."

They continued on to the renovated train station, new home to the Currahee Military Museum. People saw them and nodded respectfully. Even after all these years, Martha had to stop herself from tugging at a veil she no longer wore.

Jan Peeples, a buxom blond woman wearing a short dress that threatened to reveal more than she intended, waved to them. The cloth ribbon around her neck read MC. She handed a badge to Martha, then tugged at her arm.

"You come with me."

"I thought we would all sit together," Martha protested.

"Not to worry," Jan said. "We reserved three seats right up front for your family."

"We only need two," Eve said. "Mom passed a couple of months ago. Cancer."

"Well, I'm so sorry for your loss," Jan said. No one believed her. "Come with me, Martha. We need a few pictures of you with the mayor, Historical Society officers, and the like."

Jan hustled the guest of honor toward a raised bandstand that faced the museum and the Currahee. Martha was soon buried in a tide of reporters, local politicians, and well-wishers.

Eve rushed to the museum's bathroom for one last bladder check while Wayne spoke to some old friends and neighbors. All expressed condolences over Ruth's death. When Eve reemerged, she and her father worked their way to the collection of seats facing the bandstand. They found the three marked MORRIS and sat.

"Any news from your brothers?" Wayne asked.

Eve shook her head. "Same stuff. Still in Brazil. Never coming to the US again. John wrote back and told them that with another baby on the way and him in a new job, he didn't think we could send them any more money."

"They will not answer my calls or letters," Wayne said. "I'm still unsure what I did to make them so mad."

"It's not what you did, Daddy. It's what you did not do," Eve replied. "You did not buy into the craziness of the compound and the Fellowship. I think they're happy where they are. But it's my bet we see them again."

Wayne nodded in reply, though he did not believe her.

Jan approached the microphone and asked everyone to take their seats. Minutes later, the mayor of Toccoa strode out and made the obligatory small talk and quaint jokes while people pretended to be amused. The principal of Stephens County High School followed him and talked a bit of academics, how Martha Morris excelled despite the hardship of the compound, of her eventual enrollment in Toccoa Falls Bible College, and how much of an example she had been to so many of their students, especially the girls. Then, one teacher after another rose to speak to the crowd about how Martha performed in class and kept studying and attending, even during the years of reconstructive surgery. Martha sat to the left of the podium and smiled at the speakers and shook hands with them as they passed.

Then the provost of the college came to the microphone. He too praised Martha, though it was clear that he was uncomfortable with her chosen field of study.

"We at Toccoa Falls love Martha Morris," he said. "We are proud of her career, her achievements, and that as of last month, she is now Dr. Martha Morris, soon to start her new position as assistant professor of anthropology at the University of Georgia."

Cheers of "UGA, UGA" continued until the provost raised his hand for quiet. He droned on a bit too long, then introduced the honored guest. Martha fought tears as she stepped to the podium. She was not sure why she cried—perhaps for her mother, her lost brothers, the dead from the compound. She could only say that it felt like a day that deserved some tears.

Martha stood in front of the crowd, facing the Currahee. A cold wind whipped her long black hair behind her, and the crowd grew silent.

"I met Atsila over fourteen years ago," she began. "Many of you know the story of how that happened, and I'll not go into it again right now. Like me, she was lonely and scared and seemingly insignificant. But this girl reached across the ages to me. In doing so, she saved me in every way one person can save another. In studying her life, I found purpose and strength. Many of you know that it is upon her legacy that I wrote my doctoral thesis.

"Under the leadership and direction of Dr. Louise Beatty"—she nodded toward Louise, who sat next to Wayne—"we broke the syllabic code Atsila used to write her amazing tale. Dr. Beatty, please stand for a moment."

Louise stood and nodded to the applauding crowd. Rey, now a young woman, stood with her mother and bowed. Everyone laughed, and the applause grew louder. Louise had to draw Rey back into her seat as she continued to wave and smile. When the applause had died, Martha continued.

"If you would like to read her story in its entirety, my translation of it is sold in the bookstore inside. All proceeds do not go to charity."

A few people laughed.

"Atsila was of the Abittibi, a tribe that we believe to be extinct," she continued. "But these ethnic identities are dynamic, living things. If she were here today, I think any of the Native American nations would be happy to assimilate her and her family. While we know she was not Cherokee, we are choosing to legally treat her as if she was.

"The museum behind you has dedicated an entire chamber to presenting a replication of her writings in their original form so that others may study them while leaving her in peace. Her cave is now sealed and guarded, hopefully forever. This was all done with the consent and blessings of the US Department of the Interior and the government of the Cherokee Nation, for which we are grateful. Representatives of the Nation are here with us today."

She extended her hand to indicate two men sitting behind her, each wearing dark suits and shoulder-length black hair. More applause.

"The Nation has graciously provided some artifacts found in Atsila's cave to be displayed in the museum as well. For this, we also thank you. The Nation, as well as the faculty and staff at the University of Georgia and Toccoa Falls Bible College, have agreed, however, that Atsila's cave should be treated as what it is—the last resting place of an amazing woman who should not be disturbed. After nearly half a millennium, she is now at rest.

"Her story, which she so meticulously recorded for us, gave us insights into pre-Columbian life in this region as well as evidence of the earliest—and what we believe to be the most eastern—migration of other people groups whose history belongs to their survivors."

Martha paused and gazed across the museum's rooftop to the Currahee as shadows crept across its face.

"When you read her story, which I hope all of you do, you will likely find yourself as conflicted as I was when we first put it all together," she continued. "I could not decide if she was heroic and good or vengeful and wicked. On some days, I still waver on that point. But we are not alone in this. Atsila herself spoke of the terrible path she took and wondered if she was used for an evil purpose for which she deserved condemnation. In my most honest moments, I find echoes of her life within my own. Within the worst of us is some good, and in the best of us is some evil. This too I learned from Atsila.

"In the end, she gave up her lover and her only child to shield them from her guilt. In this, if nothing else, I choose to think of her as courageous, self-sacrificing, and full of a fierce and admirable love. She asked us to judge between her and the gods, and today, I stand with Atsila."

Martha's voice quavered as images of her own mother came to her. She saw her lost brothers, her friends from the compound who did not survive, and even Eve's cat. All gone, many indirectly at her hand.

In the back of the gathering stood Tom McClain. Several years earlier, he had retired and given up his sheriff's uniform. Today he wore a tan Carhartt coat and a black cowboy hat, which he tipped in her direction. Martha noted that Carol was not with him but fully understood why. Even after all these years, survivors of the Fellowship struggled when memories were dredged up that were perhaps best left as shuttered as Atsila's cave.

Beyond the crowd, Martha saw the lichen and moss shapes melding with shadow as they danced across the stone cliff of the Currahee. As she had done since she was a child, Martha looked for a face on the mountain. As usual, she found one. She continued as if she were talking to the mountain and not to the crowd before her.

"Today, I have a special treat for you, something that we will leave with the museum. Extremely rare artifacts are typically recovered, replicated by castings or other methods, then put into safe storage units. We seldom study the originals. Today, again with permission of the Nation, we would like to share with you an exact replica of one such artifact. Dr. Beatty, please."

The professor strode to the podium and handed Martha a box.

"Atsila was marked as I, bearing a cleft palate," Martha continued. "In my youth, I was not allowed to correct it and was forced to hide my face under a veil. As you can see now, I am whole."

More people applauded.

"Atsila did not have access to such care," Martha said. "Instead, her friend made her a mask of copper, the earliest known metal artifact in Eastern North America. We know from her writing that the mask was made in the image of her sister, Sehoy, and that when she wore it, she felt hidden and safe beneath that borrowed beauty."

Martha set the box on the podium and reached inside. From it, she pulled a shining object. Turning her back to the audience, she drew the band over her head.

"Today, I give you the mask of Atsila," Martha said, turning back toward the audience. A collective gasp arose from the crowd as a beam of sunlight broke through the clouds and struck her in the face. The reflection from the mask was so bright that Wayne had to shield his eyes against it. When the clouds again subdued the sun, he saw people staring not at Martha but at Eve. When he looked again at the mask, he understood why.

The mask on Martha's face was Eve. To the smallest detail, it was Eve. The same diminutive nose, high cheeks, lips fixed in an upturned bow. Wayne stared at Eve, then again at Martha. Gradually, applause rippled across the audience, growing louder and more insistent. One by one, people stood and cheered. The Cherokee representatives at first fought smiles; then they too joined in.

IN THE YEARS that followed, long after Martha stopped reaching for a veil she no longer wore, long after she had buried her father and two husbands in the red Georgia clay, she remembered that moment. Long after she could not recall receiving the many awards and writing the many books gathering dust in the small room she occupied in her final years, Martha remembered the unfathomable connection she felt with a girl, dead for centuries, and she remembered the face on the Currahee whose features changed with the slowness of trees. Long after she could no longer recall what she had for breakfast, after she lost the ability to describe the event to her great-grandchildren who sat beside her and read whatever news they thought would not depress her, she remembered when, from beneath the mask, she looked across the crowd to the Currahee and smiled.

Tears would stream down her face when she thought of that moment, tears that confused her family and made them wrongly believe she was sad for the losses that come from old age. Through her tears, Martha saw the ancient face etched on the side of the mountain and heard her father's voice as they sat on the Currahee, gazing out at the beautiful, fertile hills of northeast Georgia. She treasured many memories, but this perhaps most of all—that when she smiled from beneath Atsila's sacred mask, the watery image on the mountain smiled back at her.

THE END

Author's Note

I GREW UP in Toccoa, Georgia, a wonderful town nestled at the base of Currahee Mountain. Most know this mountain through Stephen Ambrose's book *Band of Brothers* as the World War II training site of the famed 101st Airborne Division and not by the Native Americans who gave it its name. The Cherokee, however, cast a long and much more ancient shadow in Toccoa, reflected in the town's name, which means "the beautiful." Cherokee and other Native American place names surrounded us: Eastanollee ("shoals"), Chattahoochee ("painted rock"), Currahee ("standalone"), and Tugaloo ("forked river"), to name a few. Other such names from my childhood include Chattooga, Chestatee, Tallulah, Yonah, Dahlonega, Hiwassee, Keowee, and Oconee. Even our high school's mascot was the Stephens County Indians.

Many will, rightly so, contest the origins of these names as well as their original meanings. What we cannot dispute is that the Native American population in Toccoa was largely either absent or effectively obscured in the years between 1954, when I was born, and 1972, the year I graduated high school and left for college. Despite being surrounded by such a legacy, I did not know anyone who openly identified as Native American. They were like the ghosts of Atsila's Abittibi. To encounter Native Americans when I was young meant driving to Cherokee, North Carolina, and visiting what at that time was an imitation cowboys-and-Indians theme park, complete with shootouts, gondola rides, and the opportunity to buy plastic tomahawks from salesclerks wearing leather costumes and dyed feather headdresses. As an adult, I recognize our loss.

In researching for this book, I revived a childhood fascination with these mysterious people who left behind such a legacy of art, culture, history, and tragedy, most intensely manifested in the saga of the Trail of Tears. Even for me, as a child growing up in the sixties, my teachers held little back, and we recognized how unfairly our government had dealt with the Cherokee. It left us with an unspoken need to apologize to someone who was no longer there, or at least was not nearby. Implied but rarely spoken within these stories is the fact that our ancestors also feared these people, who could be so fierce in battle and merciless with captives.

I also found that Cherokee religion and culture are not as cohesive as the faint and naive memories I carried. Stories relating to cosmology, gender differences, religious values and teachings, and language differ greatly between sources. I knew there was almost no hope that I could place Atsila within a Cherokee tribe or family without creating an offense to one or more of these authoritative sources, who would possibly never agree among themselves on how she should eat, dress, fight, or practice her religion.

The battle over these highly contested ethnic identities, etymologies, and genealogies must be fought somewhere else, for here, I took a less brave tack. Atsila's tribe, the Abittibi, never existed in the form described here. I created them just for this book, borrowing from histories of the Iroquois, Creek, and even the distant Apache. Having said that, genetic, linguistic, and archaeological records confirm that migrations of the sort described by Atsila occurred with regularity. Intermixing by marriage, exchanging of slaves, and gradual cultural assimilation would blur the bounds of many of these ethnicities.

Toccoa lies submerged in a sea of lost or forgotten ethnic groups whose fortifications, mounds, pottery, weapons, and trails blanket our mountains with echoes of ghosts—but not from the fictional Abittibi, though in fact a band of Algonquins bearing that name did inhabit the shores of a lake of the same name in Ontario. They were a small and mostly ignored tribe whose totems were the eagle and the partridge. In 1878, the Canadian Indian Office numbered them at only 450 people just prior to their disappearance from history. Their resurrection here is completely fictional.

What is not fictional is the famed Rock Eagle, found in Eatonton, Georgia.

> Shaped like a prone bird, the Rock Eagle Mound is a stone effigy. Measuring eight feet high at the breast and consisting entirely of milky quartz rocks, it was probably built about 2,000 years ago by Native Americans. Many believe it was built for religious or ceremonial purposes. (Rock Eagle 4-H Center 2024)

The name Cherokee comes from the Creek word meaning "speakers of a different language." Cherokee originally called themselves Aniyunwiya, "the Principal People." In this story, I use the alternate translation, "First People." Many, but not all, modern Cherokee accept the name, which is more properly spelled and pronounced "Tsalagi."

I think it is worth noting that Sequoyah, the Cherokee slave to the fictional Abittibi here, is not meant to represent the Sequoyah who in the early 1800s invented the Cherokee syllabary. Our story takes place centuries before his time. I used his name because I liked it.

The Nermernuh were likely among the first humans to cross from Asia into the Americas. S. C. Gwynne describes them as being "of the mountains: short, dark-skinned, and barrel-chested":

> They were descendants of the primitive hunters who had crossed the land bridge from Asia to America in successive migrations between 11,000 and 5,000 BC,

and in the millennia that followed they had scarcely advanced at all. They grubbed and hunted for a living using stone weapons and tools, spearing rodents and other small game and killing buffalo by setting the prairies on fire and stampeding the creatures over cliffs or into pits. They used the dog-travois to travel—a frame slung between two poles, pulled by a dog—themselves lugging their hide tipis with them. There were perhaps five thousand of them, living in scattered bands. They squatted around fires gorging themselves on charred, bloody meat. They fought, reproduced, suffered, and died. (Gwynne 2010, 27)

The fierce Nermernuh would eventually evolve into the largest, most powerful tribe on the continent, with an empire that stretched across 240,000 square miles. Spanish horses enabled them to accomplish this amazing feat as they were quickly declared to be the greatest mounted warriors in the world. We know them as the Comanche. We have no evidence that the Nermernuh ever made it into the Appalachians or to Stone Mountain. Cannibalism, though rare, was practiced among a few Native Americans, most notably the Tonkawas—ancestral enemies of the Comanche and not the Comanche themselves.

I realize how controversial it may seem to mention the slave trade among Native Americans. While the extent of the practice can be challenged, few dispute the fact that Native Americans took slaves for themselves and sold or traded them (Smith 2018, Snyder 2012, Gwynne 2010). Most of the slaves would have been captured in battle; however, the practice of exchanging hostages (or something similar) also occurred. Our Sequoyah would have held such a position. Calling them slaves can dredge up unfortunate historical baggage unless the reader recalls that the story of the Abittibi portrayed here is placed well before African people were brought to North America and enslaved.

Additional evidence of the Native American acceptance of slavery and the subsequent low status of Africans in general is found elsewhere. For instance, Cherokee laws formally denied citizenship or voting rights to those of the "African race," stating unequivocally that "no person who is of negro or mulatto parentage, either by the father or mother side, shall be eligible to hold any office of profit, honor or trust under this Government" (Constitution of the Cherokee Nation 1827). How much of this discrimination was learned or coerced by colonizers and how much is residual from Indigenous practices is for others to determine. That slaves existed throughout Native American history cannot, however, be plausibly denied.

I would assume that present-day Native Americans are no prouder of their slave-trading history than are the rest of us. It should also be noted that while a few White slaves were captured and traded, enslavement of Native Americans occurred on a mass scale (Gwynne 2010). Researchers note that while around 12.5 million Africans were forcibly brought to the New World as slaves, another 2.5 to 5 million Native Americans were similarly enslaved—a largely illegal activity that was hidden by a variety of subterfuges and euphemisms (Reséndez 2017).

By the time the Spaniards established themselves in the Americas, sophisticated metallurgy already existed in some areas. The craftsmen the colonizers encountered fashioned gold, silver, and copper using cold hammering and annealing (Easby n.d.). We have no evidence that such skills filtered into the southeastern tribes who lived near Toccoa, so, please, do not go looking for Atsila's cave.

The Cherokee village described in this work of fiction actually existed, and I possess many artifacts found as a youngster while fishing the Tugaloo River with my father and older brother. According to the Stephens County Historical Society:

> There were a number of Cherokee settlements in the area around Toccoa. Two of the largest were Estahoe, near

the location of Yonah Dam today, and Tugaloo on the lower Tugaloo River. Inhabited by more than 600 people, Tugaloo was a trade center at the confluence of Toccoa Creek and the Tugaloo River, a religious meeting place and a congregating point for the Cherokees. The town included a council house and some 200 lodges. Tugaloo Town ceased to exist during the Revolutionary War when Cherokees aligned themselves with the British forces in the area. Tugaloo was attacked and destroyed by members of the Georgia and South Carolina militias. The only evidence of the Cherokee town that remains is a large Indian mound rising above the waters of Lake Hartwell. A historic marker on Highway 123 at the Georgia–South Carolina border helps mark the spot. (Stephens County Historical Commission n.d.)

While there is no exhibit of Atsila's fictional writing at the museum in Toccoa, the 10,000-square-foot building on Pond Street is filled with thousands of historical artifacts and memorabilia, focused on the heroic efforts of those who trained in Camp Toccoa during World War II. Brenda J. Carlan, executive director of the museum and the Camp Toccoa at Currahee Project, informs me that the town is quite proud of the fact that all of the displays were obtained and preserved with no government funding. This hidden gem is well worth the trip and the ten-dollar entry fee.

In Martha Morris's final speech at the Currahee Military Museum, she (and therefore I) comes dangerously close to plagiarizing Dr. Martin Luther King, Jr., who famously said, "Within the best of us, there is some evil, and within the worst of us, there is some good. When we come to see this, we take a different attitude toward individuals" (Martin Luther King, Jr., 2000). I wish here to credit him with this piece of wisdom.

I want to make clear that this is a work of fiction, and except for a few of my friends from Toccoa who are only mildly fictionalized and Toccoa Falls Bible College, the characters contained here do not represent any specific person or institution. That said, the practice of blasting, where congregational members gather around a person, even children, and scream for hours for the devils to come out of them, takes place today, and its description is borrowed from an NPR interview with the authors of *Broken Faith: Inside the Fellowship of Faith Fellowship, One of America's Most Dangerous Cults*, Mitch Weiss and Holbrook Mohr:

> The doctrine is really pretty simple—devils are real. And if you're a drug addict, it's because you have this drug devil. If, you know, you're an alcoholic—the same. If you're having an affair, it's the same thing. There are lustful devils. And so what she would do is it was called Devils in Deliverance, where they would have people surround you and scream at you to get the devils out. Get out, devil. And it would go on and on and on. Perfect example is with a baby. If babies cried, it wasn't because they were hungry or they had a dirty diaper. It was because there was a devil inside them that was making them cry. So you would have groups of people surrounding an infant and screaming until that baby would just get tired and finally, you know, go to sleep.
>
> And that's how she started at the beginning with her congregants. Over time, it became more and more violent. It wasn't enough just to scream, to scare the devils out of people. Now you had to punch people. You had to hold them down and restrain them. You had to choke them. You had to do everything possible to get rid of that devil. And that's when it became extremely violent. That's where the people who've recounted their stories would break down to us. They would tell us about their injuries. And they couldn't go to doctors. They couldn't be treated because they knew what would happen. So they had to keep it secret. But it's those beatings that [are] really still seared into their brains now. They can't get rid of those images, those nightmares. (Weiss and Mohr, *NPR Morning Edition* 2020)

I found the legends of the water cannibals and the invisible Tsvdigewi to be irresistible cultural nuggets borrowed from the sources listed in the references section and included their stories just for fun (*Native Languages of the Americas* 2024; Sacred Texts Archives n.d.).

The reader may find some curious omissions related to flora and fauna within Atsila's story. This is because I struggled against a mountain of other fiction works depicting Native American life in Southeastern North America that included both plants and animals that were not indigenous but were actually imported, mostly by Europeans or Africans. The possible presence of dogs is another, much more complex story. From excavations in western Illinois, archaeologists found ancient hunter-gatherers collected shellfish from a nearby river and hunted in surrounding forests. There, these archaeologists also discovered dog burial sites, something that would have indicated a revered status in the community. Radiocarbon analysis of the bones revealed that they are around 10,000 years old (Grimm 2018). No such evidence exists for dogs in or around the Appalachian Mountains anywhere near this early. There are several accounts of dogs used as food sources and some protection, but these accounts are much later than I have placed Atsila's life. For this reason, I give only a couple of references to dogs, as there is sparse evidence that a tribe in this region would have them.

In my research I found many recipes for "traditional" Native American foods that included several ingredients to which the Abittibi could not have had access. The most glaring example is honey. There are no indigenous honeybees. Europeans imported them to the Americas in some of their earliest waves of colonization, and the insects spread. Other examples of plants and animals popularly associated with Native American culture that would not have been present in Atsila's day include horses, cattle, sheep, wild boar, sugar, Queen Anne's lace, poison hemlock, parsnip, and hundreds of others. Attempting to stay true to the era represented, I avoided most references to many such plants and animals that would eventually become quite important to Native American populations.

Early Native Americans may have been victims of their own success at hunting, and many potentially useful animals disappeared in the early history of humans in the Americas:

> Perhaps the two most accurately dated extinctions are those of the Shasta ground sloth and Harrington's mountain goat in the Grand Canyon area; both of those populations disappeared within a century or two of 11,100 B.C. Whether coincidentally or not, that date is identical, within experimental error, to the date of Clovis hunters' arrival in the Grand Canyon area. The discovery of numerous skeletons of mammoths with Clovis spearpoints between their ribs suggests that this agreement of dates is not a coincidence. Hunters expanding southward through the Americas, encountering big animals that had never seen humans before, may have found those American animals easy to kill and may have exterminated them. (Diamond 1997)

I drew many myths, medicine formulas, and stories from multiple sources, and I am in debt to the authors listed in my references. Of particular note is the wonderfully diverse collection of medicines made from locally gathered plants to which I give significantly less attention than is warranted.

Just to clarify, in case it was not obvious, Yochanan of chapter 2 and Dinah Whiten are the same person. This seemed fitting as Dinah is derived from a Hebrew word meaning "judgment" or "the one who judges."

I took liberty with the presidential visit to Toccoa following the flood. Within hours of the dam failure, President Carter and First Lady Rosalynn Carter heard of the disaster while attending church in Washington, DC. The president immediately arranged for a presidential jet to take the First Lady to the scene. She arrived while workers were still removing bodies from the debris. The president himself would not visit the disaster zone until much later.

A final note regarding the history of the Kelly Barnes Dam failure. President Carter was true to his promise to investigate and therefore prevent other similar disasters. The investigation did not, of course, find that the dam failure was (as found in this work of fiction) caused deliberately. The Federal Investigative Board was formed to engage the public and other agencies to improve the safety of new and old dams. They would solicit everything from photographs of the failed dam in Toccoa to stories of its construction, repairs, and revisions. They conducted interviews with people from as far away as Texas and California. On December 21, 1977, just forty-two days after the flood, they released their final report:

> The Kelly Barnes Dam failed about 1:30 a.m., on November 6, 1977. The dam went through various stages of development. The final height of the dam was approximately 42 feet above the rock foundation. The Board could not determine a sole cause of the November 6 failure (however) the most probable causes are a local slide on the steep downstream slope probably associated with piping, an attendant localized breach in the crest followed by progressive erosion, saturation of the downstream embankment, and subsequently a total collapse of the structure. (Federal Investigative Board 1977)

The Rhythm of Grace on Standalone Mountain is, of course, a work of fiction, but it plays on events that remain fresh in the memories of the people of Toccoa. Thirty-nine people lost their lives the night of the dam failure, and I am acutely aware of the possibility of reviving that pain. I hope that enough time has passed that this tragedy can be remembered in a way that honors the lost ones listed here.

Karen Anderson	Dirksen Metzger
Joseph Anderson	Ruth Moore
Rebecca Anderson	Jeremiah Moore
Gerald Brittin	Edward E. Pepsny
William L. Ehrensberger	Carol Pepsny
Peggy Ehrensberger	Paul Pepsny
Robert Ehrensberger	Bonnie Pepsny
Kristen Ehrensberger	Eloise J. Pinney
Kenny Ehrensberger	Monroe J. Rupp
David Fledderjohann	Jerry Sproull
Mary Jo Ginther	Melissa Sproull
Brenda Ginther	Jocelyn Sproull
Nancy Ginther	Joanna Sproull
Rhonda Ginther	Richard J. Swires
Tracy Ginther	Jaimee Veer
Cary E. Hanna	Mary N. Williams
Tiep Harner	Paul I. Williams
Robbie Harner	Betty Jean Woerner
Christopher Kemp	Deborah Woerner
Cassandra Metzger	

The Kelly Barnes Dam was never rebuilt.

Acknowledgments

I NEED TO THANK many people for their assistance in this book. First, my dear wife, Hart, who has amazing spelling and grammar skills. Also, Carol Killough, Barry Swiger, and Bret Lott, for reading early versions of the manuscript and offering valuable suggestions. Finally, to the wonderful people of Toccoa, Georgia. It is hard to imagine a better place to have called home.

REFERENCES

Arneach, Lloyd. *Long-Ago Stories of the Eastern Cherokee.* The History Press, 2008.

Convention of Delegates from the several districts, at New Echota. "Constitution of the Cheorokee Nation." July 1827. http://www.digitalhistory.uh.edu/active_learning/explorations/indian_removal/cherokee_constitution.cfm.

Diamond, Jered M. *Guns, Germs, and Steel: The Fates of Human Societies.* New York: W. W. Norton & Company, 1997.

Duncan, Barbara R. *Living Stories of the Cherokee.* The University of North Carolina Press, 2014.

Easby, Dudley Tate. *American Indian peoples: Precolumbian.* n.d. https://www.britannica.com/topic/metalwork/American-Indian-peoples.

Federal Investigative Board. *The 1977 Toccoa Flood, Report of Failure of Kelly Barnes Dam Flood and Findings.* December 21, 1977. https://ga.water.usgs.gov/www2/flood/toccoa/index.html.

First-Nations.info. 2020. https://www.first-nations.info/abittibi-indians.html.

Foster, K. Neil. *Dam Break in Georgia: Sadness and Joy at Toccoa Falls.* Harrisburg, PA: Christian Publications, 1978.

Garrett, J. T. *Medicine of the Cherokee: The Way of Right Relationship.* Bear & Company; Original ed. Edition, 1996.

The Cherokee Herbal: Native Plant Medicine from the Four Directions. Bear & Company; Original ed. Edition, 2003.

Grimm, David. "America's first dogs lived with people for thousands of years. Then they vanished." *Science Magazine*, July 5, 2018.

Gwynne, S. C. *Empire of the Summer Moon.* New York: Scribner, 2010.

Isaacs, Sandra Muse. *Eastern Cherokee Stories: A Living Oral Tradition and Its Cultural Continuance.* University of Oklahoma Press, 2019.

Matin Luther King, Jr. *The Papers of Martin Luther King, Jr., Volume IV: Symbol of the Movement, January 1957-December 1958 (Volume 4).* University of California Press, 2000.

Mooney, James. *Myths of the Cherokee (illustrated): Extract from the Nineteenth Annual Report of the Bureau of American Ethnology.* Bureau of American Ethnology, 1897.

Moony, James. *The Sacred Formulas of the Cherokees.* Madison & Adams Press, 2018.

Native Languages of the Americas. *Native American Legends: Yunwi Tsunsdi'.* 2024. https://www.native-languages.org/morelegends/yunwi-tsunsdi.htm.

Norton, Terry L. *Cherokee Myths and Legends: Thirty Tales Retold.* McFarland, 2014.

Reed, Marcelina. *Seven Clans of The Cherokee Society.* Cherokee Publications Inc., 2014.

Reséndez, Andrés. *The Other Slavery: The Uncovered Story of Indian Enslavement in America*. Mariner Books, 2017.

Rock Eagle 4-H Center. 2024. https://georgia4h.org/4-h-centers/rock-eagle-4-h-centers/about-rock-eagle/.

Sacred Texts Archives. *Sacred Texts Archives: The Water Cannibals*. n.d. https://sacred-texts.com/nam/cher/motc/motc087.htm.

Smith, Ryan P. "How Native American Slaveholders Complicate the Trail of Tears Narrative." *Smithsonian Magazine*, March 6, 2018.

Snyder, Christina. *Slavery in Indian Country: The Changing Face of Captivity in Early America*. Harvard University Press, 2012.

Stephens County Historical Commission. n.d. https://stephenscountyga.gov/history/.

Weiss, Mitch, and Mohr Holbrook. *NPR Morning Edition*. By Rachel Martin. February 17, 2020.

Weiss, Mitch, and Mohr Holbrook. *Broken Faith: Inside the Fellowship of Faith Fellowship, One of America's Most Dangerous Cults*. Hanover Square Press, 2020.

Yates, Donald N. *Old World Roots of the Cherokee: How DNA, Ancient Alphabets and Religion Explain the Origins of America's Largest Indian Nation*. McFarland, 2014.

www.ingramcontent.com/pod-product-compliance
Lightning Source LLC
LaVergne TN
LVHW041755060526
838201LV00046B/1007